SHADOW OF THE WAVE

STRANDED AND STALKED

A Meredith Ogden Hollywood Legwoman Mystery

PENNY PENCE SMITH

150 Hamakua Dr. #357
Kailua, HI 96734

ISBN: 978-17-372084-2-6 (Ingram Print)
ISBN: 977-83-614988-7-1 (KDP Print)
ISBN: 978-17-372084-3-3 (EPUB)

Cover design: Cynthia Gunn
Author photograph: Ingrid Taylar
Interior design and book production: Elizabeth Beeton

What our readers say about
Meredith Ogden,
Hollywood Legwoman Mysteries

Sunset West—Guns, Grit and Gossip

"The book not only told a fascinating story, but the author's descriptive writing is a pleasure to read."

"This is her second in a series and is just so much fun to read, once again, about the Hollywood/entertainment scene…not-to-be missed…."

"Meredith Ogden is a really cool character."

"I'm…hooked…brava for yet another enthralling Meredith Ogden adventure!"

"I finished it on the plane…last night … when I would have normally fallen asleep upon taxiing and stayed asleep until landing."

"…Raymond is delicious…"

"…hope the story line continues…"

The Last Legwoman—
A Novel of Hollywood, Murder and Gossip!

"…really good story…writing was beautiful…"

Don Wallace
author *The French House*
editor, *Hawaii Book Review*

"…an engaging storyteller…" *Honolulu Star* Advertiser

"…a joy to read…"

Meredith Ogden
Hollywood Legwoman Mysteries
by Penny Pence Smith

The Last Legwoman—
A Novel of Hollywood, Murder and Gossip

Sunset West—Guns, Grit and Gossip

Also by Penny Pence Smith

Under a Maui Sun
Reflections of Kauai

To Ruth Walden who covered the Watergate
Hearings as a reporter, inspired legions of students
as professor and Associate Dean at UNC-Chapel
Hills' School of Media and Journalism, was a
tolerant golf buddy and most important, a dear
and rock-solid friend—an editor who was never
afraid to say, "You missed the point.
You buried the lede!"

CHAPTER 1
OCTOBER 11, 1989
SUISUN BAY, CALIFORNIA
WEDNESDAY AFTERNOON

"Sue the F——g studio!"

Dusk settled over Suisun Bay just north of San Francisco. An occasional fishing vessel passed through; a sailboat slipped by quietly. But mostly it was the ghost ships—sixty-six of them in well-defined rows, the military's "Reserve Fleet" or "Mothball Fleet" occupying the narrow slip of water—discarded, ancient, rusted, tired and creaking warships. Like a field of ethereal soldiers standing in formation, their war long forgotten.

On a high deck of the innermost ship—sitting many stories above the waterline—perched on scrappy metal steps up to the highest cabin on the structure, Meredith Ogden rested her head on knees hugged close to her body. Caught between frustration and panic, she tugged at her thick jacket. Her throat ached from yelling—screaming—nearly two hours—from the bow of the boat.

"Hello! Anyone…Help!"

Frantic words that dissolved into the breeze across the shadows and finding listeners only in the clouds. Meredith unfolded her lithe, athletic form from the hard steps and stood to gaze—yet once more—across the water, mentally searching for a fix for the predicament she was in. Stranded on an abandoned warship was the most unexpected result of a planned ordinary movie set visit for the intrepid writer. A prominent, nationally known columnist covering the entertainment industry, she was most often seen on red carpets and in spotlights around star-studded premiers and events. Seldom stranded on an abandoned warship with only winds and threatening rain to keep her company.

How, she wondered, could a major movie studio escort an important Hollywood journalist to this isolated location, site for the upcoming blockbuster release *Shadow of the Wave*, then forget she's on board? And not even notice enough to send someone back to retrieve her. The thought left her breathless. And furious. And a little frightened. This is worse than the worst "B" movie plot, she told herself. And hardly worth spending anxiety on…and yet….

Working on an in-depth article about the movie industry's relationship with the U.S. Military, she had connected with the most prolific producer of movie and TV shows centered around armed service subject matter. Matthew Morgan's long reputation was built on his ability to locate productions on military property, use military equipment and even personnel, and generally bolster the overall character and mystique of the American soldier. His latest movie, a multi-million-dollar blockbuster with top-tier stars, would fill theaters in a few months. Much of the film was shot on the decrepit warship languishing in Northern California's Suisun Bay. "It was a cheap opportunity," he told Meredith. He had invited—urged—her to join a small band of press and executives for a quick visit to the set of *Shadow of the Wave* in order to gather a good understanding of the story's context and landscape.

Meredith didn't really need the visit to the ghost ships. She had already spent several hours with Matthew Morgan at the studio and in his Los Angeles office, but she realized that seeing first-hand how a rusty battleship might be resurrected as the backdrop for an epic maritime drama would lend color and veracity to her work. She accepted the invitation, caught an early morning flight from L.A. to Oakland in time to meet the assembled group for brunch at a harborside restaurant, then drive the hour-and-a-half to Benicia on the Carquinez Straits. From there, they divided into two watercraft launches that took them to the watery home of the National Defense Reserve Fleet, the Ghost Fleet.

The sight of the vast rows of moribund maritime giants took away the breath of most of the 13-person entourage consisting of the movie's executive producer Matthew Morgan, the studio's publicity chief, four weighty international press members, *Shadow of the Wave* publicity representative, two drivers, two other studio executives and two unidentified film distribution VIPS.

"This ship reminds me of the movie *Poseidon Adventure*," uttered the journalist from France. "Like I'm living in the shadow of the big wave." His lilting dramatic accent causing several colleagues to regard him in puzzlement. They said nothing. Movie title aside, Suisun Bay didn't seem prone to large waves.

Meredith felt her own heart pound as her imagination took over at the view—not just rusting ships but long-forgotten, perhaps never told, stories of life, death, courage, victory and tragedy. She felt the thrum of spirit and soul as the launch grew closer to the awesome lineup. They boarded the ship situated in one of many rows, the one farthest into the bay, away from land, to see where *Shadow of the Wave* had been filmed. The movie crew, long gone, had converted many areas of the ship into sets representing the story being told. Now gone, all vestiges of filming removed, the empty vessel had returned to its former abandoned shell. Like a hunched over elder, scraggly and matted grey hair, watery eyes barely seeing but trying to be welcoming. It was an image Meredith kept with her as she fought to keep grounded and work to figure out how to now escape the old gent's company.

When executive producer Morgan had prepared to give a presentation of the film to the assembly, he told Meredith she could step aside if she wanted. She'd heard the spiel before. Looking at the group assembled by the studio, Meredith was slightly amused. Besides studio personnel and a representative of the organization overseeing the ship maintenance, there was a correspondent from a major German publication, a French television network, and Clarice Duncan, entertainment columnist for a local weekly paper from a small town in upper Marin County above San Francisco. She had expressed surprise at the inclusion of the part-time journalist and the producer rolled his eyes and said, "she pestered me to interview someone—the movie was shot so close by. I remember her from a while ago with a larger paper. Know her?"

Meredith nodded. "She used to be with the old Celebrity Plus syndicate, but it was absorbed then shut down by one of the larger ones. Been a while."

A few steps down from the main deck area, Meredith settled into a room off a long hallway and out of earshot to make notes. She sat down on the empty floor and leaned against the bulkhead wall to scan her notes. There was a plethora of material. A good three-part column series took form and she began to organize it, engaged totally in the process. Suddenly she looked up to realize at least an hour had passed. She made her way back to the main deck area to join the group and discovered—there was no group. There were no voices. The launches weren't even in sight. Somehow, she'd been left behind. She felt her spine clench, her mind reverting almost to the childhood fear of discovering she'd been abandoned in a strange and frightening place and no idea where her mother or dad might be.

Yelling and frantic waving to the disinterested bay had no response whatsoever. At first she considered the possibility of simply climbing across the many ships stacked next to one another until she reached the one closest to the actual landing facility on the shore. But exploring, she saw there was at least a twelve-foot leap to the hull of the adjacent ship. Then she thought about swimming to shore. Her rusty iron home was the last ship in the bay itself and boasted a gangway to the water, but no platform or dock there. Again, the distance to the shore was too daunting and the weather too cold.

Yet, only a mile or more away was the massive expanse of the Benicia-Martinez Bridge—stretching about a mile and a half across the Carquinez Straight with enough commerce and traffic to see the addition of a second span in the next two years. Meredith looked across at the minute movement atop the span and yelled "Hey, look this way. I hear you. How come you can't hear me?" She screamed in frustration, then kicked the rusted gunwale. "Ouch," she barked, surprised at her own force, and gave up.

Breathing deeply, she talked herself away from panic, reminding herself that this was the adult world and that between the myriad of individuals involved with this excursion, rescue would be inevitable. And she repeated the words over and over.

So much for another one of those simple one-day excursions—and home in time for a late dinner, she told herself. She knew she had scant time to plan what looked to be an unplanned overnight stay on her floating bivouac. And no way to contact anyone. No available electricity aboard the ship that perched high above the water. With dusk giving way to darkness and a storm pending, she moved into the one room that seemed closest, most open and captured some light from the outside. She pulled her large bag atop a single remaining scarred and splintered table and felt inside for whatever she'd packed that would be helpful. Fortunately, she sighed, she had the foresight to think about temperatures in the San Francisco area, worn her bulky weather jacket and brought a knit cap and scarf. Her seemingly bottomless tote held an old cellophane bag of trail mix and the bonanza: a Snickers bar she bought in the L.A. airport before boarding her flight. Dinner. Those items were accompanied by a half bottle of water, a bottle of Advil, small cosmetic bag and brush for "on the go" touch-ups, wallet, a tiny slender pen light on her key set, the miniature multi-purpose "tool" her colleague insisted she always carry, and, of course, her notebook and three pens, and her constant companion—a tiny Minnox camera. She found a scrunched-up half bag of popcorn from some other event pushed deep down in her jacket pocket.

It would be a long night.

Meredith could see clouds starting to obstruct the stars and lights from the shore and felt the dampness of forecasted rain. Winds had already escalated. She strained to see what activity might be in progress in the bay, but it stretched dark and quiet. Only the metallic groaning and creaking of the tired and ancient ships surrounding her laced the air. A gentle almost imperceptible roll of the hulk. She shuddered and pulled her jacket closer and returned to the temporary camp she set up under the topmost deck where she had some shelter from the weather and illumination from a safety light, one of many above the massive water dormitories. A long-lingering suspicion of her own unknown night demons lay quietly in her mind.

Eating half the bag of trail mix and two bites of the Snickers bar, she had tamped down her anger far enough that it no longer qualified as "fury," then settled in to make the best of this uninterrupted time and distract her underlying awareness of the empty, ghostly monolith. A pen and notebook were her only back-up and she scratched out her immediate thoughts.

What will Raymond think when I don't show up at home? The domestic ground's already a little shaky.

How will I pick up my car tomorrow from the shop? And who's the asshole who keyed the angry scratch in the door of my beloved red Mustang. Inconsiderate.

Who's posing as me, and why and who was following me in New York?

*What will I tell Cece Longmore and **It's a Good Day** producers about their offer of a permanent slot on the show? So many considerations: New York, L.A., on air—becoming the personality who talks about other personalities or…?*

What about Ronnie? Can't help but wonder if he'll still harbor in the homeless camps and shadows of New York or pick up on the long-ago momentum of the super-popular young teen TV star? Or choose a new direction?

How will I get off this hulk and get home? Will I ever get off the hulk? How did this happen?

Sue the f——g studio!

A friend in need…

Midnight

T.K. Raymond dozed off watching the late show, stretched out in comfortable and familiar sweats, hoping that Meredith would either walk in the door or call to report her whereabouts. Unpredictability—particularly in travel—was not unusual for the journalist. But given her adamancy at thorough investigating and reporting of stories about the entertainment field, she could get caught in conflicting situations or certainly tough ones to resolve.

Once he asked her, "Why does a 'suggestive' situation that might not even lead to an interesting sidebar grab you strongly enough to take you off on a totally obscure chase for information? Often there's not even a story at the end."

"Because I'm a journalist," she answered. "It's what we do, what we're made of—the challenge and the thrill of it all. After all," she grinned at him wickedly, "it's why I found you so captivating so long ago." Still, since she and the detective had become lovers and then cohabitators over the past five years, both tried to keep the other abreast of plans and change of plans that developed.

By midnight, Raymond was officially worried. As the captain of a "special profile" unit of the Los Angeles Police Department, he oversaw an office of special investigators covering real estate, investments, sports and soon, corporate management. Raymond himself, and partner Marty Escobar, were the specialists in the entertainment industry—had been so for a number of years. He had a keen sense of trouble when it was brewing, especially in his own home territory. His assignments, often challenging as they were, were well matched in complexity as well as danger by many of the stories that Meredith pursued.

He meandered through her home office for the nth time, flipped through her calendar, checking notes on her desk pad, her to-do lists. But nothing suggested either an overnight up north, or any potential for an extended stay anyplace other than home. And wasn't that the fly in the ointment? "Home" seemed to have different definitions and parameters for the couple.

As a cop, he picked up the phone and proceeded to probe whatever sources and tools he could conjure to try to track the steps of the intrepid journalist with the copper blond hair and large dark eyes, quick laugh and absolute pull on his senses and desires. The airline she'd mentioned had no manifest record of her return to L.A. from Oakland. No cab company reported picking up a woman at LAX, delivering her to the Malibu area. Friends his call awakened ever so late had neither heard from nor seen Meredith. Calls to her assistant Sonia, rousing that household, uncovered nothing of any plans for extended work away. Catching the concern, Sonia had begun her own phone work, trying to unearth information from any studio contacts with whom she had personal and private contacts. So far, no information or even insight. The studio team from Suisun Bay was well out of hand for the night.

10 SHADOW OF THE WAVE

Raymond walked out on the deck overlooking the sand on which the comely home sat on the Malibu Beach shore and continued to plumb his knowledge about how they might find a clue to Meredith's whereabouts. He reminded himself that he was a detective, after all.

★★☆

Meredith sat for a long while, back against the bulkhead of her make-shift camp, knees drawn up, simply staring across the deck of the ship. For a while she dozed but revived with the groaning and creaking sounds of the iron behemoths surrounding her. They were the Reserve Fleet—supposedly the naval craft Uncle Sam could recall at any moment if a world crisis erupted. Most were old and decrepit—perfect for movie sets but not much else, she guessed. Controversy surrounded the six dozen or more vessels because most were leaking toxins from their disintegrating metal hulls and rumor had it they were to be removed and destroyed. A few were legends on the high sea like the USS Iowa that had played a life-saving role in the Korean War. The Glomar Explorer, commissioned to locate a Russian nuclear sub sunk off the American coastline.

But fascination over the ironclad armada soon paled in the echoing emptiness and imagined menaces lurking in the darkening shell surrounding her. She set out in another attempt to find an escape route, pulling a ratty fragment of tarp—a left-behind like herself—over her head to fend off the drizzle. She found her way cautiously to the ship's bow from which the deeply slanted gangway stretched down to the water level. The slender derelict ramp bucked and swayed in the wind against the massive hull and led directly into the watery black abyss below. No small docking platform or step. Remembering how rigorous the passage upward was in the calmer daylight, she found it daunting and frightening in the dark and returned, warily, feeling even more frustrated, to her small encampment. Quickly glancing to the distant bridge with its tiny twinkling but benign headlights, she screamed silently and cursed the studio for its oversight. And again, returned to her notebook and pen deflecting thoughts of imagined predators.

The security lights located high above iron hulls gave some illumination and slightly deferred the mythological accounts she read of apparitions of former sailors, or the possibility that criminals and other sinister reprobates were hiding on the abandoned hulks. Dimly shadowed halls, passageways, rooms and decks around her seemed illusory and if she gave it focus— haunted. She worked at ignoring the unfamiliar and disquieting sounds from near and far. And the bobbing of the ship in the water—something she still was adapting to.

Sometime long after midnight by her watch, she heard a rough scratching in the hallway adjacent to her camp. She shuddered then blanked it out, reminding herself she was too mature to even contemplate ghost sailors. But the bag of soggy popcorn that lay open nearby suddenly wiggled. Startled, she watched a small rodent poke its head out of the bag then pop back inside. The bag offered hidden refuge with great benefits: scattered bits of popcorn.

"Don't eat too much," Meredith cautioned. "It may be a while before the cupboard is restocked." The sight of the rat made Meredith smile and feel a little less shaky. A new friend, a reminder that life was going on. More calm, she assured herself that of course she would be found and rescued from the ship. She returned to writing notes—the only option when sleep wasn't available. She strategized thoughts about the suggested quick turn-around visit next week to the New York show on which she had been subbing for the past six weeks for Nancy

Igleton, one of the permanent well-known hosts, currently on maternity leave. Nancy would return on Monday and the head honcho, the NTS Program VP, wanted Meredith to come back to meet with him and further discuss her own potential future with the show as well as welcome Nancy back on-air.

Picking at a cuticle, sitting back against the bulkhead, Meredith pondered the obvious and colossal opportunity possible with a major network news outlet, and tried to balance her own feelings about a future. She loved her role writing the types of material that challenged her intellectually and creatively and made her proud. But cringed at the reality of her own drive and ambition. Not quite 40, she knew the media landscape for Hollywood news was ever-changing and she needed to think proactively to stay ahead of it. She enjoyed a robust—maybe even savory—home life with Raymond with no pressure to make long-term decisions. And there it was again—balance. The comfort of personal intimacy versus the thrill of professional momentum. Her inherent dilemma.

She pushed the mounting stress—familiar as it was—aside and focused on planning upcoming articles and interviews, made grocery lists, then assembled a list for the upcoming holidays and Christmas cards to be sent. Christmas made her think about her annual Palm Springs visit to Magda Phillips, her almost-mother-in-law from more than a decade before. The closest human being she knew that might qualify as a "relative," she thought back on Christmases spent with Magda and how they'd come to know one another through Magda's son "Phipps", filmmaker Trevor Phillips, whom Meredith had—reluctantly—agreed to marry years before. And how that reluctance, never expressed to the brilliantly eccentric young artist, now dead, still haunted her all these years later.

CHAPTER 3
SEPTEMBER 7, 1989
FIVE WEEKS EARLIER—BEFORE SUISUN
NEW YORK CITY
THURSDAY

Don't I know you…

"And we're out!"

The call of the floor director set Meredith to untangling the microphone from her blouse and rising quickly from the elongated desk she shared with the TV show's co-host, Amanda Borkin. Meredith unpinned her copper-blond shoulder-length hair and shook it out, exhaling a vocal gasp. Amanda glanced quickly at Meredith and gave her a thumbs up, then returned to her own activities. The day's ninety-minute talk fest was over for another day. All new to Meredith, a peripatetic reporter always, the sitting and planning—manipulating—news and content was foreign to her. She normally followed the natural development of a story—which then turned into a printed piece published in more than 300 papers and magazine, many internationally. Meredith always took her beat—Hollywood—seriously even when other types of new professionals might not. She was working to comfortably grasp the lightweight manner the *Good Day* show handled news—news of any type, most often lightly discussed including side comments and host personal asides.

It was an opportunistic assignment Meredith had accepted, more or less on a whim, without realizing the impact it would have on her daily life and work. In Los Angeles, with her one-time news partner Cassie O'Connell, producer of a major morning talk show there, she appeared one day a week with the program's two regular hosts, normally providing a Hollywood update and sharing the overall discussions with the others on camera. Russ Talbot, her boss at United American Media, UAM, the international news syndicate for whom she wrote, contacted her one day in August to ask her if she would be interested in subbing for Nancy Igleton, one of the two regular anchors on the National Television System's top-rated national morning show, *It's a Good Day*. Nancy would be away on six weeks' maternity leave. The producers had seen Meredith on the L.A. morning show and invited her to step in for the short time. Russ encouraged her to accept the invitation and a few weeks later she pulled open the door to *Good Day* studios and offices in New York City, feeling like the assignment was an interesting side-line to her work as an internationally recognized Hollywood journalist.

The first day, she was welcomed with much aplomb—big on-air introduction by her temporary partner Amanda Borkin, lunch with the management staff at a trendy Manhattan restaurant, lodging at a 5-star hotel, a personal assistant to help her step into the daily flow of the show. Including the 5:30 AM call on the studio set and the introduction to all of the support personnel associated with a highly-rated nationwide TV show.

The world of *It's a Good Day* was a beehive of activity flowing through four adjacent stage areas: the anchor or home around a living room ensemble where much of the show took place, a news desk and video screen for the twice-morning world update, a small and efficient kitchen, and a stage area for musical and other performances. The heart of the show was the two co-hosts and assorted other contributors—weather reporter, weekly cooking expert, various fashionistas, and more. Mostly the hosts sat in the living room set on a couch or in other comfortable chairs and discussed the topics of the day.

By the third morning, Meredith knew the first names of the script person, the hair and make-up specialists, the writers. In very short order, she was totally immersed into the show's heartbeat and process. By the end of the first week she also identified those who would be helpful, those who only paid some lip service, shrugging her off as a lightweight substitute for the real Nancy. And the fact that her cohost Amanda Borkin seemed to stay well distanced from everything Meredith.

A well-groomed woman in her mid-forties, high-styled chin-length hair in varied and well-integrated shades of blonde, Amanda carried her queenly position in daytime TV with confidence and regality. With a throaty voice and often-cackling laugh, Amanda was affable, always designer-dressed, and took seriously her role as the senior host of the show. It was an image not always accommodating to Meredith who was often addressed by Amanda as "Dear," and occasionally patted patronizingly on the shoulder. But Meredith also noted the frequent visit in the control room of NTS higher-ups as each morning's show unfolded over the air. She knew Amanda was anxious to underscore her own position, and the executives were anxious about the absence of the regular star, Nancy, concerned that the back-up kid—Meredith—would live up to their needs and expectations. And retain the adoring audience.

Meredith liked the immediacy of a live broadcast. Liked the attention paid to her field—entertainment news. But had not anticipated others doing the research, setting up the focus of each news item and then pre-writing questions and scripts for interviews. The show's producer Tim Felton assured her she would soon be used to the process and learn to have more control over the content. She was new to the size and weight of the medium and in particular, *It's a Good Day*, itself, the most-watched morning show in America.

And, she reminded herself it was temporary. Now, four weeks remained until Nancy Igleton returned from maternity leave. Meredith had remained in New York the first weekend although her contract allowed her to fly home to California every weekend. She relished the chance to acquaint herself with a little more of the city than she usually had on quick work trips in the past. New York had not disappointed. The pace, the energy and the diversity of lifestyles around her every time she walked down a street, were both fascinating and exciting. Tomorrow being Friday, the coming weekend would be her first time going home to L.A. in two weeks.

She walked quickly to her dressing room, wiped off the thick layers of make-up and brushed the spray from her hair, changed into jeans and a comfortable turtleneck. Grabbing a soda from the hallway machine, she headed to the conference room and the planning session for the next day's show. As quickly as a murmur of consent about details came from around the table an hour later, she was out of the chair and on her way out the back door of the legendary building where the National Television System studios were housed.

I need a walk, she thought as the large ornate doors closed behind her. A long one to shake out my bones and spark my muscles—and clear my head—like a mobile meditation. Stopping in at a nearby coffee shop to pick up caffeine to fuel the afternoon, she checked off the to-dos on her list. First and foremost, she focused on her regular newspaper columns for the United American Media Syndicate. Already done. Reviewing Sonia's weekly celebrity question/answer column. Also done. Reservations home to Malibu for the weekend. Done with gusto, she smiled with anticipation. She'd leave the next day early afternoon following the show's daily planning session. Return Sunday evening. Her contract gave her weekend round trips to L.A. if she chose to take them.

Walking, sipping coffee from the paper cup, she focused on *It's a Good Day*, what it was, what it represented for her career, its impact on her domestic life, and whether it had any role in her future. She pondered Tim's tips on how to make it more her own—even if for only a few more weeks. Deeply into her meditation, she walked down streets she knew, and meandered into some she didn't. She'd managed to wander into an unfamiliar neighborhood, one she didn't recognize—less amenable to meandering visitors. Older, less maintained buildings surrounded her. More industrial businesses, fewer shoppers and passers-by. She looked around and suspected she was in or near a neighborhood she had been told about—gradually gentrifying but still tattered, Hell's Kitchen. She gazed around reaching for something familiar, mused at her own absent-mindedness. Glancing down an adjacent alley, she saw a scruffy old man curled against a doorway. He looked up, watery eyes probing her interest, before they fell back to his hands in his lap.

Turning around to locate a street sign, Meredith faced three men shambling toward her. A

mental caution flag went up. Varying heights but consistent clothing —rumpled and soiled like discarded bedding—long unruly hair and untended beards. Two held lit cigarettes. Meredith stepped aside, on alert, to allow the trio to pass and as they approached, her sight fixed on one face—younger than the others, piercing blue eyes and even under the grit and grime, baby-faced and familiar. She caught herself from instinctively greeting him. His gaze fell on her as well and his eyes seemed to widen in surprise recognition.

Then, at that moment, he turned down the adjacent alley in a faster gait, his two companions speeding to catch up. One nodded in passing at the old man against the building. He nodded back.

"Ronnie!" Meredith suddenly blurted out. "Ronnie Milton—is that you?"

But the men hurried onward, leaving Meredith puzzled, a little shaken and out of breath. How, she wondered, was a preteen superstar from a decade ago, a TV golden boy, shuffling along a back alley in New York seemingly down on his luck, hidden in the shadows? Or was it him? He was grown up now but the man she momentarily saw had the same indigo eyes, the adult version of the former baby face, blond locks even matted with grime. He wore red tennis shoes—just as the boy she'd known did—and he clearly recognized her.

She stepped up quickly to follow the trio, but they had already turned a corner and were only fast-moving silhouettes on the street ahead. Meredith reached for memories about the young boy she had once known so long before.

The next day, Friday, after the show planning conference for Monday and before her three o'clock flight to Los Angeles, Meredith took a fast-paced walk to the block where she'd encountered the men the day before. She peered cautiously down the alley and saw the old derelict huddled against another wall, further into the shadows. Looking around for anything threatening, she cautiously made her way down the narrow road to where the old gentleman rested. He looked at her and grunted.

"Do you know the three men who came through here and nodded at you yesterday afternoon?" The man dismissed her with a wave. "Seriously," she countered. "I saw one of them acknowledge you. Do you know where they live?" The vagrant snuffed and shook his head.

"One of them, Ronnie, the younger man—I need to find him. Do you know him?"

"Don't know no Ronnie—don't know who you mean."

"Blonde guy. Had red tennis shoes on."

The bum shook his head. "Red shoes is Dancer." Meredith looked at him with a puzzled glare. "Dancer, lady. Like the movie—Red Shoes."

"Where does he…stay…live?" The old man shook his head, waved both hands and said, "Go away!" She did, but with intent, hurrying back to her hotel to make a phone call and retrieve her bag to head for the airport.

Homeward bound

The slight, smartly dressed Japanese man adjusted his glasses as he picked up the ringing phone on his well-organized desk in UAM's finance division. He answered and heard Meredith's voice. Its usual musical smile brought a wide grin to his face.

"Now that you're in town," Ito gushed, "when will you visit us? And when can we get together?" The diminutive man had a long-yet-short history with Meredith and her news buddies. He'd been the houseman for uber-columnist Bettina Grant when Meredith and Sonia worked for the woman in her Bel Air, California, home office. He brought them coffee daily and occasionally some Japanese food delicacy. When Bettina was murdered and the small team struggled to keep work flowing, and to learn who had killed their colleague, Ito stepped up to organize the office and handle the details. When the team reassembled in a new headquarters and included Cassie O'Connell, another former Bettina Grant alumnae, Ito remained the office manager, expertly plying his financial skills. Two years later he moved to the UAM New York headquarters as a financial specialist. Cassie had become producer of UAM's morning talk show headquartered in Los

Angeles—the program on which Meredith served as a guest host one day a week. And Meredith stepped up less as a gossip columnist but rather, a twice weekly entertainment industry observer and feature article writer.

"So far just two weeks in town, and going home for the weekend, but next week—can you make lunch on Wednesday—about one. We have a meeting every day until around twelve-thirty. I can't wait to see you, Ito! I hear you're doing spectacularly well," Meredith gushed.

"A dream come true," mused Ito.

"Now I have a favor to ask of you," Meredith began.

Ito laughed out loud. "Of course, you do. Go on," he urged. She told him about sighting the former boy TV star and how she came across him that day. "I don't even know how to tell you to begin, but could you see if there's a homeless shelter or soup kitchen, church or something in the area where I saw him and met the old man who seemed to know him? Maybe he hangs out someplace like that. All I know is they call him Dancer. But please, please don't put yourself in any danger!"

Ito chuckled and said, "Yes, Boss! There's nothing I like better than undercover research. And how nice to be doing it—again—with one of the world's coolest researchers!"

"Thanks, Ito. And I'm not your boss anymore but could you call Sonia and ask her to find whatever she can on the former kid star Ronnie Milton? I have to catch a plane. I'll check in Monday and see you on Wednesday!"

"Ciao!" said Ito, hanging up with an energized sense of purpose. He loved the world of show business.

Doing a quick check of her room as she closed her carry-on, Meredith noticed a new red message light on the phone, apparently arriving during her conversation with Ito. She hurriedly listened to the message. The efficient voice of the secretary to Cecil Longmore, president of the network news division, was extending an invitation to join Mr. Longmore and a few friends at his home in The Hamptons the next weekend. A car would pick up Meredith and several other guests Friday afternoon, return them to Manhattan on Sunday. More information would be waiting for her at the desk on Monday morning. Mr. Longmore hoped she could attend.

"My, my," thought Meredith. "The executive suite with a nod to little old West Coast stand-in—me!" She hung up the phone, grabbed the handles of her carry-on and left.

☆ ☆ ☆

Raymond leaned against a pillar in the gate area and studied a brochure touting some exotic location—compliments of an information counter at the side of the waiting room. As the newly arrived aircraft disgorged its passengers, he looked up and saw Meredith trudging through the passageway, dragging her bulging carry-on suitcase. She saw him and smiled her electric smile. He couldn't help but return it. He anxiously met her stride, reached out to secure her case, then slid his arms around her slender figure and hugged her tightly. She responded enthusiastically, relishing the warmth of his embrace, the surety of his strong body and his familiar scent—the comfort of their steam-heated dynamic. She'd been away two weeks, the longest they'd been apart for nearly five years.

"Turn around," he directed her, met with a puzzled look. "Every time you're gone very long you come home either bodily or mentally beaten up. Let's see...." Meredith had to laugh out loud. Cringing, she did a quick turn around and murmured, "You're right." Her mind quickly pushed away memories of their New Mexico movie set experiences from a year ago.

"Hungry?" he asked, already knowing the answer. Meredith could eat anytime, anywhere—yet, disgustingly, never show it on her tightly-built figure.

"Enough," she said. "I had a fast salad in the lunch place at work before I took my flight. The dinner on board wasn't very appetizing and I knew the time difference between New York and L.A. would make it about dinnertime here, I thought I'd talk you into some calamari...."

"You read my mind," he laughed. "The Sea Shack?" She nodded.

Finishing a meal so familiar to both, Meredith already felt back in the usual flow of life. "As always," mused the detective, "you amaze with an appetite of a stevedore, yet a body of a ballet dancer. We who work hard to maintain our svelte figures envy you!"

"My favorite food," she grinned, licking her upper lip and looking around at the mostly outdoor patio diner. "This is home," she murmured. "I miss it."

"I miss you," the detective said. "Thank God for the weekends."

"About that...," Meredith started to say, then thought better of it, instead explaining, "The New York media scene is a totally different culture, lifestyle, language. It's much more a dress-up world. The pace is exhausting. But I do see where Cassie felt a void when she first moved back here from the Big Apple." Cassie O'Connell was Meredith's gossip column partner for two years and now produced UAM's L.A.'s *Morning Coffee*, on which Meredith appeared every Tuesday.

"Do you like the pace? The culture?" probed Raymond, reaching for his glass of wine and fearful of the answer. Meredith thought for a moment.

"I like the ego trip, the accolades they toss at me, the size of the audience and the sense of importance that permeates the set. Sometimes just walking down the street gives me a shot of adrenalin and energy that surprises me...." She was pensive for a moment, Raymond a little nervous. "But it isn't here. It isn't you. And I miss it all—you all." She sensed Raymond's unease. She grinned at him mischievously. "Come on. We have catching up to do and it's three hours later according to my body clock."

As they entered the comfortable home they shared, Raymond dragged Meredith's suitcase through the door from the garage and into the red adobe tiled living room. Meredith swept in calling for Paco, her eight-year old silver-grey cat. Raymond mused as he always did that the two had a personal language of their own and if given an ultimatum, his lady-love would choose the cat over him.

As they locked the doors, turned off the lights and made their way to the upstairs bedroom, Paco launched up the stairs to follow. He stopped on the fourth step, turned and leaped his way back to his nest on the refrigerator top. It was no night to compete for space in the big bed.

CHAPTER 5
OCTOBER 12, 1989
GHOST FLEET—SUISUN BAY, CALIFORNIA/MALIBU
THURSDAY MORNING

Waves of recollection

2:00 a.m.

Winds had picked up and rain steadily pelted the ironclad hulls of the abandoned ships, orchestrating a surreal cacophony throughout the formation in the bay. Meredith had almost become immune to the sounds as well as the creaks and groans of the old tankards as she buried herself writing notations in her notebook. She winced at the realization only a few empty pages remained. Her reminisces about Magda Phillips and Phipps, Meredith's long-ago dead fiancé, renewed a guilty sense about words of truth never spoken. She toyed with them, finally committing them to the lined paper.

Well, gosh, Phipps:
    I wonder where you are? I picture you making promo films for Saint Peter—or is it St. Thomas, the apostle biblical knowers call "the First Marketing Man?" Anyhow, I'm in a pickle. Surprise! It's hard navigating the Hollywood sign and the Walk of Fame without you to guide me. Has been since you left us ten

years ago. Not to be redundant—something I've asked you and me for years—how come none of us knew you had a heart condition until…well, you know. And, sadly, only 34. You certainly got your fair share of attention with that stunt!

For a bunch of time—almost since you left—I've been a Hollywood journalist. Honest! So many trips along the light fantastic! But, right now I'm stuck, shaking like a little old lady in the middle of a Sunset Boulevard crosswalk, surrounded by ancient war ships that have a history of soldier ghosts and hidden monsters, and I don't think anyone knows I'm here and I can't get off this hulk. You'd have some great ideas. Wish you were here with all of us now. But…I'm trying to expunge all the bad things I've thought and done over the years, hoping it has some leverage in Heaven. Otherwise I'm afraid I'll shrivel up and die and become food for the rodents on this derelict. Sounds downright religious, huh? So here's the thing I've carried for a long time. It won't hurt your life now so maybe you'll understand and forgive me…?

Three points: I loved you then. I love you now. You're a part of my life and one with the world in which you and I shared them—the seedy streets of which I still walk—the one of Fame outside Grauman's Chinese Theater. Hollywoo-woo as you called it. But I could never have turned down your proposal. Never. But I also could not see myself as a married lady. The idea of marriage—to anyone—meant expectations no one seems to escape: a house in the Valley, grocery shopping every week, probably a dog, and…groan…a kid or two. Couldn't do it. Maybe just too young at 24. But even now, I still shudder at those possibilities. I hope you forgive my innocence then. Altered reality now.

So since you left us, I've become quite close with your mom. Amazing insight she has. We're the closest thing each other has to you. I still grieve at your leaving and am thankful—more than you can imagine—at your foresight and generosity. You made my life easier with your bequeaths—especially since we hadn't even set a wedding date.

I have moved along. I know you'd want that. A couple of relationships, none too serious, until recently. Still shake at the idea of marriage but it helps that he's older (Oh Phipps—I'm almost 40!) has a nice son, daughter-in-law and grandson. The family name is already carried on. Seems as indifferent to wedding bells as I do. Maybe I'm broken, but the idea of formalizing an already lifelong commitment is like double jeopardy.

☆☆☆

While Meredith ruminated through her own previous heart choices, Raymond ruminated over the perils her choices and decisions about story chasing had posed and no doubt would continue to pose for them both. He suspected some of those were afoot now. He thought of his many lectures and cautions to Meredith and her colleagues—Cassie, Sonia, even Ito—and how quickly the words had disappeared into thin air. Visions of past danger and trauma encountered during investigating newspaper stories flashed through his memory: entrapment in a burning room by her former boss's killer, the beating she and Cassie both endured in New Mexico, and...and...." He silently cringed.

What irony, he thought, it wasn't just Meredith's musky, enigmatic—not quite classical—beauty that was so addictive to him, but her independence and single-minded focus on her work tracking down the core truth of a story she pursued. And the life choices she pursued. Like him. She had insinuated herself into his investigation into the murder around her. Called on him for help, partnered in research, and made clear what else she had in mind. So, he figured if he worried about her now, it was his right and responsibility. But, he flinched a little, his worry.

CHAPTER 6
SEPTEMBER 9, 1989
MALIBU, CA
SATURDAY

What's up with that?

"So, let me understand. You won't be coming home next weekend?"

Meredith reluctantly shook her head. "There's some kind of a thing going on at the home of the News Division President in 'The Hamptons,'" she exaggerated the last words. "I had a private invitation to join a 'few friends' and I think I should go considering the attention they're giving me—and the money they're paying me." Her *It's a Good Day* contract called for six weeks, five days-a-week appearances and trips home to California on the weekends.

Raymond straightened his shoulders and shrugged. "Price of fame. Gotta do it, I know. Believe me, I do."

Meredith swallowed subtly and said, "Why don't you fly out, spend the weekend with me and see what life in The Hamptons is about?"

Raymond shook his head. "I'd do it in a second, but…I've kind of got a similar conflict here. My boss—Department Chief Bernie Bristow—you know him— is having a small barbeque at his new Playa Del Rey house—yeah, he finally moved west after all the carping about the better air here than in downtown—he's invited my unit and a few other folks. Next Saturday. I was hoping you would be there with me, but I understand."

It almost disturbed Meredith that Raymond was always stoic. He never whimpered, complained or begged. He simply acknowledged and accepted. She stared at the ham sandwich in front of her. Finally, she nodded. "Life has a lot of sides to it. Some get in the way of others," she posited. They avoided looking at one another for a while and chewed on lunch.

"So, what's this about tracking down a kid TV star—some hobo in Manhattan?" Raymond broke the silence, his voice buoyant and collected again. "Is this a real 'story' or a curiosity you need to chase down?"

"Do you remember the TV show—*The Kids Next Door*—went off about eight or ten years ago? Had a young boy as one of its big stars, Ronnie Milton. Great kid. I got to know him well. I ran into a derelict guy on the street a couple of days ago and I KNOW it was Ronnie. I don't get it. He had a long run, obviously plenty of money, was bright and optimistic—had his sights set on the future. Ten years ago. Now he's a vagrant, roaming the street. How? Why?"

"I should know you'd find a story," chuckled Raymond. "Even being on an intense top-rated program, you'll find a show biz story to chase. I'm actually glad. It keeps you grounded. Sonia called and asked if there was anything I could find in police or other official files. I called a source downtown who looked–stayed late Friday to fax it over to me. We found some things—it's a surprising story. Not a good one, I'm sorry to say. But I only have the law enforcement's official documented side of it—that's part of the public record. I'll pass copies on to you. But it's only a tiny kernel in the whole stew, I can tell. Please be cautious how you approach this one—if it's a real story, if the guy you saw is Ronnie. It's strange."

"Strange how?"

"The kid's father was a long-time union organizer. Some industrial union—maybe motion picture, not sure. His mother was a bookkeeper for the same union. But somewhere in the flow of events there had been some troubles within the organization. Was there a connection? I don't know. Two years after the TV show ended after six years, Ronnie was about twelve by then, both parents were killed in a freak auto accident on the Palms to Pine Highway from Temecula to Palm Springs. Car went off the road and tumbled—et cetera, et cetera."

Meredith looked stricken. "My God, that poor boy. He was close to his family and there were no other brothers or sisters. What happened to him?"

"The last information I have is that his maternal grandmother took him in and was raising him in Glendale. They investigated the accident but got nowhere with any kind of blame—figured it was a slightly rainy night and the father, who was driving, misjudged one of the tight turns. No alcohol, no mechanical evidence, no troubles to be found that would suggest anything different." Raymond looked down thoughtfully and toyed with his fork.

Meredith scratched her head and groaned. "Next week I'll try to track down the young man I saw. I swear it was Ronnie."

"It's old news and he may be destitute or mentally unstable after that," Raymond suggested. "Twelve years old is a terrible age for a kid to lose both parents. I know that from when Lilli died and both Will and I spent some time with therapists." Will was Raymond's son, now in his twenties. Both were left to rebuild their lives when Raymond's first wife Lilli died at a young age of breast cancer.

"Well, it may not be him that I saw, and this is all just time wasted."

"There's one other small item you should be aware of. It's about your Brentwood townhouse." Raymond referred to the homey two-story unit Meredith owned and in which she had lived—with him for two of ten years—until he sold his own Malibu beach cottage and bought the larger home where they both now resided. The twenty-one-year-old daughter of a friend of Meredith's was currently living in the townhouse with a roommate, paying a nominal rent while the two finished their last year of school at UCLA. They were scheduled to graduate and vacate the townhouse in a couple of weeks.

"Your neighbor there, Norman, called a couple of days ago to say he'd seen someone nosing around the back porch while the girls were at school. That afternoon Margie called to say that someone had been in the unit. Taken nothing but had strewn her lingerie all over the bedroom. Her roommate was gone all day so you can imagine the panic. Marty and I went over immediately and sure enough—someone had been in the young woman's drawers, so to speak. She or her roomy apparently left the back sliding door unlocked. No damage, no fingerprints but a lot of fear. For good reason. Norman didn't see a face so no identification. But I had a tech install better locks and I gave them a big lecture on securing their doors and some other safety stuff."

Meredith ran a hand over her face and moaned. "Too much going on. I'm glad Norman's still there but it may be time to sell the place. Margie is leaving soon when her program ends. I'm not a good landlord. Don't really want to be."

"Up to you. It has been a special place for you and you'll have to make the decision what to do with it now. I hope that doesn't mean moving back into it." He looked at her hesitantly eyebrow raised.

"Get serious!" she chided. "You can't get rid of me that easily…." Her words were cut off by the doorbell and Sonia arriving for a short work catch-up while Meredith was still in town.

CHAPTER 7
SEPTEMBER 10, 1989
EN ROUTE TO NEW YORK
SUNDAY MIDDAY

Wings from the past

The drone of the engines and the dimness of the aircraft cabin at night lulled Meredith into a state of numbness as she returned to the East Coast. She muddled through the conversations with Raymond and Sonia over the past day and a half, then began to read the materials both had provided about Ronnie Milton.

"I found this information in our files, the only place I had time to search," Sonia had explained. "And everything stopped a long time ago—you were still Bettina's legwoman and really only starting your own articles for the news syndicate. But Ronnie had finished his series *The Kids Next Door* and was just starting his first pure starring role. Very different character. He was 12 by then. But apparently he'd lost his parents in a recent accident. Filming had been delayed by about 90 days. Then he got sick, our files don't say with what, but enough that he was rushed to the hospital and then all I could find was that production was shut down again. Nothing more. Until I can get to the industry library in Hollywood next week, I can't find anything else. There's nothing that says whether the movie ever went back into production or ever got made or released. Or what happened to Ronnie."

Learning more about the young man was a welcome distraction from the mixture of excitement and anxiety about the next four weeks as a network TV celebrity—the bridge between a bold, growing careerist with new horizons to conquer, and a committed, experienced professional with a well paved career path already in place as an entertainment observer.

The materials mostly confirmed what Raymond had recounted about the former TV star but gave no insight into where his career had veered. During his years on the TV series, the young actor had also appeared in two movies. In Sonia's notes, not even a "Whatever happened to…" or "Where is he now?" mention appeared in the media. Strange for a kid who had been one of the darlings of the young teen magazines.

The young Ronnie Milton's face came back to Meredith from when they flew home together from the remote filming of his TV series near Phoenix, Arizona. Meredith spent two days interviewing the stars and covering the away-from-home shoot. Ronnie, Meredith and another cast member were flown back to L.A. on a small single engine plane at the end of the session, the young boy, dressed in a sophisticated polo shirt, khakis and an aviator jacket, was white-knuckled in his total terror of flight, especially in a small plane. In the terminal before takeoff Meredith had spent an hour assuring the boy and trying to deflect his attention from the upcoming flight. During the conversation he told her how much he was looking forward to going back to a "normal" school life and his hopes to play varsity basketball. As they buckled seat belts aboard the small craft, he winced and said, "You know, this is one reason I'd like to retire from acting for a while, anyhow. Everyone wants me to travel and I hate it!" His small hands were in a death grip on the armrests.

Meredith began asking him questions about himself and about his family. The tension in his face and hands seemed to lessen gradually. She had spent a good amount of time focusing on his bright expressive blue eyes and his soulful face. He told her of his affection for his mother who still worked in her bookkeeping job but had cut back to three days a week to spend more time with him, and his grandmother who volunteered to be on set with him every day he worked. How protective of the family his father was and the security systems around their house to keep unwanted people out.

"I think," he said, garnering all his youthful wisdom, "they are worried that people want to get too close to me, probably because I'm a celebrity." Meredith had smiled at the combination of nascent ego and innocence. They talked of cast friends and competitors, about the "nice" directors and the bullies and about how young Ronnie would love to just go to school for a while. "I get tired," he sighed.

"Of the fast pace and routine?" Meredith asked.

"Of it all," he said and turned to gaze out the window as the small plane descended into the Burbank airport.

Now, on another flight twenty years later, Meredith thought about the scruffy young man she had seen one week before on the Manhattan street and wondered, if it was indeed Ronnie Milton, what took him to such a desperate place.

CHAPTER 8
SEPTEMBER 11, 1989
NEW YORK
MONDAY AFTERNOON

"In the name of the…"

Ito quickened his step, surprised as always, how fast Meredith could walk when focused on a destination, even after the tedious weekend round trip flights and associated jet lag the next day. The two hastened down a narrow alley-like street toward the unadorned entrance of a small, shabby church. They had cabbed to an intersection about two blocks away and hoofed the rest of the distance. Meredith's suggestion from a lifetime of caution from chasing nuanced stories. Ito reveled in the suspense. At the side door Meredith stopped and took stock of their surroundings. Featureless, austere, impoverished.

"This is it?" she asked, glancing around. Ito nodded in confirmation and knocked on the weathered door. A middle-aged black man with short, well-groomed hair and a firm build wrapped in dark jeans and dark shirt and clerical collar greeted them at the door. He had an open ebony face and a ready smile but alert, aware eyes. He spotted Ito and smiled even more deeply. He waved them into the hallway and down into a cramped office.

"Please," he motioned toward two meager chairs sitting in front of an old but spotless wooden desk. The room was stacked with well-organized books, ledgers and file folders, but the walls were painted bright sky blue and were clean. Meredith subtly glanced around amazed at the light the walls lent to the room. Ito thanked the man and introduced her. They all shook hands. "My name is Paul Mercer. I'm the priest here at St. Bartholomew. Ito called and stopped by last weekend. I hope I can help you find and identify the young man he mentioned. Calls himself Dancer?"

Meredith nodded and elaborated. "I just think he may be someone I've known from earlier times—as a young boy named Ronnie—and I'm curious to find out if he is that boy. I noticed him on the street last week and his face seemed so familiar and it took me by surprise. An old man sprawled against the wall in an alley a couple of blocks away said his name was 'Dancer.' That's because he wore red tennis shoes."

The reverend rubbed his hands together and thought for a moment. "Why do you want to find him—other than renewing old acquaintances, I mean. You described him as a street person, so I wonder what possible reason there is to disrupt his life or yours?" His words were not cruel but curious and guarded.

"I don't want to disrupt his life," Meredith answered, choosing her words carefully. She'd down-dressed hoping to diffuse her normal shine, and wore jeans and a plain grey turtleneck, no makeup, her usually haloed copper hair tucked well out of sight under a slightly large Dodgers baseball cap. "I once wrote many stories about him—in another life. He was…well…kind of a special kid and I lost track of him only to see him apparently living if not ON the street, around the street near here. I felt…compelled to check it out, find out he's doing okay. Of course, it may not have been him. I wouldn't write about him—even if it is him—certainly not without his permission, and probably not at all."

"I called two dozen shelters and churches in the neighborhood," Ito spoke up in explanation, "and when I talked with the person who answered the phone here at St. Bartholomew's, she seemed to recognize the name. So rather than press over the phone, I came by here last Sunday in time to catch Reverend Paul after the morning service. Thank you for your candor, Reverend, and we don't want to hurt anyone. Honestly." Meredith affirmed with a nod.

The priest rested his chin against folded hands and shrugged. "Well, there is a young man called Dancer who is visible around our church. I would…cautiously…introduce you to him…if he's around. Not here, but some neutral spot. I don't know his history. I don't ask. He comes here to play basketball and he helps out with the soup kitchen on some days. I can't say if he's the person you are looking for." The holy man, a stone cross looped around his neck, pursed his lips and looked at both Ito and Meredith. "I'm willing to ask him if his real name is Ronnie—or was once called that. And If so, if he'd be willing to talk, quietly and under wraps with you. I'll let you know."

Meredith thanked the man and handed him her card with the number of her studio office and hotel written on the back. "Come and celebrate with us anytime" he responded. "We celebrate Mass every day at eight in the morning, and several services on the weekend." He smiled and handed both a thin informational brochure. They acknowledged and left quietly.

"Lunch still on for Wednesday?" asked Ito.

"Of course—we can reconnoiter," said Meredith. Ito thought he'd better look up the word "reconnoiter."

CHAPTER 9
SEPTEMBER 11, 1989
NEW YORK
MONDAY AFTERNOON

I have a little shadow...

"So how's the glitz and glamor of network TV?" asked Meredith's UAM boss Russ Talbot. The imposing man relaxed his 60-something fashionably-suited body into his chair, his head of thick silver hair catching the light from the window behind him. Meredith and Ito cabbed from the church to UAM's headquarters, waved "bye" to one another at the elevators in the lobby of the massive network headquarters—he to his own office, she to Russ's. Settled into a well-stuffed visitor's chair in his office, Meredith accepted a scotch on the rocks and looked around, noticing how much more comfortable he was with her now than when they first negotiated their one-on-one relationship in the five years since Bettina Grant's death. There'd been much parlaying over those years. With Russ's acknowledgment then guidance she'd reached a powerful position in the entertainment industry media circles. The word "gossip" was hardly murmured around her now.

"The studio as the stage is confounding, the performers so self-aware and on display—even at their most modest, but news is news. I'm worrying more about how I dress, what image I present even when I'm working out or getting coffee. In TV, it's about the news deliver-er, not the news or how well it's communicated."

"And how does that work for you?" asked Russ.

"Strange, a little conflicted. The attention is exciting. Being a female in the TV news business is a plus—important because people do notice you. It seems you build up value and equity in your own profession much more noticeably. In the print media, no one knows who I am, what I really look like or where I go. Just what I write. Well. No one's suggesting this is anything but a six-week carnival ride."

The seasoned news pro only smiled. He knew Meredith's ambition and her power to make things happen. "Don't be so sure," he prompted. She looked at him, curious. He shrugged. "Meredith, somehow, things just happen around you. Most of them good—but let's not forget New Mexico! Don't discount anything. Your TV on-camera presence has been noticed by a lot of important people. This New York thing came about because you're good on your one day a week on the L.A. TV show."

"Yeah, and it's L.A.," she said with a dismissive wave of her hand, then stopped for a moment and reconsidered. "And Cassie produces it. She knows how to showcase and motivate me. I'm comfortable there. There seems to be a pecking order at NTS, or at least a perceived one. I'm not sure I fit in New York media."

"Does anyone?" laughed Russ. The two chatted for a few more minutes and made a lunch date for the following week "to talk about your upcoming contract renewal." Meredith shuddered dramatically. Russ gave her a sidelong look as if to say, "Like you have anything to worry about." But she would, anyway.

As she entered the hotel lobby at five o'clock straight up, digging through her bag for her key, she felt a presence behind. Turning quickly she was face to face with a short, solidly built man—square body, square head, big square hands, one of which reached out to introduce himself. Startled, she pulled back. "Sorry," he apologized. "Didn't mean to frighten you. I'm Buster Bolles. Private Investigator. Former NY Police."

Meredith cringed. Now what?" she thought, reaching a hesitant hand forward to shake his. "What's this about?"

"Relax," he smiled. "I'm a friend of T.K. Raymond—out there in Lala Land. He asked me to connect with you. He's concerned about a story you're researching and asked me to check in with you. Let's sit down for a couple of minutes and talk about it."

"I.D.?" she said before moving. He pulled a worn leather wallet from the interior pocket of his tired brown blazer and flipped it open to an equally tired official ID card. "I'll just take a couple of minutes. Bar's right over there." Meredith looked at her watch, remembering that she had to turn lights out at eight in order to rise and be ready for the cameras at six the next morning. She hesitated at Buster's invitation, then realized his connection—Raymond—and nodded okay.

"This is nothing anyone needs to be worried about," she explained, sipping on a ginger ale. Buster took a large drink of a darkly amber beer. "I'm just curious if someone I saw nearby is a boy I once knew under very different circumstances." She purposefully withheld information, hoping to dispel any suspected need for the thick man to get involved.

"Gimme a little more detail and I'll just keep an eye out."

"No need. As Raymond points out, the whole experience could end up being a dead end." But she gave him a few scant details and then made her apologies, explaining her strained nighttime hours and the need to prepare for the next day's broadcast.

"You bet," said Buster, smiling and handing her his card. He tossed some bills on the table and ambled out the door as she watched, waiting for the elevator door to open. She thought about the strange man, then about Raymond. Tall, straight up, tight body conditioned frequently and well, generally California-cosmopolitan and dressed smartly, even in running shorts or jeans and a denim jacket. Or his perfectly tailored Armani tux. "Yum," she said out loud, surprising even herself.

CHAPTER 10
OCTOBER 11, 1989
SUISUN BAY GHOST FLEET
EARLY WEDNESDAY MORNING

When you gotta go…

3:00 a.m.

She had to pee. The ship railing wasn't an option with the wind and rain, and the idea of even damper clothing throughout the ordeal made Meredith shudder. So she steeled herself to explore the passage adjacent to her tight, covered encampment under the deck overhang above her. Pulling her jacket close, she fumbled in her bag and found the small penlight on her key chain. Snapping it on, she moved hesitantly down the short flight of steps into the corridor that led into a large black hole of unknown darkness. There had been shuffling and thuds emanating from the maw during the long night. Some had interrupted moments of near-sleep and had deeply distracted meditation. Now nature called.

"Please stay put," she turned and admonished the tiny rodent in the popcorn bag. "I need your company and your bravado. I wish you could tell me where the head is." She followed the thin wavering stream of light from her tiny torch. A heavy thud ahead forced her to crouch against the cold passageway wall. She took deep breaths as time passed. Finally, with no more sounds and nothing else unnerving coming her way, she crept forward. The emptiness and shadows of the life she imagined that once occupied the walls kept her on edge. She hoped she need not descend into the deepest-most innards of the hull in search of the latrine.

Midway down the passage, with the help of her light and eyes adjusting to darkness, she found what appeared to be a bathroom, multiple urinals and a long line of water spigots and sinks. No water was available in any of the facilities, but she shrugged and thought, *whoever put me in this situation can clean up after me.*

Feeling slightly more confident as she returned to her base, she peered into several of the rooms along the hall. In one she noticed some debris apparently left behind by the movie company when it cleaned up after production. She moved quietly into the room and with her meager light looked around. Some mussed up paper, wood dowels and a crimped but long dusty red rag in a corner. She carefully picked up the fabric and held it away from herself, fearful of spiders or worse. Its only inhabitants were age and dirt. She wrinkled her nose and shook it, relieved to see nothing threatening. One more tool for daylight, she thought to herself.

"You better be here," she spoke to the popcorn bagged rodent as she returned to the small camp. A slight wiggle answered her and she let out a sigh of relief. Then settled herself against the wall again to ponder how to find escape when daylight returned.

CHAPTER 11
SEPTEMBER 11, 1989
GREEN PARK HOTEL, MANHATTAN
MONDAY NIGHT

Sleep tight...

"You think I need a watch dog?" Meredith purred—tired, happy to talk with Raymond—but not up to a long discussion—another one—about taking chances in her own investigations. It was an old subject with them. Her depleted room service tray sat outside the room door and, wrapped in her hotel robe, she curled against the bed pillows, phone clenched against her ear, a half-full wine glass in hand.

"Here's the short version," he explained. "You're chasing after some itinerant kid you MIGHT know from years ago. Bad part of town, a church basically for the homeless. And you're on call, in person, from five-thirty a.m. until after mid-day as well as writing column materials and keeping tabs on Sonia here in L.A. Based on experience and history, it can't hurt for someone to have your back—at least some of it—at least from a distance...," he paused. "I would take care of that up close and personal if you were here."

"Mmm...," she sighed with some erotic emphasis, then chuckled. "So what aren't you telling me, Raymond. You seem a little...circumspect? Why worry about some minor street observance that, as you say, could and probably is nothing?"

"I talked with the investigator on the Ronnie Milton case today. I vaguely remember stories of it because it was entertainment industry-oriented—the industry union involved was one of ours—the case was just being closed when I came aboard. The lead guy thought there was something about the union books and whistle blowing by the mother having some connection to the parents' fatal car accident. That was troubling to some in the department. But no one could prove it or link anyone from the union to the accident. The case languished and fell into the archives. And Ronnie was taken in by his grandmother and just disappeared—totally—very soon afterward." Meredith pursed her lips and chewed on her thumb nail.

"The notes said she was moving him with her to somewhere in New Jersey to help him heal and find some normal family life," Raymond went on. "Last anyone heard of either of them. Why not let Buster check it out there. Keeps you out of the mire and focusing on your own TV assignment. The show will be over before you know it and you want to make the best of every moment."

"Well, if I get the chance to sit down with the mysterious young street guy, I plan to do that, but sure. Buster—and Ito— have my back otherwise. How's that?"

"Go to bed, Meredith," said Raymond but she could hear the affectionate smile in his voice. "I'll hold the phone up to the patio door and you can hear the surf. Then pretend you're here with me and…."

"Tell me…," she murmured.

CHAPTER 12
SEPTEMBER 12, 1989
NTS STUDIOS, NEW YORK CITY
TUESDAY MORNING

Breaking news

As Meredith entered the studio hallway, still awakening her mind and body to the work ahead, she was greeted by her producer Tim Felton, anxiously pacing the reception area, waiting for her. He beckoned hurriedly. "Meredith—a quick word. Come into the conference room. Someone you need to meet." She followed him, curious, also aware of the time and the work ahead before she went before the cameras.

"Meet Rick Santaros," said the producer. Meredith's eyes snapped to attention. She pulled herself up straight. Rick Santaros was a role model in the field of live news. Most often reporting from international turmoil, wars and political zones, Santaros was in his forties, dark hair, medium stature but tautly built, with intensely dark eyes that brought unquestioned credibility when he spoke. They shook hands. His grip was sure yet welcoming.

"A real pleasure," he beat her to the greeting. "I'm always blown away by what you do and how well you do it with people who literally terrify me." Meredith hoped she wasn't blushing. Santaros smiled. "I'd rather sit down with Muammar Gaddafi than with John Wayne. I'd never know what to say."

Meredith laughed heartily and said, "Knowing Duke Wayne, you have a good point!"

"We have just a couple of minutes," interjected the producer. "I want you two to work together on a developing story. Not a quick news break, but a longer piece for…say…Friday, depending on how the story unfolds. You both must have read this morning that the son of Bill Trubo, producer of *Saturday Night Laughs*, has been taken into custody by the Iranians. Supposedly spying for the Americans. Trubo says the boy—well, he's twenty-seven—was in the country to do research for a Master's degree in Anthropology he's working on. State Department's already on it, military weighing in. I'm told it won't be a simple negotiation or solution. That's all I know. Rick—you've got the ground in the international polemics. Meredith—we need your partnership from Trubo's Hollywood arena. Think you two can put together a cogent and deep-broad piece? You know you aren't alone. Every news outlet in the world is digging into this one. But I'm hoping you can provide a strong picture with both your connections…?" He looked from one to the other.

"Isn't that kind of an overkill?" asked Santaros. "I mean, by Friday, all the network news will be covering the story with a microscope?"

"We want more of a full-look feature," Felton answered. "Maybe five minutes or more on the regular news side of the show. With Meredith here we have some Hollywood access and perspective and Rick…well, you know the sources and back roads to the intelligence community…."

"Got it," said San but with some hesitancy, in his words.

"Sure," Meredith added curiously, but her internal investigative engine kick starting while grasping the reality of working as a partner in major network news.

"Okay. You two work it out and get on it," said Tim. "Meredith, we have a show to do." He left briskly. Rick Santaros and Meredith looked at one another and laughed.

"Lunch after you finish up here? Millie's—down the street?" he asked. She glanced at her watch, "See you there about one-thirty." They both nodded and Meredith hurriedly walked out of the conference room and headed to the make-up room.

☆☆☆

Millie's was a popular local restaurant and grill a few blocks from the studio and Meredith arrived right on time, shaking her hair from the morning's styling and hoping her casual clothes would be acceptable–jeans to which she added a white silk shirt kept for emergencies in her dressing room and a borrowed blazer in place of a windbreaker. Looking around she realized she had nothing to worry about. The word eclectic ruled. Brooks Brothers pin stripes to sweatshirts and ponchos, no one noticed how the others were dressed. A cool contemporary room was appointed with unadorned, minimalist tables and chairs. Bright modern paintings filled the walls. She breathed a sigh of relief and caught sight of Rick sitting at a slightly sheltered table, clearly one of the more desirable ones away from the traffic. He waved her over.

A small notebook sat in front of him. She pulled her own from her bag as she sat down. "Eaten here before?" he asked. She shook her head and he passed her a menu. "I like the calamari," Rick added.

"Chicken Caesar salad and a bowl of clam chowder," she said as the waiter arrived pen and pad in hand. "Oh, and a side of corn bread," Meredith added living up to her own reputation as an eclectic and enthusiastic diner. Realizing Santaros seemed a man of few words, Meredith followed suit. "Where do we start?" she asked.

"With a deep breath and a glass of wine," he answered, smiling at her. "I've already ordered the latter. And you don't look like someone who could eat that much lunch food," he mused.

"Thanks. My appetite is legendary and, boy, can I use a breather. Pace is a little daunting for a print journalist," she admitted.

Santaros laughed, then added, "Fresh off a broadcast, I find it's always good to decompress for a few minutes. You've already put in a full workday." The wine arrived at that moment and was set before each of them.

"Thanks," she smiled, reaching for her glass.

"How's the new assignment?" he asked.

"Going well," she answered, sitting tall and glancing about the room as if she knew everyone in it. "You live here in New York, Rick?" she asked.

"Sort of. Keep a studio apartment for when I'm here. Mostly I'm on the move. My real home is in D.C. but even that's just a two-bedroom flat. Right now, I'm only back on American soil for the next month. Probably why Tim pulled me in on this."

"Well, it's good to have the opportunity to work with you. I don't get many award-winning political correspondents as news partners," Meredith said as an aside. "And I have some material since this morning. But have you heard anything new about the status of the boy? Still in custody?"

"Yeah. No change yet. State Department still saying 'discussions are taking place.' But a couple of other sources tell me this whole thing is just a grandstand. A very visible opportunity to stalemate any other talks going on—mostly sanctions conversations. High profile."

"From my informal conversations with some of the *Saturday Night Laughs* folks, I got that they believed there was a comedy skit a couple of months back that was considered a deep affront to Ali Khamenei. Although he is supposed to be more amenable to American culture than was his predecessor, he supposedly really disliked how he was portrayed and scripted. Lots of hate mail to the network, show and producer. Apparently, some came from 'official' sources and went to the State Department as well—even the White House. People I talked to thought the abduction of the Trubo kid was retaliation for the humiliation the Iranian clergy felt," Meredith explained, grateful for Sonia's friendship with several of the cast members that resulted in the information.

"Seems almost frivolous," said Rick. "I don't doubt that it could be true, but you don't usually hear of this kind of major international dust-up made to slap back at an American comedy show."

"What do the feds say about it?"

"Officially, I've been told quietly that a meeting is set up between Trubo in D.C. on Thursday with the Iranian Ambassador and U.S. heavies."

"I assume to demand an apology…or…"

Rick shrugged. "Well, I'd hope that was it, but there'll be more asked, of course." He pulled a folder from his satchel on the floor and handed it to Meredith. "Purloined copies of the wire demands from…

"Purloined? By you?" Rick shook his head. "Never."

"I have more as well. Here's the official memo inside the network—also purloined but not by me—of the official position memo from Trubo to his crew and performers. Basically, talk to no one, say nothing." Meredith handed over a sheaf of papers.

"It's a start," murmured Rick. "If we have a long segment on Friday on the morning show, we'll have to fill it out. I'll go to work to get a sit down in Washington—with someone."

"And my next-door neighbor in Malibu is Trubo's brother. I talked to his wife this morning during a break and she has promised he'll call me tonight. He's in D.C. with Bill. But Trudy will make sure he calls—she's a good neighbor and friend, says she'll work to get Bill himself to talk with us or at least give a family statement. Hopefully we can get some inside perspective on what the boy is going through. Ditto the family. Trudy herself can paint a colorful picture."

"Wicked," said Santaros with a mischievous grin. "They told me about you—wicked and faster than a speeding bullet." Meredith smiled as the food arrived and was set in front of them. The rest of the conversation, amid enthusiastic food consumption, centered on logistics, and assignments. They agreed to meet again for coffee on Wednesday afternoon and regroup in light of the scheduled official political meeting on Thursday. "If we're reporting on Friday, we'll have to write on Thursday night and update first thing Friday morning. And we need some of these faces on camera." Meredith nodded, her focus already set to figure out the on-camera issues. Lunch ended. They left to tackle the rest of the afternoon.

When she returned to her room a while later, Meredith had a message from the priest not really admitting who the young street person was but inviting her to meet with them at a coffee shop in another part of town. She called back to confirm, then alerted Ito. The meet was set for three p.m. Wednesday afternoon.

At five she pulled on her navy blue travel sweats and went to the cramped workout room in the basement of the hotel. Longing for an aerobics studio or swimming pool, she made do with the weight machines and the treadmill. Not many guests using them at that time. Back in the room, she ordered room service and went to the shower. She mused that someone had said how enjoyable she might find six weeks in New York. Like a vacation. "Ha!" she laughed out loud.

CHAPTER 13
SEPTEMBER 13, 1989
NEW YORK
WEDNESDAY EARLY MORNING

Another million people...

At four forty-five a.m. Wednesday morning, Meredith slid into the studio-provided car en route to the network, facing another packed day. Through the morning processes, she set aside thoughts about the other major issues on which she was working. Always able to compartmentalize, she needed to focus on the here and now for live TV. As she stopped by her dressing room after the script meeting at eleven, a light rap on the door brought Rick Santaros into the room.

"Apologies but I can't make time this afternoon so I came by. Notes...," he handed a folder to her. "Nothing really heart-stopping, but some color from Jen Lipscom, the White House press secretary. Had a short but friendly call with her for a few minutes this morning. And I talked over coffee with the Chronicle's Middle East correspondent who says, Iranians gonna get 'tough'—hates *Saturday Night Laughs*—and wants it off the air. That's the quid pro quo. Lipscom says the admin is pretty sure they can calm the thing down. Two sides of the same coin. So. It's early yet and let's keep the pressure on."

"And I talked with Trubo's brother Mark last night—I'll fax notes to you," Meredith added, "Haven't written them legibly yet. I'm supposed to talk with Bill Trubo, himself, tonight. We'll see if he calls but, in any case, between Trudy and her husband Mark, we have some good all-around color. I talked with our producer for my L.A. show and she's agreed to work out camera time if we get Trubo—or anyone else from *Saturday Night Laughs*. Of course, she'll also run some footage of her own. What about the D.C. end of it?"

"Arranged through the news producer—if we have something. I'll let you know." Rick turned to leave giving a hurried thumbs up. "Talk later." And he was gone.

Amanda Borkin appeared suddenly leaning against the door frame. "Sparkin' with the big dogs," she laughed. Meredith waved dismissively. "Nice break," smiled the cohost. "You go, honey!" And she left.

☆☆☆

Meredith and Ito enjoyed a comfortable and familiar lunch together and exchanged personal updates. "No new special person?" she asked him. He only smiled mysteriously. "Nothing I'd talk about." But he said he loved his job, the pace in New York and the adventure— "Every time I step out of my apartment." Meredith understood, finding herself swept up in the energy and movement when she walked down a street.

"Still, I do miss the air of Los Angeles, the movie stars! The sense of optimism," said Ito. "Anything is possible there—I proved it." They both laughed. "And how do you like Malibu for a homeplace?" Meredith talked about the lifestyle change since she had moved the year before from her long-time refuge, a lovely verdant townhouse in Brentwood, several miles inland from the ocean. They'd closed the editorial offices in West Los Angeles as each member of the group moved to new duties. Meredith and Sonia now worked out of the Malibu house—the quintessential upscale Southern California beach life.

As they finished lunch and moved toward the door, Ito grabbed her arm. "I want to go with you to meet with the Reverend and the boy." Meredith vehemently shook her head. "No. I don't want to spook him with a stranger—if it is him."

"But you shouldn't go in alone. You know that. If T.K. Raymond has taught you anything it's to have back-up."

"This is just a sit down, Ito, with no future purpose. Not even certain it's the person I think it is. Really just something to quell my own curiosity. No story—yet. And no intentions. And with a priest."

"Okay, but I don't like it. What could go wrong?" he asked cynically.

"You just don't want to be left out of it!" She retorted. They both laughed, Meredith harder than Ito.

. . . − − − . . .

5:00 a.m.

Curled tightly against the bulkhead, her knit cap pulled around her ears and scarf wound tightly around her neck, Meredith felt left out of the real-time world. She attempted sleep—once again. From time to time she nodded off but inevitably a metallic creak or groan brought her attention back to reality. She now dismissed most of the sounds, but from time to time she swore she could hear whispers. And those unnerved her. Sometimes she imagined a giant wave crashing over the ship. And they set her mind to wondering how this predicament happened.

Was it truly happenstance? An oversight or case of poorly managed operations by the studio? How could someone not notice a press representative of her stature? And those questions made her wonder if she wasn't overly self-impressed. Maybe she—honestly—wasn't considered too noteworthy to be neglected. I'm being paranoid, she whimpered to herself. She wished she carried the heavy, bulky blasted bag phone, too much to tote around generally, and she kept hearing there were smaller more efficient models soon to come. She held out in hope. Meanwhile, she began to search her memory for whatever she knew about Morse code, tapping out what she could remember of the "help" signal. SOS, she told herself. Save Our Ship. Three quick knocks or flashes, three longer ones and then three short ones again.

She flipped on her small penlight and tried the sequence. But the light was so tiny, who would ever see it? And there was no traffic around the ships. But daylight was only a couple of hours away. Surely there would be waterside business—sailboats, fishing boats, military vessels. But could they see the light? Especially in the weather plaguing the entire scene. The skyway bridge so close and yet so far now boasted the soft hiss of increased daylight traffic, but no additional help in seeing Meredith.

She settled back against the wall and tried once more to rest, checking again to make sure her fellow camper was still lodged safely inside the popcorn bag. To convince him to stay put, she pinched off a tiny portion of the Snickers Bar and pushed it into the bag. Then mused that her long-time feline companion, Paco, would have his own thoughts about a rat within capture distance.

CHAPTER 15
SEPTEMBER 13, 1989
NEW YORK—ST. ALBAN'S SOUP KITCHEN, BROOKLYN
WEDNESDAY AFTERNOON

I remember you...

The general purpose room of the simple, unadorned St. Alban's outbuilding was, for Meredith, daunting in its largeness and emptiness. Without people gathering or working, it was an echoing abandoned shell with a clean but decades old black and white vinyl tile floor. But in one corner, seeming to huddle against a simple card table, was Father Paul Mercer and the street person Meredith had seen the week before. He looked up to acknowledge her presence. The short, ample woman, hair tied in a bandana, who escorted Meredith to the room, disappeared as though she'd never been there. Meredith squared her shoulders and walked across the empty hall to the seated twosome, her footsteps lightly echoing on the ancient tile.

"Father?" she acknowledged. He smiled and motioned to her to sit in an empty chair. As she did, she looked at the other inhabitant—her young street man. He kept his head bent, his eyes focusing on his hands. Red sneakers were visible at the end of long legs tucked under his chair.

"Hullo Miss Ogden," he spoke up almost a whisper.

"Ronnie."

"Ronnie has agreed to talk with you," the priest added. "But only with the condition that nothing gets written and discussed about him or this discussion outside of this room."

"Of course," Meredith affirmed. "That was the deal." She looked over at the young man who finally raised his eye to hers. "I just…wanted to…understand, Ronnie. How are you here? Now? Like this? The last time we met you were a confident, outgoing, bright kid and nothing but promise ahead of you." He nodded in agreement.

"Life happened," he said without rancor or drama. He handed Meredith a fat file folder. "Most of it's in here." She perfunctorily thumbed through the pages, newspaper clippings, other reports and accounts, death certificates. A decade of the detritus left behind from a series of tragedies.

"I know about some of this," she admitted, "but…from the top of the heap to basic…seclusion? Wasn't there another alternative? I know your parents died in a car accident on a rainy road. You were about to star in a new movie—two years after your series went off the air. Your grandmother became your guardian…and then? Nothing. No movie, no more teenage superstar Ronnie Milton."

Ronnie rubbed his hands together and stared at them, clearly uncomfortable. "So here're the Cliff Notes, Miss Ogden. But it's not all bad." He exuded a deep sigh, sat back and began his story. "My mother was an accountant—bookkeeper—with the Technical Trade Associates. Not really a union but a key consultant to a bunch of the film industry trade unions. My father was a member of one of them. Which one doesn't matter. Mother found some—discrepancies—in the association's books starting from before she came to the organization. Apparently a stream that continued into her time there. She dug in a little and discovered funds going into personal accounts of union management, bribes, pay back. I never really understood the particulars. She brought it to the attention of her bosses and well, it went up from there and somehow ended up—accidentally, she always said—with the FBI. Stuff happened and the head of one of the most powerful unions ended up indicted and through all kinds of negotiations went to jail. For a long time.

"Needless to say, my mother left her job—didn't really need to work by then. My income was…well, substantial. Dad was studying law—a dream of his. Then, the union boss in jail…well, he got caught in the midst of a prison fight and was killed. His son, Sonny Bota, a real brute of a guy, made it clear he'd get his 'familial revenge.' The police and feds hung around as protection for quite a while and finally decided the guy was blowin' steam and they had no justification to protect us." Ronnie stopped for a moment, held up his wrist showing a worn shiny leather wrist band fastened like a pet collar. "My dog Charlie disappeared one day and this collar was hung on our door knob. I believed Sonny's threats even if no one else did. I knew he'd stolen—or killed—Charlie." The young man took a drink of a soda sitting in front of him. Meredith was mesmerized—and saddened—by the recitation.

"Two weeks after I had signed on for the Western movie—supposedly my first teenage starring role—my parents died in the accident. That night, my grandmother took over. She was a tough old broad. And so smart. Street smart. I'd actually heard Sonny making the threat, on tape, from the FBI. She listened to it, quietly packed up both of us, hired an attorney to close out my family's and my 'affairs,' as she called them. It was all such chaos and sadness. I don't remember much of it, was in a complete emotional fog and was glad to get away from it. Official story was I'd had a 'breakdown.' Within a week I was in New Jersey with a revised name and 'some time off.' Eventually, I went to high school there in a small town outside Edison, New Jersey. I was under the radar, removed totally from Hollywood and anyone or anything I'd been involved with before. My grandmother died my senior year, just before I graduated. She had never stopped watching for Sonny, who we heard never gave up his threat of revenge. Once or twice we thought someone showed up in the area that might have been part of the old vendetta. But I felt certain the house was being watched about the time I was to graduate. I saw quick glimpses of the guy—the same one—a few times and felt like I was being followed. So, one night just before graduation, I put anything I cared about in my back pack, left in the middle of the night and arrived at Union Station here in New York shortly after and have been here since."

Meredith stared at the young man and flinched. "Wow. Ronnie. I'm so stunned by this story I'm almost speechless." The blue eyes and always sweet face of Ronnie Milton broke out in a wide grin. "I spent enough time with you Miss Ogden I can't even imagine you speechless." He laughed and so did she. The moment broke any barriers that might have existed between them.

"Don't you miss at least part of your old life? You were so...out there," Meredith said, trying to find words that captured his star presence from a decade earlier. "I mean you had loads of fans, and people supporting your work, of course—and I'm so sorry—loving parents but I'm sure a lot of loving friends as well. A very secure financial foundation. And anyway, you're a smart and enterprising young man. I remember you had actually written and directed a short film at age 10."

Ronnie shrugged. "I had a lot of folks fawning over me. Parents of course. Mostly because, as you say, I had a very secure financial base. But you know, Miss Ogden, I feel like you and I have had this conversation in part before. I'm basically a loner. I was caught up in a system that made the wheels go around for me. But I always felt overwhelmed."

"I do remember you telling me that, sitting on a small airplane, frightened about the flight."

"My fear of flying hasn't changed," he snorted, "but neither has some of the other stresses. And, as I mentioned, not all of what has happened is bad. I found some things I love. Working with kids. I help out with the services for the homeless. I live at the church."

"But the losses, Ronnie. How do you deal with them?" she shook her head. "Parents, grandmother and yes, even the lifestyle and friends. Not as rewarding as your current life but losses just the same."

"Some of it," he answered slowly with much thought, "has worked itself out, reconciled itself. Time. The rest, well, Father Paul really worked with me to understand and accept that." Meredith nodded quietly.

"How do you live, though? Are you paid, do you have friends and travel or go wherever you want?"

Ronnie laughed and the priest smiled. "I have all I need as a home at the church. My friends are…well, you saw some of them the other day…but they're steadfast and uncomplicated. And I'm out in the world a lot more than it may seem. My work is very fulfilling. And, money is never an issue." Meredith suddenly got it. The young boy was wealthy beyond every day needs from his years on a top-rated TV series—and residual income from the reruns still charming that—and a newer— generation of viewers. She smiled her understanding.

"And Sonny and his vendetta? Still dogging you?"

"We haven't seen any evidence of anyone recognizing or looking for me since I arrived here five years ago."

"I won't reveal your secrets, Ronnie. I just knew I knew the blue eyes and sweet face I saw on the street," Meredith murmured.

"It's a good story isn't it?" he smiled wistfully. "I imagine it must be frustrating to have that at your fingertips and not able to tell it." He stated the obvious because he knew the Hollywood scene so well. But there was no rancor or chiding in his voice. "I like to write now, myself—just stream of consciousness stuff, but I remember what a good story-teller you are. I even watch you some mornings while you're on that talk show. I wish I could let you tell the story. Maybe someday when we're sure it's safe and we can blank out the actual names and places. I really am happy and settled. This is my home now, me."

The amply-built woman with the bandana-held hair suddenly appeared as if from the air to announce, "your car is here father." The group stood up. Meredith couldn't help herself. She walked around the table and hugged Ronnie, who affectionately returned the embrace. "Thanks for remembering me," he said. "I have good memories of the times you spent with me on the set. And really of keeping me calm on that frigging small airplane!"

The Reverend Paul Mercer looked on paternally as the group turned to leave. Meredith handed them both a card bearing her local numbers, and smiled at the priest. "I know. You have Mass every day at eight, and several services on the weekends."

"Y'all come!" he invited.

CHAPTER 16
SEPTEMBER 13, 1989
GREEN PARK HOTEL, MANHATTAN
WEDNESDAY NIGHT

"…always there to remind me…"

"Miz Ogden…?"

Meredith did a fast turnaround to see the bulky figure of Buster standing behind her in the hotel lobby. "Again?" she whimpered. "What now?" She had spent the last half-hour in the business center drafting up the Trubo material, incorporating Rick's notes and also new information—quotes from the *Saturday Night Laughs* cast members.

"Sorry," said the portly man, his hands deep in his khaki pants pockets. "You need to know you were followed today. When you met with the priest."

She looked at him. "You mean by someone besides you? Why?"

"Just doing what the big guy asked, T.K. But you were followed by two folks. Not includin' me. So you should rethink what you're up to. Why would someone follow you?"

He got Meredith's attention. "I can't possibly be the reason for someone tracking the people I was meeting today. That just cannot happen." She fervently hoped she wasn't the link between Ronnie and the predators from long ago. But why, she wondered, would they connect her to the boy? And why now—after so long?

"Here's a Polaroid of the first guy on your trail." Buster pulled a wrinkled badly framed shot of Ito from his pocket. Meredith felt her stress level fall almost noticeably. "Oh my goodness. I told him not to follow me. But he's stubborn—and protective. He's not a threat, just a concerned colleague."

"Well then there's this one," offered Buster, bringing out another instant photo. This one was unfamiliar, a whip-thin heavily garbed figure with an overcoat, large round sunglasses and a knit cap pulled low and tight around the face and the coat collar up high hiding the features. "Couldn't get a full front and can't tell if it's a male or female. All I know is he or she is white. Recognize the face?"

Meredith shook her head. "No, no - but, crap! If I led anyone to the person I was meeting with it would have terrible consequences." Her heart pounded as she contemplated the disastrous possibilities for Ronnie.

"They weren't following your meet. They were following you. Followed you to the meet and back here afterward. Took off as soon as you entered the hotel."

"Took off to where?" she asked, startled by the realization.

"Cabbed to a Holiday Inn in midtown. I got someone on it there. Says the guy left the hotel immediately in an airport van. Didn't seem to be checked in."

"Why?" Meredith's mind searched every story, every situation in which she was involved. Nothing seemed important enough to merit anyone tracking her actions. She pulled Buster by the sleeve and guided him away from the lobby traffic. In the overhang of a large potted palm she turned to face him. "Not a word about this to anyone, hear me?" her voice was low and in command.

Buster continued to look at her without even a minor flinch. "Yes, ma'am. But there's a reason someone's tracking you. You gotta know that."

""But I don't know why. Nothing I'm doing is remotely covert or even interesting. It's all just in the everyday news."

"I don't know. The guy's apparently headed out of town. I'll let you know if I learn anything different, but in the meantime, I'd feel better if you were locked safely in your room for the night. May I walk you up there?" She hesitated then agreed. If Raymond knew and had enlisted the guy, she figured she'd trust him. He escorted her up the elevator and to her room. As soon as her key was in the door and it swung open to an empty suite, Buster flicked a finger salute and hurried down the hall.

☆☆☆

Meredith's call from Bill Trubo came in as promised while she ate her room service dinner. "I'll do whatever the legal beagles at State tell me," said Trubo. "Whatever is needed to get my son back but it's a nasty tightrope. The show's been on for a long time and has a strong reputation and loyal base. I probably won't again take on the High Ayatollah or whatever he'll be called next. But I can't gut the heart and soul of the show. And I doubt the network wants it gone, so…the feds are coaching me how to handle the conversation tomorrow. And I also know they don't 'negotiate with terrorists.' I'm not sure this situation fits into that, but I hope we find out. I'll sit down for your cameras. Rick Santaros has that set up. But it could be the biggest whitewash you've ever heard. I want my son released safely. I want everyone to understand that. If I cancel you guys at the last minute, so be it! Capisce?"

"Got it, Bill. I'd like to use a couple of your quotes about doing whatever is necessary. Okay with that?"

"Of course— that I want my son released safely." They said goodbye and Meredith assembled her materials. Cassie, her L.A. show producer, had already recorded Bill's brother Mark on camera with a carefully scripted plea for the safety of the boy who was innocently trying to research a thesis. But Bill's wife Trudy told Meredith, "Off the record, the kid is a spoiled brat and I wouldn't be surprised if he thought he COULD spy— for the fun of it." Meredith blanched at the comment.

She ran for thirty minutes on the lonely treadmill in the hotel basement, showered and phoned Raymond. Buster had called him and he knew about the person tailing Meredith.

"Just for your information, the person boarded a plane for LAX. Coming here."

"I don't get it, Raymond. Nothing I'm doing is covert enough for anyone to be sneaking around to learn about it."

"What about this Trubo interview?"

"It's all coming out in the major media anyhow. Doesn't need any secret espionage by me."

They puzzled the issue and then moved on. Meredith told him of her meeting with Ronnie Milton and the priest but reminded Raymond that it was completely confidential and off-the-record. "But could you possibly check on a name —Sonny Bota—son of the union guy who was indicted and jailed for embezzlement as a result of Ronnie's mother's discoveries."

"See, you do need me," joked the detective, slumped into the rattan sofa on the patio, comfortable in running shorts and a t-shirt, salt air and sand, shoes off. "Let me see what I can find. It's maybe the only way that I can get this big-time TV star to pay attention to me now."

Meredith could only laugh. "You have no competition, Raymond...."

...Happy to meet you...

Meredith moved erratically through her room at the Green Park, preparing herself for a full and pressured day on Friday. She felt somehow schizophrenic with her thoughts dashing between concern for the Trubo story, Ronnie Milton, Friday's *Good Day* and the upcoming house party in Montauk—The Hamptons. She was glad to have a single focus when her phone rang and Rick announced he was in the lobby and would meet her in the bar.

"It's good they had the intelligence meeting this morning," he said. "Unless something really unexpected happens tonight— and be prepared because it could and probably will—we're set for tomorrow's news segment. Scheduled now for the eight a.m. news slot. Ready?"

Meredith laughed. "Oh sure. Nice to report serious news like a serious reporter—not chuckling and chatting about it from a couch. And boy, it's different from writing it for the audience to read for themselves."

He plucked a stuffed olive from his martini and tossed it at her. She gasped in surprise as it landed in her lap, then giggled. It was the first time she'd allowed herself levity since she arrived in

New York. "Be yourself. Relax. You got this," Rick told her. "Even I'll admit, though, that making such a huge deal out of it for this morning show seems overkill," he shrugged. "Tim seemed adamant about making it 'a breaking news feature.'"

"By kick-starting it three days early? Couldn't this have been done by you and the other regular news department after the intelligence meeting today?"

"I think they wanted to find a way to bring you into the picture by making it an 'important' hard news feature."

"I made a few phone calls. Nothing earth shattering."

"Contacts and meeting deadlines," he smiled.

"Business as usual," Meredith retorted. "Don't misunderstand—who would give up an opportunity to share a story with the nation's most recognized foreign correspondent? But making this huge issue of it?"

"You're imagining too big a picture of this. I'm only involved because I happened to be in New York and putting me on the story makes it look like an even more exclusive expose. It's all network politics. All about the *Good Day* show. And its ratings—even before you arrived. "

"So, you're saying I'm a ratings magnet? Hard to imagine that?"

"I'm just guessing here, Meredith. But it seems to me they're looking for a new hook, something that will bring in new audiences, enliven the format. Forget about this conversation. Just enjoy the spotlight and do something totally silly for the weekend," he countered, changing the subject and focusing on his wine glass.

She explained that she would be at The Hamptons for the weekend as a guest of Cecil Longmore. He raised a dramatic eyebrow, then told her he, too, had received an invitation. "I may drive up for the day Saturday, but I have to be in D.C. on Monday and probably headed to Europe from there."

"I know nothing about The Hamptons. Including where it is. Should I dress for dinner?" Meredith exaggerated an elitist accent. Rick broke out laughing. "Well, I'd tell you to wear your beach clothes. But with Mrs. Longmore and some of the others, even beach casual is a parade and a competition." Meredith flinched. He said, "Just get to know some of the network community. You're a high-ticket item right now."

With a martini under her own belt she blew a quiet raspberry. "I'm going," she admitted, "because it's politic. But mostly because I'm desperate for some ocean air."

"A better reason," he said, finishing his drink and standing up. "See you tomorrow morning. And don't let them pull your hair so tight away from your face. You look a little trussed up sometimes," he said.

"Funny, that's how it feels," she responded. He shook his head and walked out of the bar. She smiled, relaxed. Laughter and jokes had been a long time in coming to her in New York.

Buster Boles in the shadows of the nearby hallway also noted the relaxed and happy smile on her face as she headed toward the elevator.

✭✭✭

"So, it's the big-time tomorrow," chuckled Raymond, the television flickering but muted in front of him in the living room. "Major news maven, side by side with NTS's hot shot political correspondent."

"Probably the first time since I came to New York that I actually got to be a real journalist and not a talking head sitting on a divan," snickered Meredith.

"But you look great on the divan every day."

"Big deal. I'm trying to figure out why it seems important—it shouldn't be."

"Well, there's the money, and the recognition."

"There's that," muttered Meredith, also a little concerned that the network TV show was edging into her own consciousness as something important.

"And there's always 'welcome home' ceremony in Malibu to look forward to. And only eight days away for the next visit!"

"Too many days and a lot can happen in those eight days here in NY. Nothing seems to flow in any kind of familiar way…a real test of flexibility."

"That which doesn't kill us only makes us stronger?"

"Belch!" she snorted.

"Speaking of happenings," he interjected, "we've been digging into the Bota case. You know the father died in prison years ago. Getting close on the kid—Sonny—chasing after any family members and where Sonny is located now. He's in the wind it seems. We may have found an elderly aunt but she's in a nursing home and we couldn't get in to see her until tomorrow. So—Film at 11, super star. We checked on the manifest from the LA flight yesterday but no Bota or any other suspicious name came up. We don't know who was on that plane after they followed you all day."

"Well, at least whoever it was is in L.A. now. After the broadcast tomorrow, I go to Montauk—The Hamptons. I'd rather come home but Rick Santaros today confirmed my own belief that I should go for political reasons. I just want to go for the ocean air! I miss it…I miss you, Raymond." Both were quiet for a moment. The TV in the Malibu living room flickered silently and the sounds of the street in Manhattan were muted by closed windows and air conditioning.

"Who all will be at the weekend?" Raymond finally broke the quiet, almost hesitantly.

"Don't know. Some will be in the car that picks me up tomorrow. We'll see. But you have a party Saturday as well, right?"

"Oh yeah. You know how outgoing I am without your sparkle in a crowd. But I know most of the folks who'll be at Bernie's barbeque and we have a new member of our 'special cases' team who Bernie has asked me to pick up and bring. So…someone to talk to."

"Eight days," reminded Meredith as they concluded the conversation.

"Not soon enough," Raymond affirmed, closing off.

CHAPTER 18
OCTOBER 12, 1989
SUISUN BAY GHOST FLEET
THURSDAY MORNING

Child's play?

5:30 a.m.

Meredith gazed over the bow railing at Suisun Bay, damp greyness swirling around her like a cloak. Not yet sunrise, the rain had finally given way to fog and overcast with diminishing winds. Somewhere she heard a distant foghorn and the muted hiss of early travelers across the distant bridge. Not quite two hours before sunup and, she hoped, more activity in the bay. Contemplating how to proceed in her determination to escape from the rust bucket once the sound of live boats became evident, she identified two important tools: a tiny penlight and a long, soiled scrap of red fabric.

She toyed with the light's small on/off switch, figuring it could only be seen in the dimmest sky. The red rag would be the better advantage once daylight arrived. Two realities emerged: she had to be close to the water where vessels passed by, and the timing mattered—with the penlight before full dawn, and with the long fabric after. Trepidation stalled her determination, remembering the swaying gangplank from the top deck to the waterline below. Yet, thoughts of the ship's noisy but unseen inhabitants in the depths of the hull bolstered her determination and she began to rehearse SOS tactics. First, maneuvering a staccato on/off beam from the penlight to mark—three short bursts, three long bursts and three more short bursts. I wonder if the batteries will last longer than a few attempts, she thought to herself.

Standing in the soft glow of the safety lights above the ship's top deck, she snapped the red rag attempting to strike SOS Morse code bursts, but she ended up laughing at herself. No way would anyone decipher the flapping fabric as any kind of code. She reached for the soda bottle, only a couple of inches worth of liquid remaining, and took a tiny sip. She saw a slight quiver in the popcorn bag and felt a small sense of comfort knowing again that she still had company.

She worked with the red fabric looking for ways to make it useful. Some repelled her—waving it around and yelling "Yoo hoo!" So, she rehearsed swirling in alphabetical forms—SOS— only backward so anyone looking toward her would see the correct message. She laughed heartily understanding it was the best she could conjure, feeling like a nursery school kid in craft class.

☆☆☆

Malibu Beach
5:30 a.m.

The beach breeze in Malibu was crisp and exhilarating for Raymond as he jogged down the sand, the sun not yet hinting of its arrival. He often used his runs as meditation—not particularly formal, but an airing out of the issues tucked inside or put aside that needed attention. This morning, his full focus was on Meredith and her mysterious whereabouts. The sand flicking under his feet, the soothing tumult of the surf and the soft calls of the seagulls created the cadence he needed to organize the steps he would take in his own search now that the day was awakening along with the access to resources and people.

Breathing heavily and wiping the sweat from his face with his sleeve, he mounted the steps to the house and went directly to the phone. His first call was to his own colleague, Marty Escobar. He barked instructions at the younger man, only coming out of a sound sleep, himself. "Find out the law enforcement agency in the area—sheriff, highway patrol—I don't care. Whoever has jurisdiction and knowledge of the Bay. Give them the situation and how to reach us. Tell them to consider it a missing person case. That's what we're calling it here in L.A." Marty scrambled, understanding well the weight of the drama unfolding and its importance to his colleague. He'd been on the front lines of it from the start of the relationship, knew its intensity.

For Raymond, his thoughts returned to the heightened moment of realization with Meredith. "What do you have in mind?" he asked her the first night of their liaison. Her answer was, "Everything." Now, "everything" pretty much wrapped up their life together.

Raymond took a deep breath and called a friend/colleague in the Coast Guard, at home, and stationed in Long Beach. A long way from Suisun Bay but he needed a landing point. All the military services structures were complex with far flung webs. He needed to know who to contact in the direct vicinity, someone who could do something helpful.

Breaking news

The shrill ring of the phone brought Meredith up from her deep sleep and as she felt for the phone, she saw the time was two-thirty a.m. She mumbled a "Hello."

"Well, the best laid plans…," came a familiar voice but she had to shake her head to focus and realize who it was.

"Rick, what? What's happening?"

"The Trubo boy is suddenly off the grid, totally. The Iranians aren't saying where he is. The feds are totally closed-mouthed. They say they have no information on his location now, or if he's been taken."

"And this just after yesterday's supposedly successful start of negotiation?"

"Yeah, well. No surprise."

Meredith turned on the bedside lamp, swung her legs from the bed and sat up. "Let me think," she gulped, rubbing her eyes. "I have Bill's private number in D.C. I can see if I can reach him and if he will at least give me info or even a quote. I know I can't get him in front of a camera this morning. If that doesn't work, I'll call his brother Mark and Trudy and see what they can add."

"You got a tape recorder?"

"Of course," said Meredith, pulling herself to her feet, looking impatiently toward the shower.

"Sending a car for you in thirty minutes."

"Good thing they have hair and make-up people waiting," snapped Meredith as she dropped the phone in the cradle.

Forty-five minutes later she and Rick huddled over the news desk, flipping through their notes, updating and reorganizing their script. "Aside from his profanity," sniggered Rick, "You got a good interview with Trubo. Surprised he took the call and is letting you use it."

"His vocal permission is on the tape," Meredith added. "There's nothing really compromising in what he says—it's a complex situation." Rick shrugged.

Coiffed and powdered, Meredith rode on-air conversational shotgun on the couch with Amanda when the morning program began. The tousled golden-red-haired cohost seemed unusually distanced from Meredith, almost disinterested in what the producer considered the "big story." At five minutes before eight, Meredith walked across the massive studio from the homey talk-set to the news area. There, she joined Rick and the regular news anchor already behind the desk in front of a large mural of the universe. A small earpiece was affixed behind her hair on one side of her head.

Commercials concluded, the cameras were focused on the three. Morning headlines wrapped up by the anchor, he introduced both reporters—Santaros with his title of NTS Political Correspondent, Meredith as "award winning celebrity journalist." They unfolded the story. Midway through the news presentation—as Santaros was presenting the official information and perspective after Meredith's explanation of the personal background and context, she suddenly heard an unexpected voice through her earpiece. Mrs. Trubo from Malibu wanted her to know the family had received word the boy was on his way home.

Meredith jotted down a note and slid it over to Rick. He continued talking to the camera but scribbled for her to continue on with the next segment. She did and with the camera focused on her, Rick quickly exited his seat to make a quiet call. The assistant gave Meredith an off-camera motion to stretch her recitation. Off script and embellishing a usually concise narrative with more color about the *Saturday Night Laughs* program, history and cast, Meredith felt the electric charge of the challenge.

With a light tap on her elbow, Rick returned. Concluding her comments, she announced, "And Rick, you have breaking information about this situation."

He picked up the dialogue with a vague statement about an unconfirmed report that the young hostage had been released and was on his way home, then asked Meredith what she knew. She could confirm that the family had received the same information. They concluded with the assurance of updates as the story unfolded.

As the action swung back to the regular anchor, Meredith and Rick quietly exited the set. He gave her a finger salute as she returned to the talk show sofa where the rest of the morning program would continue. Toward the end of the show, during the last commercial, Meredith was again handed a note which she acknowledged when the cameras were on her again. "A spokesman for the State Department has confirmed that the son of the *Saturday Laughs* producer is, indeed, en route back to the U.S. NTS News will have updates as they are available," she announced. Amanda sat stony-faced through the announcement, pulling off her earpiece and tossing her head dismissively and leaving immediately when the cameras went dark. As Meredith exited the set, she caught sight of Rick, talking with a colleague down the hall. He called out, "Good show, Meredith," then winked at her.

"Back at'cha," she smiled, then hurried from the studio to her dressing room to decompress before the soon-to-begin planning meeting for Monday.

It's the weekend

Precisely at four, NTS News President Longmore's hired car arrived to pick up Meredith. Already settled into the comfortable limousine interior were the Producer of the *NTS Evening News* Murray Detmier, his wife Valerie, and Sal Minao, Technical Director for the *It's a Good Day* show who was joining his wife already at their seasonal hideaway in Montauk. Meredith wondered how and why she had been included in this gathering. She barely knew anyone except for Minao who worked on her show, and *A Good Day* producer Tim. Except for herself, Meredith quickly assessed, all other invitees were couples.

"You'll love The Hamptons this time of the year. We're all there to take advantage of the last bit of summer and welcome early fall," cooed Valerie Detmier.

"And let off some steam with some great scotch," added her husband. Valerie threw an icy glance at him. "You'll get a chance to meet some of the rest of the crew. Your producer Tim and his wife will be joining us, and tomorrow night Cece and Billie, his wife, will be hosting a barbeque get together for anyone left in the area from NTS News. You'll get a chance to see everyone at their most…relaxed." Valerie glanced at him again.

Meredith felt on-parade for the perusal of the riders. Questions about her background and work were put forward. She answered politely but perfunctorily. Her friend Gloria's words echoed back: "Be one of them." She'd only had four hours sleep and a full day of work. What she most wanted was some rest. Fortunately, the group convened at a restaurant in Montauk for dinner, casual and unpressured. She met the other house guests who had also spent a full day at work so the conversation was light-hearted. Her hosts, the Longmores, had shown her to the guest suite where she would stay, and she begged off a night cap in favor of going to sleep.

Early the next morning, awakened by the sound and smell of the ocean, she rose before most of the other guests. She'd not really appreciated the property and its location in the dark the night before. So, pulling on sweatpants, t-shirt and jacket she quietly found the door to the beach. The house was enormous. It reminded her of the small inns along the Monterey Coast. Three stories, distressed wood—crafted to perfection—sitting almost sideways on the lot so that both the front and the back verandas had ocean exposure.

Walking for about an hour she inhaled the salt air and unique fragrances of beach plants and wildlife. She smiled at the sight of several small birds feeding along the foliage, and sea birds she didn't recognize on the sand. She was sure the wingspan of the silhouette soaring above her was that of a hawk. As different as the sensory delights were from her own California ocean life, she found herself homesick. A lot of change very fast, she told herself, but could feel herself already adapting to the dramatic culture shift. The promise of it all was heady and the realization surprised her. She'd had no thought of relishing the New York experience.

Most of the guests had already passed through the breakfast smorgasbord as Meredith came in from her walk. Only Billie Longmore, wife of Cecil— "Cece" —the legendary President of NTS News lingered at the food counter. Billie was easily in her 70s. Her sparkling silver hair was pulled into a casual, almost frivolous, pony tail. She wore little makeup that morning and over dungarees and a flannel shirt was a large apron that read, "Yes I did." She smiled at the younger writer and handed her a cup of coffee. "I'll bet you could use this. Cece told me about your day yesterday. Congratulations, though. I always feel we're lucky just to get through one of those without major glitches."

Meredith murmured a humbled "Thanks but a lot of the strength of our story was Rick's. I was glad to offer the 'Hollywood angle.'"

"Good heavens," crowed Billie. "The Hollywood angle is half the world these days. What a great position you have and Rick wouldn't have had a good story without your portion of it."

"He was kind," chuckled Meredith. "I've watched him reporting from some of the most troubled spots of the world. He'd have had his story wherever he was and truthfully? It was a little intimidating working next to him."

"Well, don't let him kid you," Billie said, sitting down across the broad dining room table from Meredith. "All these globe-trotting cowboys are just running away from themselves." She chuckled and Meredith was reminded that Billie had been a pioneer field correspondent for various news organizations years before. Certainly long before women had entered the field as solidly as they were doing it now.

"Running away is easy to do in the news field, isn't it?" Meredith opined. "My significant other warns me against running off in pursuit of some incident that seems interesting but might not even be a story. Totally diverting my time and energy!"

"It's what we do. How we live," said Billie with a warm, earthy laugh and Meredith knew she liked—and trusted the woman.

"How about I show you some of the sights today. We'll have lunch in town. Most of the other guests have plans of their own until Cece's barbeque tonight. That is—if you have the time and the inclination to spend the day with an old tour guide." Meredith heartily agreed, suddenly the questions about how to gauge the weekend disappeared. She accepted some scrambled eggs and toast and as the two were picking up their dishes, Rick Santaros walked into the room.

"Hi Billie. Meredith. Can a guy get a cup of coffee and something to chew on."

"Rick! So glad you came. You know the drills," said Billie, waving her hand toward the kitchen.

"You also have an extra bunk for me, Billie? I hadn't planned to spend the night but knowing Cece's barbeques, I won't want to drive back to Manhattan after. A couch will do."

The older woman smiled affably. "We always have an extra berth for you Rick. Take the atrium. Bath's down the hall and it's a pull-out couch, but it's comfy and you'll hear the surf and have your own entrance." With that the two women left to gather themselves for the day. Rick Santaros grabbed a bagel, spread some cream cheese on it and sat down to read the paper.

"I take it you haven't been out to The Hamptons before," said Billie as she and Meredith pulled from the drive of the Longmore's house.

Meredith shook her head. "I've worked a lot in New York—as support to what I do from Los Angeles. Meetings with my media syndicate, covering stories. But aside from the three-day visitor pass in Manhattan, I don't know Montauk from Montana." Billie laughed heartily.

"Don't let it overwhelm you. I'm glad I have the chance to spend some time with you. I'm afraid the rest of them would probe you to death. A young, beautiful, smart and accomplished woman in their midst. And one mired in the real world of celebrity. My God, bring your umbrella! Don't let them rain on your parade—or try to take it over."

Meredith scowled, puzzled. "How would they do that? And why?"

"Because that's the media business here in New York and there'd be little guilt about co-opting what—to them—is a possible charismatic resource that they'd like to own and control. Why do you think you're here?"

"A good question. I don't really know. Russ Talbot at UAM recommended I do it, but once I got here, it seemed impolitic to ask any more about it," answered Meredith.

"It was probably 'good politics' to accept that invitation as well. And it was. But enjoy the attention and make the most of it. Don't lose sight of yourself in it though."

"I'm a temporary substitute for Nancy Igleton and in two more weeks I'll be heading back to Southern California, focusing again on movie stars," Meredith laughed robustly.

"We're all just simple kids from…somewhere," Billie said with a chuckle, "some of us caught a brass ring and put on better clothes and big airs and became 'New Yorkers.' I know your background, and you hold your own—but don't forget to do it among these hounds. "

"The whole New York gig is a little enigmatic," Meredith admitted. "Including that I ended up doing this morning show when there are several dozen TV faces right here, more recognized. And then an invitation to a high-profile, private party in The Hamptons. Of course, I'm flattered, appreciative and wouldn't miss it for the world. Yet…curious."

"Meredith, they'll test you—tempt you—with the idea of bringing in a new member of the network news team. They don't even know how that would look if it happened. It's their way. Choose how you want to be part of it—or not—and stick to it. I'm sure you're used to it, but they can be sharks."

"Interesting—and thanks for the insight, Billie," Meredith said as her host pulled into a parking place at a block of shops. The day progressed through lunch and myriad conversations with the older woman about career, history, relationships—new friendship bound for longer term.

Yet, an errant thought lurked in the back of Meredith's mind…be careful. I haven't seen the full dimensional view of this whole escapade yet. And I'm surprised the whole experience is a little seductive considering the ego stroking—and the money.

Can't we just be friends?

He spat out a string of expletives, realizing how chaotic life was without Meredith in the house. He rummaged through his closet trying to decide what clothes would be appropriate for a "casual" barbeque at his boss's house. Most of his "special profile cop colleagues were located remotely from the usual police department facilities—and their oversight and activities. Beer after work at a local sports bar was the usual and sum-total of socialization. Their boss, Bernie Bristow, earlier in the year, had moved his personal residence from downtown L.A. to Playa Del Rey on the coast. He also spent a lot of time in the office Raymond managed. Bernie liked the west side.

For Raymond, who was used to very high-profile social events with Meredith—star-studded red-carpet affairs—shifting his recreational focus to his own back yard was unnerving. The Hollywood spotlight always seemed safe because it was always for show and Meredith's focus. He was the quiet arm piece who went to amazing events without having to perform or reveal any of himself. How quickly things had changed for the fifty-one-year-old detective-turned-unit boss. Was it only four or five years ago he was a loner, living in his small beach cottage, a widower with a son long-gone to academic pursuits and a quiet social life with occasional but rare "dates"? His crime investigation work was his total focus…until the wily gossip reporter barged into his life through the high-profile murder of her boss. And the rest was…well, history, he mused. And life changing.

So, Bernie's barbeque was a challenge. Overly exposed—naked, he thought. I'll feel naked. In an empty house and coming up—at a party of my own peers.

Especially since the boss had asked Raymond to provide a ride to the festivities for a unit newcomer who arrived only two days before and was still figuring out the terrain.

The newcomer was a specialist in corporate crime/forensic accounting and Bernie explained actually worked for Major Crimes, but would reside in Raymond's unit, live by its schedules and rules, and in most respects, not work *for* Raymond, but rather, *with* him. Still, this was a valuable addition to the concert of "high profile" investigative specialists in the team. Until she walked into the office on Friday.

Enter Margo Flaherty!! A jarring reality for Raymond who had neglected to ask Bernie who was joining the office. With numerous weighty cases filling the days, Raymond hadn't inquired further until the tall, willowy red head walked into his office a day earlier, with her customary subtle sashay, and shocked him into instant backpedal.

"City boy!" she greeted, reprising a label she'd given him in the heat of a shoot out on a remote New Mexico movie location eighteen months before. Then an FBI team leader of a corporate drug trafficking investigation, she was part of a federal case to which he was loaned to determine if he was a fitting—or willing—potential member of an elite FBI unit. The Los Angeles Police Department had bigger plans for him and the FBI link-up never happened. Margo with her team retreated into their own usual cocoon, long gone from the glare of the movieland spotlights.

But the history was longer than the New Mexico dust-up. Margo and Raymond were classmates in a law enforcement training class some years before. Raymond's wife Lilly only a short time before had died from breast cancer. Margo was the super-smart, ingenue—flamboyant in style and tongue and intimidating to most of her peers. The class days were long and complex in St. Louis, a town foreign to both. At an impromptu pizza and beer-joint party, jazz thumping in the background, Raymond sat distanced from the social center, absorbed in his own issues. That reticence intrigued Margo and she soon found herself sharing a beer and the outskirts of the garrulous crowd with him. The combination of loneliness, study pressure, fascination and the plain pleasure of collaboration created a mutual three-day cocoon. Raymond considered it an educational, distracting, three days in a foreign town with a pleasant collaborator, concluding when the plane took off for home. Margo considered the quiet, focused, smart and sensual man—with an obvious success path ahead—more than an out-of-town wonder. It took several months of subtle repudiation, excuses and rebuffs to end the velvet blitz by Margo. All from coast to coast. They finally agreed that it was a fun rendezvous and finished. "I get it, T.K.," she finally gave in.

Several years later Raymond reported to an FBI safe house in the San Fernando Valley to start the investigative work on the drug case and Margo Flaherty greeted him at the door. Team leader. All business. Except when she wasn't and then she was just the least bit flirtatious. But not threatening. She saved his life in New Mexico then headed out to her own turf. He to his. One time she was included in a strategy meeting about the case, which, ironically, Meredith and her news partner Cassie

O'Connell attended with vital evidence. The environment in the room was charged because, as one of Raymond's colleagues commented, "Women seem to sense predators."

So the super-charged red head would now be working in his office and he'd be escorting her to a party. The only way it could get worse was when he told Meredith how his Saturday was unfolding. And he surely would tell her.

Ah, Saturday night…

Meredith worked the room as she would any VIP social event, spending time and bantering with each of the 17 dinner guests. Some she already had met; others were new to her. She sat down to dinner with the *Good Day* producer Tim Felton and his wife Dani and relished perfectly seared fish with fresh grilled corn on the cob, a lush green salad and fluffy homemade rolls. Alone with Dani, Meredith forked a bite of cheesecake and commented how organized and streamlined the show's production process seemed. Dani took a deep drag on her beer and snorted. "Well, Amanda doesn't make it easy with Nancy gone."

"Losing a valuable partner leaves a pretty big hole. It takes time to adjust," Meredith suggested. The show seemed, to her, like a cohesively tuned mechanism with established roles well played. Now, she wondered.

Dani shrugged and shook her head. "Nancy's the real go-between from the couch ladies and the production team." Meredith choked back a laugh at "couch ladies"—the description of the two co-hosts that would probably have them both firing their well-honed news vocabularies like semi-automatic rifles. "Without her...," Dani went on, "well, Tim's life is constantly challenged."

"I didn't notice discord going on. Things seem to be on an even keel," Meredith answered working to neutralize the conversation.

Dani started to laugh. "The after-work phone calls Tim's getting from Amada. Nancy used to mediate that kind of thing before it got as far as the producers."

"What kinds of things," Meredith probed, curious.

"Just stupid insecure stuff. One time she raised holy hell because the producers hired a new wardrobe person. Amanda didn't like her, said she spent too much time working with the weather girl—who was pregnant at the time and actually needed extra help with how she dressed."

Meredith thought about Dani's role as producer's wife, the backstop when the talent—or anyone else on the show—wanted to vent. Part of the job for Tim. But Dani went on. "She was angry about the special segment you got with Santaros. Big time news handed to the sub, the California sunshine kid. And video even repeated on the network's evening news. Like Tim had anything to do with that."

"Who did?" asked Meredith.

"Tim's boss—Detmier. Tim says he was adamant, so...."

Meredith shrugged. "Well, I'll be heading home in a couple of weeks and Nancy will be back to being the peacemaker." Dani took a long chug from her beer and added "Let's hope."

Diplomatically excusing herself to score another white wine, Meredith wanted to find less thorny conversation. Company gossip was a rabbit hole she preferred to avoid. Rick Santaros had arrived with some attention from the group. Meredith made her way quietly to where Billie was pouring a drink. She offered the open bourbon bottle to Meredith who shook her head and pointed at the wine carafe. "Was Amanda invited this weekend?" she asked, pouring a glass.

Billie nodded. "Oh sure, but she had other plans. She isn't very social away from the workplace." Meredith nodded and lifted the wine to her lips. Looking quickly around at the roomful of new people in her life and feeling claustrophobic.

"Going out for some ocean air," she said as she turned and slipped down the hall toward the terrace on the other side of the house. The elegantly restored wood in the moldings and door frames caught her attention as she passed along the corridors. The entire house had been initially designed and then obviously restored to the genial atmosphere of an earlier time. An etched glass door opened easily and welcomed Meredith to the soft patter of the surf and the gentle darkness of night. She walked across the wide veranda and down the few steps to the sand. There, she opened her arms, tilted her head back and took a deep breath. Lowering herself down on a step, elbows on her knees, wine glass in hand, she breathed in the chilled salty air.

"Pretty nice, isn't it?" a gruff voice shocked her out of meditation. The wooden step bounced as a heavy-set man sat down next to her. She recognized him from the party—not sure of his title but a mover and shaker from the network news department. She also recognized the sour odor of booze—lots of it, seeming to emanate from every part of him—more than the night breeze could blow away.

"Ocean air is always refreshing," she answered.

"Nice addition to the couch team," he said.

Puzzled, she asked, "What do you mean?"

"You," he said, and she heard the whiskey slur. "Perky. Good kick in the ass for the two vipers." Meredith felt him slouch closer to her and she quickly began calculating a politic exit. But he beat her to the draw and tossed a clumsy, heavy arm around her shoulders. "We need new blood, show's getting tired but for sure you're not!"

Meredith jerked upright, looking toward the house, but the thick body blocked her way, so she started toward the water. Rising from the step, he stumbled after her. "Hey, no offense— just some friendly camaraderie…"

"Thanks for the compliments," she said, stepping sideways, feigning cordiality, "but I'm going back inside now."

"Don't rush off," he said, thick-tongued. "It's a beautiful night—too beautiful not to be friendly!" His meaty arms encircled her waist, turning her roughly face-to-face as she struggled to free herself. "Get to know your colleagues," he murmured. Her self-defense training taken after New Mexico came to mind. She drew both arms back and exploded them in one giant push into his chest. He groaned, stumbled backward, swearing, "Damn, no need for that, honey," he spat. "I'm someone who can help you!" She twisted angrily, headed to the steps, but he grabbed and caught her jacket. "And I can hurt you, too!" She spun toward him, her fist clenched tightly, swung her arm back ready to burst it into his face, knowing it would end the contest.

"Stop, Meredith," came a quiet whisper. "Don't do it." She turned quickly, fending off the large figure whose hands continued to clench at her jacket. Rick Santaros came out of the darkness. "It's not worth it to you or him," he quietly commanded. He firmly pulled her away, then equally as firmly grasped the older man by the shoulders and spoke to him. "Hy! Hy, let's call it a night, what d'you say?" He turned Hy toward the house and urged him up the steps to the veranda, there, gently pushing him into a padded lounge chair. The large man slumped back, breathing heavily, never muttering a word. "Just lie there for a while buddy. Take a nap," Rick said.

Agitated, Meredith trailed up the steps and stood in the doorway. "He won't remember this tomorrow," Rick said to her. "He never does. He's a drunk outside the studio. But he's a giant at his desk and soon to retire. And you don't want the gossip or the notoriety, either. Let's leave it alone. No harm, no foul." She only shook her head, trying to shake off the adrenalin as she turned back into the house. Adjusting her denim jacket, she walked slowly down the hallways, sorting out anger, shock, confusion and what to do next. Indecision alone propelled her into the large living room throbbing with conversation and music.

Refilling her wine glass, she took a deep breath and regarded the social melee surrounding her. A sleep-inducing discussion about network employee policies was making her cringe as Rick arrived silently at her elbow. He jovially pulled her away from the throng and said simply, "If you're feeling like you need to escape this jungle dance early, I'm out of here tomorrow morning—back to the city. I'll be in the dining room at ten, ready to leave. You're welcome to ride with me instead of waiting until the four o'clock limo—if you want." Anger still broiling her over the patio encounter, Meredith started to mention it, but Rick only shook his head. "Not here, not now," he murmured and turned away.

Reverting to her automatic social demeanor, Meredith moved through the group, smiling, adding a comment and lightly interjecting herself into the group. She gracefully wended her way to Billie, leaning against the archway into the room. "Time to fold my tent for the night," Meredith said congenially. "Nice party, thanks for including me."

Billie regarded her closely. "You okay?"

Meredith nodded, smiled and said. "I am. But tired."

"Sleep well—Cece has arranged a sailing adventure for the day before everyone heads home."

"Sounds great," Meredith responded. "See you in the morning." She moved to the stairwell to the second level and her bedroom suite, mounting the steps while tamping down her roller coaster anger and frustration. Rick's voice kept returning, "not here, not now." The words repeated themselves even in her sleep.

CHAPTER 23
OCTOBER 12, 1989
SUISUN BAY, GHOST FLEET
THURSDAY MORNING

...Comes the sun

6:30 a.m.

Meredith's eyes snapped open to the sounds of activity. Restless sleep had finally overtaken her before daybreak. She pulled herself from the slump against the bulkhead, rose creakily to her feet, propelling herself anxiously to the ship's railing. The light of dawn had not yet arrived in full, but was eminent and although the rain had stopped, the fog was only starting to lift.

And one of her emergency SOS tools—use of her pen light for Morse code—needed a dark sky and someone to notice. Timing was everything. Pulling her jacket tighter, she reached for the light and rushed to the ship railing that faced the open bay. Boat traffic was still scarce—a shadowed outline too far away, the whine of an unseen high-pitched engine approached then diminished. Determined, she flicked the SOS Morse code over and over until the early morning light blotted away the message. Disappointed, she pocketed the light and slogged back to her midship encampment.

That was stupid, she chided herself. A tiny penlight—Morse code? Stupid! Kindergarten reasoning. Digging into her tote, she pulled out the inch-thick remnant of the Snickers bar and broke off a small nibble. The rustle of the popcorn sack interrupted the silent symphony of self-pity and she nipped off a crumb, shoving it into the bag. Someone else needs a treat this morning! She thought.

The length of red rag lay curled next to her bag. I guess that's the next option, she grimaced, losing some hope with the failure of the Morse code beam. The morning light continually brightening, the fog lifting gradually, she packed up her few belongings into her tote, picked up the red flag (we'll call it a rescue flag, she told herself), and trotted confidently to the deck entrance of the gangplank leading down to the bay. Pausing at the top, she studied the ramp, narrow and quivering slightly. She could work her way to the bottom, the water, and be closer to any passers-by. She could stay above on the ship railing, waving her flag and hope it could be seen. She troubled a variety of other options including swimming across the narrow bay.

A compromise took her a short distance down the ramp from the top, her tote settled arm's reach above, the plan being a quick scramble back to the safety of the deck should wind, rain or failure happen. With a deep and dejected breath, she began the choreography with the fabric—swooshing SOS over and over, first with her right arm, then her left. She could see more of the bay with the fog lifting, but the sight—and lack of notice— only depressed her more. The hours, though short, seemed long. Hope, not very.

Arms sore and tired, she sat back and stopped the dance, defeated and grappling for a new strategy. The thought of spending another night on the groaning hulk, creaks and whispers wafting from the inner corridors, was unacceptable. I can't fathom it and won't do it, she said out loud to herself. But there was a full day ahead and something would change. An optimist always, she just had to figure out how to make it happen.

And at that moment, a large graceful sailboat came into her view, heading toward the ship. Sails down, it was under power and definitely aimed her way. It came about quickly, then bobbed parallel with the ship's side and the gangplank, but still several yards away.

"You alright up there?" a male voice called out, and a large man swathed in weather gear appeared at the rail of the sailboat.

"No, I can't get off. I'm stranded. HELP!" she shouted, waving.

"Say again—you need help?"

"YES," she shouted. "HELP!"

"Can't get any closer, myself, sorry, but sending out a call for help!"

"PLEASE," she shouted. "NOW!"

She saw the skipper lean out over the water and she sensed— more than saw—him giving her thumbs up. Then the engine surged and the boat took off. Meredith felt tears streaming down her face. Rescue? Maybe? She didn't trust her own sense of confidence. Slumping down, she allowed herself to relax before feeling compelled to begin the red flag dance again, the feeling of anger and blame toward the studio again bursting forth.

CHAPTER 24
SEPTEMBER 12, 1989
MALIBU, CALIFORNIA
THURSDAY MORNING

Who's in charge here?

8:30 a.m.

Sonia clinched the phone between her head and shoulder and held up a cautionary forefinger to T.K. Raymond. He was pacing in front of the desk Sonia intensely occupied—Meredith's desk in the oceanfront home he shared with the absent Hollywood columnist. High anxiety charged the room and he ground his fist into the palm of his other hand, staring out the panoramic window at the endless sea outside. His face handsome but creased with trouble and worry. His dark hair, lightly sprinkled with silver, had not yet seen a comb that morning.

Calls sent out from his office to law enforcement agencies in the Suisun Bay area, and his appeal to his Coast Guard buddy put some wheels in motion but delivered no information yet.

"So, Terry," Sonia spoke up, her words hard and accusing, "This august group of important and apparently smart people, just didn't notice that one of the most prominent members of the press in the industry wasn't on the boat going back to shore? Or even more absurd, not at the airport! That she'd just disappeared and no one noticed it or tried to find her? Or was there something more sinister afoot—did she fall over the side from the fo'c'sle?"

A rare moment of amusement. Raymond wondered how Sonia knew what or where a fo'c'sle was on a ship. He heard the studio publicist's whimpering response filtering through the speaker, "We don't know. We're contacting everyone who was there and asking questions. We'll find her. We will. We'll get to the bottom of this!"

"Call me every 15 minutes, Terry! Give me an update," Sonia directed, a rare and surprising commanding tone of voice for the usually courteous right hand/assistant to Meredith Ogden. She slammed down the receiver into the phone cradle. "Assholes!"

Raymond checked the time on Meredith's small desk clock and walked quickly into the living room to pick up the house phone. Moments later he leaned into the office and announced, "I'm going to shower and clean up. I've set up a command performance with Stan Smallet, the studio's VP of Marketing, at 10:30. We'll get to the bottom of this clusterfuck! Do you want to be there?"

Sonia thought for a minute then shook her head. "I think someone should be here in case we hear from Meredith." She cleared her throat and smiled wryly. "I think you can handle an interrogation, Detective Raymond." He bounded up the stairs to the second level to change clothes.

Choose your battles

"I never said you couldn't handle yourself," Rick Santaros argued firmly. "I was just warning you that the battle you were about to—handle—wasn't the right battle."

Meredith waved a shrimp-speared fork, smirked and commented, "I have to wonder what kind of battle is appropriate if not being assaulted by a power-hungry drunk!"

The muffled clatter of the cozy New York neighborhood restaurant-bar surrounded them as they closed out the morning's journey from Montauk to Manhattan. Rick suggested they grab lunch before he dropped off Meredith at her hotel. Earlier that morning, she had opted not to join the NTS group on a boating excursion but instead accepted a morning ride back to Manhattan with the TV correspondent. The thought of spending time with "Hy"—Hiram Bushman—the beach predator, convinced her to avoid further engagement with the rest of the guests. Rick's words from that night about provoking Hiram echoed in her memory: "Not now, not here."

"'I'm having a hard time sorting this all out," she told Rick in the car. It had been a troublesome, sleepless night for her.

With the passage of twelve hours, her fury had eased but her annoyance was deeply seeded into her psyche. "No one has the right to mistreat a female colleague by sexually harassing her— just because he's powerful and can do it—has done it— I assume, without penalty before!"

"I understand, Meredith. I do," Rick had reasoned along the way in the car. "Remember, I'm not part of this tribe. These groups are like small villages. They fight and bicker among themselves but an outsider who takes on one of the village idiots might well lose his or her own head!"

"I can't believe that kind of bullshit is even tolerated," Meredith snorted. "Being boorish and abusive is one thing but then rationalizing it with threats—and then having a colleague rationalize it. Wow!"

"I didn't rationalize it—I just tried to calm things. And you've never seen that kind of hypocrisy and abuse in Holly-wood? I don't believe that!"

"Sure. I see it all the time, but it's hard to imagine that it's so tolerated in this little 'village,' as you call it, that it seems like everyone knows it will happen and then tries to explain it away."

Anger and angst were finally spent by lunch after nonstop conversation during the drive. Later, parked in front of the hotel, Rick opened the trunk and retrieved Meredith's bag. Catching the handle, she turned to him. "Thanks. In spite of the boor and his awful breath last night, I appreciate your intervention—and perspective. And it was fun to share the spotlight—the big news spotlight, even if it was a manufactured one—and meals—with one of the stars! I usually only get to write about you guys!" She grinned.

"My pleasure," Rick responded. "Manufactured 'breaking news' or not, I'd share a story with this news maven anytime." He bowed slightly, repeated, "Anytime," and abruptly leaned over and kissed her cheek. "Ma'amselle. I'll be overseas for a while but reach out anytime and I'll be there…and let me know if these assholes are giving you a hard time…." He looked at her with the deep brown eyes that seemed more soft and welcoming than the cameras ever caught. She got that he meant his words.

Meredith wagged a forefinger at him, smiled mischievously, then shook her head—mostly in a reminder to herself. "It's been a treat, Rick. Honestly. Safe travels." She turned more quickly than she intended and walked briskly into the hotel.

Sunday morning coming down...

The towel hanging over the railing on the patio overlooking the beach ruffled in the brisk breeze. Raymond sat at the dining room table inside and watched the waves playing in the wind and took a long swallow of milk. His head was foggier than usual, thanks to the jovial gathering at Bernie's house the night before—and the margaritas he'd consumed. But through the throbs and mental mist, he grappled with a problem he knew was only bound to escalate. Margo.

He wondered if he was imagining the problem—or she was inciting it. A brilliant agent and operative, bold, strategic and enterprising, Margo had made a strong mark in her work with the FBI in circumnavigating the wily halls of corporate America. She'd been instrumental in the take down in New Mexico the year before. And in saving Raymond's life. She was a valuable asset to the department. But their long-ago history and her flinty personality made him uncomfortable, especially when she aimed her pointed coyness toward him. Which, it seemed to him, was whenever he was around and not surrounded by coworkers.

The night before, he had picked her up from her newly acquired apartment in Westwood to give her a ride to Bernie's barbeque. "Nice to have a date," she had remarked as he arrived. He shuddered, but she did nothing to encourage concern. Throughout the evening he avoided her. Much of the time he spent talking to Marty, once his partner in celebrity crime, now the lead on that form of high-profile work. They kicked around investigation ideas for the Ronnie Milton case and more pressing current pending crimes. The margaritas seemed to show up—as did Margo from time to time in the normal course of socializing with her new colleagues. Raymond always found an excuse to move into other conversations but accept subsequent tequila offerings. By eleven o'clock, he'd learned that another coworker lived in Westwood and would be leaving a little later. Quietly saying his thanks to Bernie and wife, he brought the colleague over to Margo. "I need to get going, Margo, but we don't want to cut your evening short so Dan, here, also lives in Westwood and has agreed to give you a ride home. That'll give you some more time to spend with folks in the department." He quickly turned and headed out the door leaving Dan to get acquainted with Margo, noticing that Dan's wife joined the conversation.

Raymond drove home quickly and sighed with relief as he pulled into his garage, thankful he was able to drive without impairment after his evening of margaritas, and that he'd managed to avoid what he feared would be an awkward midnight confrontation with the wily redhead agent. And that he had avoided the embarrassment of being picked up by one of his police colleagues for driving erratically. He, of all people, knew better. Margo had shown none of his imagined flirtatiousness toward him, but he felt guilty about his own self-doubt and unwillingness to be a good colleague and overlook history. He rewarded himself with a shot of richly aged scotch and collapsed into bed.

Milk seemed soothingly appropriate the next afternoon. He told himself that the Margo problem had to be sorted out. Having a conversation was one step. But he'd had similar conversations before, and they always ended up uncomfortable and going nowhere. He intuited Margo was feeling a kind of envy or rivalry over the attractive woman who now occupied his home and bed? But he shook his head as he asked himself, is this just my own imagination and ego flaring up? But he needed to solve the problem— didn't want his department and his position poisoned by the underlying attitude Margo brought to it—or maybe only he did— and he didn't want his life challenged by it. Life with Meredith had enough of its own challenges.

The phone rang late in the afternoon. Marty greeted him with, "I'm glad you got home okay. Thank god Sally drove me. Let's not encourage Bernie to do that again soon!" Both laughed heartily, Raymond feeling glad someone else had over-enjoyed the margaritas. "I got through to the director of that nursing home where Sonny Bota's mother is now living," Marty announced. "I'm going over tomorrow but the director said the old lady is so demented she probably won't even understand the questions. Want to ride along?" Raymond quickly agreed, hung up and figured out his schedule in order to dedicate the time.

Hey, sailor…

No other craft had approached the hulking ship where Meredith sat wearily and now only intermittently waving her red flag. No response had yet developed from the promise of the sailboat skipper, and Meredith had not managed to attract the attention of any other passers-by. She was hungry, thirsty, fog-damp and tired. Mostly she was dispirited. She pushed herself up from her crouch on the gang plank planning to return to her nest—which she had optimistically decamped at least two hours before—and rethink options. As she climbed up the top-most section of the gangway, she heard the whine of a motor coming closer. Turning, she saw a small motorboat aiming in her direction. She turned and waved the red flag frantically. The boat slowed, turned and slid next to the gangplank. Meredith's spirits rose.

"Are you in trouble?" called a swarthy man, dressed in a soiled sweatshirt and ripped jeans. He slowed the boat and grabbed onto the gangplank.

"Yes!" Meredith called. "I'm stuck on this ship and need to get off. Can you give me a ride somewhere?"

"Sure," he called out, waving her down the gangway. She bumped down gingerly and he held out his hand to help her climb into his boat. She gasped a loud sigh of relief as she regarded his simple vessel. No fancy riggings, a small cabin and tools or equipment stacked against the transom. She sat down with a sold thump on the bench. He thumped her bag next to her. "Thank you. I've been stranded on this thing for nearly a day. Wasn't sure I'd ever get off."

"Wow. I've never heard of anyone stranded on one of those ghoulish hulks," he whistled. "Where to?" he asked, revving the motor and moving forward. The question caught her short. "God, I don't know. I didn't think quite that far." She breathed heavily for a moment or two, then said, "Nearest Coast Guard station, I guess. Or sheriff?"

"Coast Guard? Or sheriff?" her rescuer asked, frowning.

"I don't know where else to go that would help. I'm Meredith, by the way."

Silence filled the air before the skipper spoke. "That's fine. But I'm working so I have to make two short, nearby deliveries first—maybe an extra half hour? Sorry, it's the best I can do. My name's Duck." Meredith nodded, first amused by the name, then slightly taken aback but not wanting to abort the only alternative she'd been given to staying on the ship. The movement of the motorboat was refreshing after the cumbersome roll of the war ship and the constant creaking and grinding of its girders.

Fifteen minutes later, the motorboat slowed and approached a small industrial-looking warehouse with a neglected dock. Duck pulled up, climbed onto the landing and tied off the boat. He carried a shoebox sized package, tucked it under his arm and headed to the building. "Be right along." Meredith looked around the small boat, noticing little in the way of creature comforts—not a live-aboard for sure. Just a small motorbike of some kind tucked under a seat and some snack bags. She laid back against the gunwale and closed her eyes. True to his word, Duck was back and starting the motor no more than five minutes later.

"One more stop," he told her. "Then I'll drop you off." Meredith fidgeted, anxious to get onto terra firma and figure out how to get home. Another fifteen minutes passed and a stop at another nondescript building with a clumsy dock. They'd shared little conversation, mostly Meredith explaining why she'd been stuck on the ghost ship. "Never heard of that before," murmured Duck. "But there's all types of rumors about real ghosts, some felons hiding out—even vagrants squatting there. How in the hell they get on board—you got me." Duck made another very quick delivery and was back in the boat pulling away, soon heading into a small channel that narrowed into an inlet heavily shrouded by trees and brush.

"Where are we?" asked Meredith, beginning to feel fearful and anxious. *Please let me think clearly enough to manage whatever comes next*, she cautioned herself.

"Don't get crazy," Duck said. "This is a small public marina. There's a restroom and I'm sure a phone somewhere here. I can't go to a Coast Guard station. Okay? This is the best I can do." He guided the boat onto one of the few docking berths and stopped. He jumped out and held out a hand. "You have to get out now."

"But, where am I?" Meredith implored. "You can't just leave me." She sat solid on the bench.

"You have to get out. Now move!" She stood up shakily and took his hand, jumping over the side and onto the dock. She watched Duck as he stepped back into the boat and started the motor. "Good luck!" he yelled. On pure impulse, she reached into her bag for her tiny Minnox camera and snapped one picture, then another and another. Duck gunned the motor, backed up the boat, made a tight turn and took off at a speed more than she had seen since she stepped on board.

Where in the world is...

Seven glum faces sat around the conference table in the offices of Stan Smallet, Marketing Vice President of Global International Entertainment (GIE). T.K. Raymond sat at one end of the table, Smallet at the other. Between them were the Director of Security Bill Willums, studio Head of Publicity Chuck Toller, Terry the publicist for the film, *Shadow of the Wave* producer Matthew Morgan, and the ghost ships press trip coordinator/intern, Nate Bills.

"We'll get this puzzle solved," Smallet insisted. "Terry's been on the phone all morning tracking down everyone who was on that junket."

"It's still in the wind," said the blondish-haired young woman whose job had been to escort major press members to the movie location on the ghost ship, and make sure all had the best information and experience possible in order to say good things about the movie. "But I haven't been able to reach a couple of key people. We put everyone on two boat launches at the end of the session. Each group transferred together to a specific limo on shore. One went to the Oakland Airport. The other to the San

Francisco Airport. Nate escorted everyone to their respective launches…Nate?"

The young intern, nervous and talking with a shaky voice, cleared his throat and began to explain. "I made a list of who was on each of the launches but there was some switching around at the last minute and it got a little confused." He looked down at his list. "Originally Meredith Ogden was on my list for Oakland. She said that's where she'd originally flown into. But then someone…I think it was the French guy…told me she'd said she was going instead with the San Francisco group. When we got to the dock in Benicia, one of the other European guys in the Oakland group switched to San Francisco, said he wanted to go into the City after all. And Terry decided to stay behind with Matthew and the crew from the company taking care of the ships, to wrap up after the event. The young man shook his head in frustration. "It all just got confused and in the midst of it, I lost track of Meredith, I guess."

"Did you see her get into the San Francisco limo?" Smallet interjected.

Shrugging self-consciously, the intern murmured, "I'm not sure. The Oakland group kept asking questions and changing their minds. The woman from the local paper wanted to stay behind with Matthew but," the boy looked over at the producer, "he said 'no.' I just lost track of the San Francisco limo and before I knew it, they'd left. No one seemed left behind so I assumed all was well." He looked ready to cry.

"So, when was the last time you actually saw Meredith Ogden?" Raymond pushed into the conversation, working to maintain professional objectiveness, not allowing his personal unease to emerge.

"Me? Well, probably before Matthew began his overview presentation on the deck of the ship."

"That was the last time I saw her as well," added the producer. "She'd already seen my presentation so stepped away to make some notes. That's what she told me."

"Who told the French reporter that Meredith wanted to switch airports?" Raymond continued, holding himself in professional command.

"We're trying to reach the reporter, Claude, now," said Terry. "But he changed his own plans and went into San Francisco on his own. We've lost track for the moment. He changed his original flight to New York and his office is trying to locate him."

"What do the limo drivers say about who was in their cars?" asked Smallet.

"There's another problem," winced Terry. "First, we questioned the launch skippers but neither of them really knew who was on their boats, it was a short ride. And the limo driver to Oakland left early this morning on a fishing trip with his brother and isn't due back until Sunday night. His wife thinks they may stay at one of the motels up in the Sierras but they hadn't made any specific reservations. She'll check in as soon as—and if—she hears from him."

"The San Francisco driver?" pushed Smallet.

"Said she wasn't in his car," murmured Terry.

"And the other passengers in the Oakland car? Any one of them see her?"

Terry cringed visibly. "We can't reach anyone yet. Two of the riders haven't check into their offices—one went on to another meeting out of town. Their staffs are trying to locate them. The German correspondent rented a car and headed…we aren't sure where yet. The columnist from the local area hasn't returned calls yet. She just has an answer machine. And the guy in charge of the ship isn't expected back to his office until late this afternoon. I'd hoped he was going back to recheck everything but he's in Oakland at a meeting."

"Someone must have seen Meredith after Matthew's presentation," Raymond said, looking at a series of flow charts he had started to scribble. "Because, someone told the French reporter to tell Nate she was switching destinations. Who was that?" Blank stares met him from around the table.

"So right now, all we know is that Meredith wasn't noticed again after Matthew's presentation and possibly after she left the ship and before boarding a rebooked flight from…San Francisco? None of the airlines showed her on a passenger manifest so we can assume she never took a flight. We've contacted the Contra Costa County Sheriff's Department, the various police departments. It's still early, but there's a lot of ground to cover." Raymond drew his lips into a tight line and scowled. The remainder of the group seemed to stare grimly out the window or at their notes on the table in front of themselves. No one spoke.

Long and lonely road

Well, I guess I should be thankful he was even willing to get me off that ship, Meredith rationalized. At least I'm on firm ground. But where?

A small, log building sat on the ground above the docks. Well-kept up it was welcoming, but when she had climbed up the wooden ramps it seemed little used. She explored and saw very minimal services, assumed there was a public phone somewhere. When she found it, she also found it hanging by wires, pulled mostly out of the housing, clearly damaged by vandals. Her heart sank. She looked down the road leading from the marina, but saw only a long narrow road and no other buildings. Damn! She thought. She tried the phone in pure fantasy, finding no connection of any sort, the wires dangling around her hand. She kicked the side of the building.

Restroom—working? With water? She questioned as she rounded the building's corner, following the sign that read, "Women." She flinched again—a padlock on the door. Why? She wondered—if this was a public marina. Pulling at the lock she realized the bond was solid, then reached into the inner depths of her tote to find the small tool Cassie had gifted her after their capture in New Mexico. Fingers probing the entire mechanism of the bathroom lock device, she found the small screws holding it to the door. Fiddling, fiddling, she chanted to herself as she worked the smallish screwdriver on her all-purpose tool—as Cassie had called it. Surprising herself, the screws budged—with some tough prompting—and the flange adhering to the door frame lopped forward. "Yay!" Meredith gasped and pushed the door open.

Making her way into the stuffy and gritty restroom, she was thrilled that at least there was running water and a real commode. Cleaning herself up as much as she felt inspired to do, washing her face, combing her hair back into a damp and lank ponytail, she found a drinking fountain and after letting the water run for a few moments, she drank heartily. Now what, she asked herself. The first time in nearly 24 hours on solid ground, she felt a little dizzy from the lack of movement and sat down on a wooden bench overlooking the marina. I'm so tired, she mewed to herself. She glanced at her watch to see it was mid-day, eleven thirty. The bench was wide, long with a back and even arm rests and protected by the building overhang. She stretched out into a resting position and placed her bag under her head. Just for a minute, she told herself. The buzz in her head disappeared into soft breathing as sleep overtook her.

The harsh call of a gull broke through her slumber and she drowsily rubbed her eyes, struggling to identify her surroundings. Sitting up, she looked around to see if there was any suggestion of human activity but saw none. Only a lonely seagull sitting atop the restroom roof. "Thanks a lot!" She chided the bird. "How about calling for help!" She realized it was a Thursday afternoon and few recreational boaters would be using the marina facilities. Then she began to worry about Duck who was probably engaging in some kind of illegal activity—given that he wouldn't expose himself to the Coast Guard or any other lawful organization. Good idea to keep moving, she told herself, noticing that it was two in the afternoon. She'd slept for two and a half hours!

Using the restroom once more, she found an empty pop bottle, rinsed it carefully then filled it with water. Checking the laces on her sneakers, she sighed, pulled her tote over her shoulder and looked down the narrow, long road away from the marina. No buildings, no signs—just scrub brush and trees. It had to lead somewhere, though, and better than sitting waiting for Duck to decide she might have seen too much, she concluded and started the walk, hoping her erstwhile rescuer would not turn into an erstwhile stalker. She was reminded of her New York stalker and began to ponder the puzzle as she trudged along.

Who's that girl?

"Did your friend find you?" asked the solicitous desk clerk at the Green Park Hotel as Meredith entered with her weekend bag in tow.

"Friend?" she puzzled. "I've been away for the weekend. What friend and when?"

The well-coiffed young man in his spotless blazer, white shirt and tie scowled. "I think it was late yesterday afternoon. Woman, long straight black hair, bangs, said you were expecting her and wanted to go to your room. We called but there was no answer. She sat in the lobby for about an hour and then just disappeared."

"Do you have a security camera?" asked Meredith. Not everyone did these days, but more and more customer service places were installing them. The young man shook his head.

"I can sketch the hair and glasses," he offered.

"Hold that thought," she said, hurrying to the elevator and heading to her room. She opened the door cautiously, looked around before entering, and moved quietly toward the bedroom to make sure no one was waiting there. Checking the closet and bathroom, seeing no one, she dumped the contents of her pull-on bag out on the bed, then dug through her purse for Buster Boles' card.

While she efficiently separated clean from soiled clothes for laundering, she listened to the phone messages waiting for her. Her best friend Gloria Masner—coming to New York tomorrow, could they get together? Cassie O'Connell with a question about her return to the L.A. morning show "...and other stuff." Raymond wondering how her weekend had gone—sounding a little more subdued than usual. Life seemed to be back to normal—at least in the hotel room.

Later, in the lobby bar, she and the chubby disheveled private investigator mothered the report of the "friend" who had come to visit. They had asked the desk clerk to describe—and sketch—what he recalled of the visitor. He was an art student and proud to be of service. Meredith regarded the sketch and said, "No idea who that is. Tell me again what the person following me looked like." Buster did his own sketch of what he recalled of the person he tracked during Meredith's visit to Ronnie Milton.

"I'm no artist," he muttered. Meredith heartily agreed but there was nothing in the person he presented both verbally and in his scratched image on the cocktail napkin that Meredith recognized. "There's not much he or she had to be recognized," he sighed, taking a drink of his beer. "Nondescript hoodie, jeans, shades, and so on." Neither of the two gave much credence to coincidence. Buster left to ponder how to proceed in his assignment from Raymond: protect the girl.

Meredith returned to her room, ordered room service, and given that it was six o'clock, started returning calls. The last was to Raymond who answered out of breath. "Literally just in the door from a run," he gasped.

"Happy Sunday," chimed Meredith, always bolstered by Raymond's voice from afar. "How was Bernie's barbeque?"

"Fine," answered Raymond but without great enthusiasm, and followed by silence.

"And?" said Meredith.

"Well, I drank too much tequila, got home but have felt it all day. Just now clearing the fog from my brain. I think I shook off the headache a while ago."

"Tsk," chuckled Meredith. "Not the usual behavior from the always-unflappable detective. Knowing you, though, you didn't act silly at the party."

"No," he mused. "I was the picture of decorum. It's my MO when you're not around."

"And when I am. And how's your new team member?"

Raymond took a deep breath and dove into the subject of Margo. "Well, there's the surprise for us all. She's the agent you met—the one who shot my would-be assassin in New Mexico—Margo Flaherty. Bernie neglected to tell me who was joining my office. Not MY team, by the way, just the office. She has a desk there but works more with another unit. They haven't a space and right now her cases are on the west side, so…."

"So, you're in charge of the fiery redhead now. The one who wore a heavy black woolen suit to the meeting in the middle of a sizzling L.A. summer and who seemed to have something to snark about the entire time?"

"Yeah. That one."

"The one who couldn't keep a critical eye off me or Cassie…."

"That one too. But she has a full case load and seems to have bonded well with others at the unit so maybe she'll be a ghost."

"And if not, well…you'll work it out." Then Meredith chuckled. "You sound either guilty or scared."

"Both. I had to pick her up and take her to the party last night, but I found her a ride home, and although I drank too much, I got home fine alone."

"Good boy."

"So how were The Hamptons?" he changed the subject.

"Montauk was really lovely. Loved being at the ocean and breathing the air. The Longmore's house was gorgeous and huge. Mrs. Longmore—Billie—was incredibly accommodating and friendly. The rest of the Hampton weekend I wouldn't do again."

"What…? Why?"

"The conversations were snorers—I'm not engaged in nor care about network policies and the future of some of the programs and so on. Although I admit I should be and should have been more attentive. Shoulda-woulda. I was semi-accosted by a drunk VIP but Rick Santaros stopped me from thrashing him with my new-found self-defense skills. I accepted an early ride back to Manhattan this morning to avoid any further dismay."

"Um. I think I'll wait until I see you to hear that whole story. I guess I don't need to ask if you had fun."

"Not exactly the word I'd use, but I did learn some things I guess it's good to know." She told him more about the entire weekend—the people, comments about *It's a Good Day*. "When I heard Amanda Borkin's comments to our producer about me, it resonated with how she treats me. I have a strategy—I'm going to interview her for an upcoming column. I can make it a two-parter and write more about live morning shows. I've never written about them before. Oh, and some strange person stopped at my hotel asking to see me. She hung out in the lobby but finally left when I didn't show."

"Any idea who?"

"Not a single one, but I'm sure Buster will be calling you with an update. Could be nothing…."

"But…?"

"No idea at all. Maybe you two can figure it out." She quickly added, "And now I think my book chapter on these adventures into broadcast celebrity can be closed for the week. And a good thing. Gloria is coming to town tomorrow for some kind of conference and wants to 'drink wine and talk.' And Cassie asked me to call tomorrow to 'clear some air' on her side of things. Know anything about any of that?"

"Ominous," exaggerated Raymond. "I'm clueless but it sounds like a busy time." The air was quiet for a while. He broke in with, "I've been thinking. Rather than you hassling around to fly across country for a day-and-a-half, how about I take a few days off—I have it coming and there's nothing heavy pending right now. I'd fly to New York maybe Thursday and leave on Monday. You can show me your new digs and the hot spots in the world of talk show celebrity?"

The air was silent again then Meredith's chirpy voice said, "You're not doing this just to keep an eye on me?"

"No—although an eye is a start."

"Then I'd love it!"

"We'll have Manhattan, the Bronx—la la la la—Staten Island—lalala…," Raymond sang. Badly.

"What generation are you from? That was from *The Eddie Duchin Story*—circa 1956!"

"My mom's favorite movie. She played the music over and over."

"Good night, Raymond. Think of all the ways we can make use of those lalala places over the next four days." She only heard a dramatized gasp at the other end of the line.

Expanding the brand

"Amanda, can I have a quick word with you?" Meredith stopped her co-host as they left the set at the wrap of Monday's show. The tall celebrity stopped and regarded Meredith almost imperiously.

"Sure. What's on your mind?"

"I'm writing a two-part feature on the morning talk shows and I'd like to interview you—at length. Are you interested in a sit-down interview one day soon?"

Amanda again regarded Meredith only more inquisitively now. "Will I be the only host interviewed?"

"I'm not sure yet, but probably the only featured interview."

"Kind of a nice inside look at our team and family?"

"I don't know yet. I don't do puff pieces, so context, contributed by everything else I learn will count."

"Will I have the ability to review the story before publication?"

"No, Amanda. I never allow that. I'm not a hatchet wielder but I do like to print the information I see, hear, find, and have been given. If there's a question, I get confirmation or verification—and a response from whoever is in the lens."

The well-coiffed and garbed talk show host stared at the ground a moment, then responded. "Yes. But if we come across a subject or question I don't want to talk about, it must be off-the-record." She paused for a moment, then added, "How many newspapers are you in?"

"Over 350 news outlets and your off-the-record works fine," said Meredith, noting the older woman had begun to preen somewhat. Still, she thought, this will be a doozie of an interview and I'll be challenged every moment to keep it moving forward and not to overreact to the snipes.

Monday had begun as it usually did for the early morning crew and for Meredith. The show proceeded smoothly and the planning session afterward was complex and technical as Mondays often were—anticipating the week's show foci. The assembled show participants and producers huddled around the giant conference table pondering, sparring and determining the week's subject matter. Once completed, her own assignments in hand, Meredith retreated to her hotel to write her newspaper column for the week and plan to meet Gloria for an early dinner, just after her friend arrived in town. She also had the troubling call to return to Cassie. And another new one from the priest friend of Ronnie Milton.

Mondays, mused Meredith. The same all over the world—New York as well as Los Angeles.

CHAPTER 32
SEPTEMBER 18, 1989
GREEN PARK HOTEL, MANHATTAN
MONDAY AFTERNOON

Don't blame me

"You couldn't have talked to me first?" came the angered growl from Cassie O'Connell into Meredith's ear all the way from Los Angeles. Meredith pulled the phone receiver away from her ear and took a breath.

"Cassie! Cassie—what's this about? I don't know what you're talking about!"

"Joining that vile group of people on the couch in New York—full time. Leaving us here?"

"Whoa!" Meredith squeezed her eyes shut and shook her head. "I'm totally confused. I'm not joining anyone in New York full time. I have three more weeks of subbing to do and then I'm back to normal life in L.A. Where'd you get the idea I was leaving?"

Silence from Cassie's end of the line. "Cassie?"

"I had two fan letters saying how much they will miss you now that you've join the *It's a Good Day* show. Those I could shrug off. But when two legitimately qualified replacements for you on our show sent in resumes because they'd heard you were gone, I had to pay attention."

"Jesus, Cassie. You should have just asked me before boiling over. I'm not leaving anything except *It's a Good Day* in three weeks. They don't even like me much! And I miss my home territory. Take a deep breath."

"Then where did these reports come from?" Cassie persisted. Her voice had lowered and calmed. At her desk at the studios where her show was produced, she slumped back into her chair and felt a large sense of relief.

Perched on the edge of her desk chair in her suite at the Green Park Hotel, Meredith propped her chin in her left hand and tried to imagine where the rumors had emanated. "I don't know. I can't even imagine. In fact it seems like everyone's so nervous I'll lower the show's ratings, they're practically dragging Nancy Igleton back into the studio in her robe!"

Silence again. Finally Meredith spoke up. "Who exactly told you I was leaving? I mean who specifically? Because I don't know who would know that even if it was true! But it's not!"

"I'll have to dig out the resumes. I tossed them at first and then realized there was too much chatter about this to ignore it. I'll find them. One was a local TV news person. The other some kind of newspaper reporter—I think one who has covered Hollywood, but I'm not sure. I'll look it up."

"So how are you doing otherwise," chuckled Meredith. "How's the house at the beach town? And Bob and the dog?"

"Stop it," laughed Cassie. "You're just jealous because you're stuck in a fancy hotel suite and appearing on one of the country's most watched national morning shows! And doing big time network news features with a famous international war correspondent! Is he studly?"

"Studly? Well, off camera he's kind of nerdy without being obnoxious. Actually, a pretty nice guy and quite unassuming. I was surprised. I enjoyed the collaboration."

"Huh," mused Cassie. "Collaboration. Okay. I'll buy that." The two talked for a few more minutes about on-going news. "Are you coming home next weekend?" Cassie asked.

"No. Raymond wants to come here for a few days. It's a good idea. He needs the break. I don't need the hassle of a very short round-trip cross-country jog and I need to see him!"

"Just don't forget the rest of us—we're waiting for the return of the gossip girl! Besides, I need a lunch pal and a wine-drinking collaborator!"

"You have some resumes—maybe there's someone qualified there," snorted Meredith. "Don't forget to check out the names on the resumes you got. I'm curious."

You've got a friend

"Ronnie is gone." The priest's deep slightly graveled voice stated gravelly. Meredith could tell he was working to control more ardor.

"Gone where?" she asked, confused but intent.

"Just gone. He came to me a couple of days ago, anxious because one of his street friends told him someone was outside the church the day we all met. That they had followed us to the location and…well, you get the gist. Ronnie hasn't been back to his quarters since."

Meredith moaned. "Shit. Yes, someone did follow us—actually three people. None of them interested in Ronnie at all. Ito was there. You know him. A private eye my significant other, also a detective, hired to keep an eye on what he worried was a dangerous situation, and then an unknown person we haven't been able to identify—but was tracking me, not Ronnie. As far as we can tell, there was no interest in Ronnie at all. Can you reach him?"

"I told him to keep in touch. We have a long and trusting relationship. But I can only hope he'll follow through."

"I'd really appreciate it if you could try to put his mind at rest. I never ever intended to compromise him in any way."

"I think he knew that but…he's just being cautious."

"And to add insult to injury—I'd like to talk with whoever saw the person following us. If it was our unknown stalker, Ronnie's friend might be able to give us more detail about his or her looks and whatever."

"I'll do my best," the priest acknowledged. "But I can't promise Ronnie will check in again." After a moment's silence, he continued. "I'll say some prayers that you identify and are safe from this stalker—as you called it."

"Thank you, Father."

"Come and visit us."

"I know. You have religious services…."

Meredith glanced quickly at the clock on the suite desk and realized Gloria would be arriving in less than a half-hour. She rushed into the shower, intent on reviving herself after a long day that had begun more than 12 hours before. She slid into casual slacks and a brown turtleneck just as the phone rang to announce that Gloria was on her way up to the suite.

✫✫✫

"So, the conference is just down the street," Meredith chuckled. "Where are you staying?" The two were dining in a small chic restaurant not far from the hotel, curved over the small table, surrounded by palms, a bottle of wine sitting between them.

The elegant brunette sitting opposite Meredith wore a dark blue silk blouse with houndstooth trousers, sterling silver hoop earrings and her hair pulled into a tight knot at her neck. She raised a well-sculpted eyebrow and named a nearby hotel.

"Jeez, Gloria," Meredith said to her oldest friend, former college roommate and current best pal, "I have a convertible bed in the living room of my huge suite. Your meeting is only a short walk away. Stay with me."

Gloria screwed her face into a scowl and thought about it. "Yeah. That would be fun," she finally said.

"Just know that I'll be scurrying out about four-fifteen," Meredith alerted. Gloria winced but smiled. "I'm out early myself to the first meeting I have so you'll be a good incentive." Both women chattered about events since they'd seen one another a few weeks earlier. Meredith took a sip of wine, wiped her mouth and looked at Gloria.

"So, what's so troubling you had to come all the way across country just to talk about it? Not George, I hope?"

"No, no…never, but…," Gloria seemed to shudder visibly, set her own wine glass down and cleared her throat. "Do you remember sitting on the grass the first warm sunny day of spring our senior year in college and talking about whether we had the maternal instincts to ever become mothers?"

Meredith nodded, searching her memory for the time and moment. "Kind of. I better remember sitting in the Polo Lounge years later talking about how bearing children simply didn't have a place in either of our future scopes…are you pregnant, Gloria?"

The brunette gasped loudly and said, "God no! But…well…about children…."

"About children…," Meredith repeated, knitting her brows, tilting her head and staring at Gloria, perplexed.

"Do you remember meeting George's younger brother, Sam?" Gloria began. Meredith nodded. She'd met him once a long time ago. "Well, Sam married very young, kind of in a drug fog to a…what we might call an 'unstable' woman. Part of his youthful drug days. They right away had a kid and the mother took off.

Soon after she signed off all connection to the baby and Sam was left as a single dad. He was only 23 and it actually helped him straighten himself out. Little boy is eight now. Sam died in a private plane crash a month ago. He was a contractor and on his way to a building site in Wisconsin when the small plane went down. Now his little boy Trey is an orphan. The mother disavows any knowledge of him, lives somewhere in South America. We've had one tumultuous month trying to sort out options, legal issues and our own desires. But we're taking Trey, adopting him…gawd, Meredith. I'm an instant mom and I never intended to be any mom!" Tears brimmed in Gloria's eyes.

Meredith could hardly talk. "But, Gloria, what a wonderful thing to do! Wow. How can you not?" Gloria just shook her head and fumbled into her purse to pull out a packet of photos. She handed them to Meredith, who quickly dissembled the stack and looked carefully at each image. "He's adorable, Gloria. And so scared and burdened. You can see that in his eyes and his demeanor. You can't blame him." She looked up at her dearest and longest-time friend who seemed to have shrunk into her chair, tears streaming down her face.

"What are you crying for?" asked Meredith, "the losses for this little boy, the loss of your own self-made independence—which I know well, and also cherish…or…?"

"I think mostly the shock of it. I wouldn't have it any other way. Trey is adorable, smart, well-mannered and yes, terrified and so sad. I don't know that I—we will ever be enough to help him be the person he was or would have been…."

"Jeez, Gloria. He can't lose in your household. One of the things we used to say when we talked about this was that IF—and that was such a big IF—we ever had kids, we would want to be in a personal, professional and economic situation to give the child the best possible opportunities and options in life. Do you think

Trey could have landed any place better than in the home of George and Gloria Masner? You have all the tools, the money and frankly the love around you to make this work for everyone. I'd say—enjoy it. It's a great new challenge. And I can't wait to be an unofficial aunt. I think an eight-year-old can't possibly be any more bothersome than some fifty-year-olds I know. Or forty-year-olds or even eighty-year-olds—wait'll I tell you about the fun time I had in The Hamptons. Now, drink your wine and tell me about your plans to arrange the house and your schedules!"

"Not until I get a hot fudge sundae," sniffed Gloria between a laugh and a wine guzzle. "I knew you'd slap me out of it!"

"Let's order two sundaes from room service at the hotel because I have to get to bed in the next hour if I'm going to get up at three-thirty and be productive tomorrow! Yes, we can also order a bottle of good wine! This is a celebration! My good friend Gloria is going to be a mom- without ruining her body, losing sleep for a couple of years over nocturnal feedings, not even losing her job! Does it get any better than that?"

The two women were placing their empty desert cups on the tray outside the hotel room door when the phone rang inside. Meredith hurried to pick it up, expecting to hear Raymond's voice. It was about that time of the evening. Instead she was greeted with a very static-laden line and a light-hearted voice asking, "Hey—how's the newest couch lady doing?"

""Well…" she answered still puzzled over the distant voice.

"It's Rick and I'm just calling to let you know that your intelligence sources were surely correct about the Trubo kid."

Meredith laughed and said, "Well, coming from you, Rick, that's important, but which intelligence are you referring to?"

"I'm sure you know the would-be anthropologist got home to New York safely and that all is quiet on the politics front with the two super powers fighting over him?"

"Yeah, I kind'a heard about that. Over and over! His dad's taking credit, I hear."

That brought a loud guffaw from Rick Santaros. "Well, I had the opportunity to chat briefly with one of the ambassadorial folks from Iran today and well…your neighbor was correct. Apparently, the kid was really rude and arrogant and everyone was glad to be rid of him!"

"And was he a spy?"

"Probably only for MTV. But keep an eye on the sketches on *Saturday Night Laughs*. I'm not sure of the negotiating points agreed upon. So how are you doing? Hopefully not karate chopping network executives again?"

"No. And not appearing in serious news segments either. But I'm going to write a two-part series on morning shows with Amanda the center point. Maybe she'll settle down…," and the commentary between the two continued for a few more minutes. Gloria raised an eyebrow when she heard the name "Rick," but finished preparing for the night in her pull-out bed. "Hey— thanks for the update." Meredith concluded the conversation. "Gives me something to talk about tomorrow when things get boring on camera," sighed Meredith. "Don't know where you are, but stay safe. 'Night."

"Not the nocturnal call I expected to hear," smiled Gloria.

"Tell you about it at dinner tomorrow," said Meredith. "Not what it might sounds like." She realized she seemed defensive but before she could continue, the phone sounded, again, and she knew it would be Raymond. She said, "Night" to Gloria and took the call in the bedroom.

CHAPTER 34
SEPTEMBER 18, 1989
EAGLE ROCK, CALIFORNIA
MONDAY

Crazy

"The old woman is pretty demented," Marty told Raymond as the two parked the car in the lot of the compactly designed nursing home in Eagle Rock, California, east of downtown Los Angeles.

"She know we're coming?" asked Raymond.

Marty shrugged. "The director and on-duty manager, Angela Rayburn, does but I don't know if they told Martha or even if she would understand." The two men walked through the front doors of the attractive stucco-and-red-tile-roofed three-story building and made their way to the front desk. Soon the manager was walking them down a long corridor to one marked "Martha" and the number "26."

Inside, a wizened elderly woman sat in a lounge chair facing the window that overlooked a wide expanse of green lawn and flowered gardens. Her long and languid grey/brown hair tied back at her neck haphazardly. She wore a beige housedress that spoke adamantly to the 1950s, and what some of Raymond's generation would call "sensible" shoes. She looked up slowly as the group entered her room. "Hello Martha," said Angela energetically. "It's such a lovely day today and I see you're enjoying it."

"Can I go outside?" asked Martha.

"Not now. But these two nice people would like to say hello and ask you some questions."

"Bah," bleated Martha. Marty and Raymond quietly looked at one another. I kind of agree with her, Raymond thought to himself.

"Now, Martha…."

"Hello, Martha," Marty jumped in quickly. "My name is Marty Escobar and I hope you can help me locate someone I would really like to find." Martha simply continued to stare out the window.

"Are you Victor?" She suddenly asked. Marty took a deep breath. "Victor was her son's legal name," Raymond murmured.

"No, Martha, but I wonder if you could tell me if you have seen young Sonny. Sonny Bota, your grandson?" The old woman pinched up her face and spat. The manager rushed to wipe up the glob on Martha's lap. Martha turned and looked at Marty, spitting a loadless wad toward him. He drew back at the mere sound.

"He's an ass. Where is he? Not here. Hasn't been for a long, long time—too busy running around wagging that thing of his at anyone who'd notice it. No wonder he got sick."

"Sick?" asked Marty gently. "What kind of sick?" Raymond subtly moved close to hear the scratchy voice of the old woman.

"What kind do ya think? What kind happens to assholes who wag their winkies at strangers?" She shifted her gaze back to the windows. Raymond gently pulled at the sleeve of the manager and took her aside.

"Do you have a record of Martha's visitors over the years?" The young woman nodded. "Yes, but I didn't see a Sonny Bota on there when Detective Escobar first inquired. "You're welcome to look at it."

Meanwhile, Marty persisted. "Your grandson, Sonny—do you remember when you last saw him?"

"Sonny? Ha ha! His fancy mama called him that because he got teased over his real name."

"What was his real name?"

"Earwig."

"Earwig?" puzzled Marty. But the old woman just laughed and nodded her head over and over. The group gently prodded the old woman for a little more information over the next few minutes but she simply closed her eyes and went to sleep.

Raymond pulled Angela, the manager, to the door and asked, "Is she screwing with us or is she really that fractured?"

"Good word," said Angela. "Maybe both, but yes, she's that fractured. I think you've got all you'll get today. She was actually more lucid than normal." Raymond beckoned to Marty who was still staring at the snoozing figure. "Let's look at this list of visitors over—five-ten years."

"Well, recently—I mean in the last few years, only the social worker has been here to see her. I don't think there's any family left. And, we're hoping social services can find more of her financial resources. We're not a public facility and so far as we can tell, she'll be out of money soon so we'll have to move her into a public home."

"Who's been paying her bills all along?"

"An accountant but he's gone now. Died last summer, and the bank has been very helpful working with the social worker, but…well…."

Raymond shook off concern that he couldn't solve and then said, "May we take a look at your visitor history for Martha?"

"Sure," said Angela. "'I've only been here three years, but it goes back a lot further."

An hour later the threesome wrapped up conversation. Marty carried a file folder and Raymond looked troubled.

"So, she supposedly had enough money to carry her for at least 50 years, has been here 15 and is out of money?" Angela nodded. "But there's no one to talk to about what happened. The old accountant is gone. His practice was solo and is closed. And there's no family left, or at least no one has been able to locate the grandson, Sonny.

"Earwig," smiled Marty.

"Let me look at that list once more," Raymond said, stopping the exodus from the office. He opened the file and spent a few minutes flipping through the pages. "Earwig." He murmured. He thumbed a page in the back of the stack. "Who's this Elwin W. Manabota?" Angela shook her head.

"Way before my time," she said. "I'm not sure anyone here would remember. That visit was more than five years ago. Maybe one of the assistants, but he's off today."

Raymond looked at Marty who said, "Got it. I'll check him out tomorrow. Angela, I'll call you about it."

"Also, if you wouldn't mind, Angela, can you find out the name of the deceased accountant and give it to Marty?"

"You bet," she said enthusiastically. "I'd love to solve Martha's home-stay problem!"

The two detectives were in the car driving back to the office when Raymond suddenly looked over at Marty with a grin. "Let this be a lesson to us—no waggling our winkies! We could get sick."

"I could get dead!" sighed Marty. "You know my wife."

CHAPTER 35
SEPTEMBER 19, 1989
GREEN PARK HOTEL, MANHATTAN
TUESDAY AFTERNOON

I see you

"I don't want to embarrass you by how we look," said a contrite and shy sounding Ronnie Milton.

"Don't be silly. Where are you and how do I find you?" asked Meredith from her hotel desk an hour or so after she had returned from her day's work at the studio. She was on high alert and sharp concern now that the disappearing boy had suddenly surfaced.

"I'm here, Miss Ogden. At the hotel, but the valet let me use his phone to call up to you. I'm with my friend Tito and we don't look so…well, you know."

"Ronnie, come up to my room and stop apologizing. The hotel can stand a little color in its lobby! If anyone gives you trouble, have them call me. We'll tell them it's for a role you're playing!"

A few minutes later an almost reluctant tap at her door saw her nearly running to open it. The two young men standing in the hall seemed ill at ease. "Nice digs," said Ronnie.

"You haven't seen anything yet," chuckled Meredith. "They're really spoiling me. Come on in." Both boys looked around and one whistled. "You must be really important," said Ronnie's friend. He was a solidly built Latino with hair to his shoulders, clean shaven and intense dark eyes.

"Not important, just considered special for no real reason." said Meredith. Ronnie laughed.

"You've always been special. Father Paul said you wanted to talk to us about the person following us when we met a couple of weeks ago."

"Following ME, Ronnie. Nothing to do with you, honest," Meredith corrected, ushering the boys to a seat in the living area. "We know he or she was on to me because they were seen by a private eye tracking me for no good reason except that my… boyfriend…who's a detective in L.A. thought it was a good idea. Long story. I get beat up a lot." The boys looked at her with wide eyes but said nothing. "Anyhow, the person you saw followed me to the meet with you, Ronnie, and then back to my hotel. I'd hoped Tito might have seen more detail and can give us a little more of an identification. You guys want something to drink?"

Ronnie looked around and said, "A beer?" Before Meredith could even protest to herself, she realized that the "boys" were grown men now.

"Sure," she said and went to the mini-bar fridge and brought out two bottles. "This is what's on hand. I can call for something different." Neither objected and reached for the beverages. Meredith decided to join them and opened a bottle of her own. No one asked for a glass.

"So, Tito. How much of the person outside the church did you see? Male? Female? White? Black? Brown? Asian? Young? Old?"

Tito thought for a minute, set his beer down and scowled. "Well, for sure a woman. She was covered all up with a hoodie, jeans and sunglasses. No hair showing but I saw a lock of what's probably bangs fall forward at one time. Kind of red-ish. She pushed it back under the hoodie. White girl. I could see her face around the sunglasses—big ones—and her hands. She had long fingernails—real long and pointy with kind of a purple-ish polish. Probably a little bit old. I noticed some of those… wrinkles maybe…around her mouth. Couldn't see anything else."

"Did you see where she went or came from?" Tito shook his head. "Didn't notice her arriving. Only after she was there. She walked off around the corner before you came out, then got in a cab that headed uptown."

"Was there any kind of logo or identification on her hoodie jacket? Or jeans?"

"Just one of those turtle things. Said 'steadfast' but lots of people wear those. They're cheap and left behind at every thrift store in the country. Old school. I didn't notice a purse but probably kept her stuff in the pockets of her jacket. Don't think she had a gun. Reason I looked so closely was 'cuz I was worried that she might be carrying if she was stalking Ronnie."

"Well, she wasn't. Honestly. Please go back to your regular lives. Ronnie, Father Paul was worried about you." He blushed and nodded. "If it's any help at all, my detective friend is well acquainted with your old case in Los Angeles and is looking into the whereabouts of Sonny Bota today. My friend tells me Sonny just plain disappeared off the planet. No one has seen or talked to him in the last five years."

Ronnie looked more anxious. "Will you let me know if he finds out anything?"

Meredith agreed but added, "I'll tell Father Paul. We'll keep some distance between us if it makes you feel safer." Ronnie smiled. "Do you two want something to eat?" They both declined.

"Take a raincheck?" asked Tito enthusiastically.

"Any time," Meredith agreed, silently glad to have the time she needed to finish up her day's work before Gloria returned from the conference—yet glad to have reconnected with Ronnie and know that he was safe and well. But she quickly made notes on the conversation before she lost track of any detail.

☆☆☆

"So now you know about my little secret emotional melt down—my last grasp at total independence. What's going on with you, Meredith? Are you making New York your home?" Gloria buttered a sliver of bread and gazed with curious eyes at her dinner companion.

Meredith paused midway through a scoop of lobster bisque. "I keep getting that question. Have I given the impression I am even considering a move?"

"Well, you are here and for a long time and into a pretty committed assignment. You already have the start of a social circle—between Ito and the gang at the studio and the hot foreign correspondent. I can't help but wonder."

"You're giving me way too much credit for aggressive ambition," Meredith sighed. "My boss, Russ, suggested I accept the morning show gig. 'It'll give you a new perspective on another side to our news industry…,' yeah. And the air is rife with snap, crackle and poop! And rumors, resentment, attempted assaults and oh my—arrogance and self-awareness! Other than that, the gig is sensational." Meredith sounded bitter and tired.

"That bad?" quizzed Gloria, looking closely at her friend.

Meredith thought a moment, then scowled. "Actually, New York is enigmatic—the energy is contagious. It catches you unaware and pretty soon you can't do without it. And the greedy side of me can't help but think how seductive the salaries are in the on-air world but…." She shrugged. "I hope I'm more practical than that."

"But, you are in front of one of America's biggest female audiences. That should count for something."

"Yeah, selling cosmetics and pain relievers and how cute and fun I look today!"

"And the spot on the national news with the adorable Rick Santaros?"

Meredith laughed out loud. "Well, it was fun to think of myself as one of the serious news folks, but both Rick and I immediately understood that our moment of partner-fame was manufactured to bring attention and ratings to the *Good Day* show. And, as Rick said, take advantage of him being in town and my Hollywood connections. Passing currents. Nice guy."

"So, from last night's phone call, no long-term connection?"

"Not the kind you're referring to." Then Meredith explained the brief episodes from assembling the news feature through escaping the Montauk gathering. "Nary a hint nor suggestion of personal connection on either side. I'm not on the market. I didn't get he was either."

"Darn," sighed Gloria. "It was a saucy thought but I'm glad. I hate to see clouds over Malibu Beach." Raymond was the best friend and former college roommate of Gloria's husband George. The two couples were close.

"Calm your over-spiced imagination. Raymond's coming out here for four days at the end of the week."

"Whew. At least you two are one thing I don't have to stress over," said Gloria and reached for her wine.

CHAPTER 36
OCTOBER 12, 1989
HIDDEN HARBOR, SUISUN BAY/MALIBU
LATE THURSDAY AFTERNOON

Road less taken

Not a building, car or person had come into sight along the narrow road on which Meredith had been trudging for the past hour. The thick jacket and scarf that had been such a comfort during her long stay on the water now seemed a burden as the day warmed up. She tied the jacket sleeves around her waist and stuffed the scarf into her tote bag. But weariness and boredom were taking over again and she was dogged by the feeling that she'd lost valuable time by allowing the luxury of a nap.

Fueled by the need to find a way home, she trudged along the road at a brisk pace until it winded her. Then, stepping through the weeds and underbrush alongside the road, she sat down under a tree. I'll take a moment to rest, she thought, leaning her head back against the rough trunk. Gloria's new stressful drama came to mind from nowhere, but reminded of her own challenges. No kids looming, but confusing future options. She laughed at herself for sitting in the woods, abandoned and lost, and wondering if she should be a TV celebrity in the fast pace of New York. Or, focus on being a credible and in-depth observer of the evolving media industry with all of its glitter and gloss by using her loved and celebrated writing skills? "Where" to excel was the biggest question. NY meant a long-distance relationship with Raymond, and the traditional longevity of such arrangements was iffy. But even living and working in L.A. had some potholes. There had always been some tension between their two professional careers, although both would quickly admit that their relationship had been nothing but beneficial and sometimes lifesaving for one another. But if the TV soaps and series were to be believed, no one made a very good life partner to a cop. Meredith wondered if she could continue to be one as her career path accelerated.

She also wondered what he was thinking about her. Another irresponsible jaunt in search of a story? Kidnapped? Taken a quick break to be alone without every-day demands? Killed? She shuddered guessing at Raymond's thoughts.

But all meanderings went aside as she heard the chuff of a distant engine. Duck? She shivered but then realized, no way. Too far inland and she'd seen stacks of packages that she knew he still had to deliver in his boat. But the vague sound of civilization brought hope and urged her to get up. She rose from the leafy, rocky ground, brushed off her trousers and began toward the road. MOVE! She told herself.

And stumbled on a root upended among the ground leaves. Toe caught under the tough appendage, she was hurtled forward and scuffed to the ground. Catching herself with both hands, nettles and wooded debris cut into her palms and she slid forward scraping her torso and stomach. "Damnation," she hissed, sitting upright with difficulty and looking at her lacerated palms. She wiped them on her jeans and noticed the rips in the fabric of one knee and more gashes on her ankle.

"Great, just great," she whined to herself, but with anger and determination she thrust herself onto her feet, reclaimed her bag and adjusted her clothes and set out once again for the road, fending off tears that stung her eyes. Tears of frustration.

✮✮✩

Also frustrated, Raymond had returned to his unit, leaving Stan Smallet and his staff and crew at Global International Entertainment nervously hustling to find the missing ghost ship visitors from the day before. And ferret out where the elusive Meredith Ogden had gone. The detective spread maps of the Suisun Bay area across the table in his office, and talked by phone to various area law enforcement agencies.

Literally no one had witnessed Meredith Ogden leaving the ghost ship or setting foot on land. Raymond had followed up with an old Coast Guard friend who called in a few favors and got permission and an escort for a crew to search the ship. The search was promising but delivered no Hollywood journalist in the flesh.

"Looked like someone had left a popcorn bag behind. A Snickers wrapper. There was a dilapidated tarp wadded up under one of the deck overhangs and some other miscellaneous paper stuff left around on the main deck. Someone, however, had used the latrine, but because of how many people had been on the ship that afternoon, it could have been one of many. Sorry T.K. I've got a boat just stopping along the bay shore asking questions, but it's like she disappeared into thin air."

The harried look on Raymond's face and the slump in his shoulders had Marty Escobar concerned. "Hey—come over for dinner later? Or grab a beer?" he suggested in the afternoon. But Raymond demurred, feeling he was better off at home that evening at a phone number familiar to Meredith. Margo approached his office and swung vivaciously in the door, but as soon as she saw—felt—the heaviness in the office, she waved and left.

CHAPTER 37
SEPTEMBER 19, 1989
GREEN PARK HOTEL, MANHATTAN
TUESDAY EVENING

Chatter

Gloria waved goodnight—and goodbye— as Meredith left the living room of the suite and headed to the bedroom. "Kisses to Raymond," called Gloria. "And thanks again. This was so fun. We haven't had a girls' trip in a long time. We need to do it more often. I think we just need to connect more often."

"The boys can watch Trey," chuckled Meredith.

"Only fair," said Gloria. She would be leaving immediately after her early afternoon workshop the next day and would not see Meredith in New York before boarding her plane for home. Meredith, on the other hand, would be leaving the suite for the show long before Gloria would be awake and conversant. So, this was farewell. Meredith turned suddenly and hurried over to hug her friend.

"Thanks, Meredith. See you in L.A.," she smiled. Gloria saluted.

Wednesday unfolded relatively quietly for Meredith after the frenetic activity of the Hampton weekend followed by the two-day visit from Gloria and the other developments around Ronnie Milton and Meredith's follower. She finished her weekly column for the media syndicate and faxed it over, reviewed the copy of

Sonia's Q/A column that had arrived by fax. Written a few lines and made some phone calls around subjects to be covered on the TV show, and checked in with Cassie.

"Sherie Silberman and Clarice Duncan," said Cassie as soon as she heard Meredith's voice.

"Who are they? Well, I know Clarice Duncan but Sherie?" Meredith responded.

"Neither have ever been on my radar," said Cassie. "Sherie has been a holy pest. She's done some commercials and says she's written some articles for that little weekly tabloid in Beverly Hills. Mostly an advertiser pub. Not much else."

"Huh," murmured Meredith. "I don't know her. She give some references? And can you fax me a picture of her. Just curious, I guess."

"Her references are mostly producers or directors of her commercials, and the editor/publisher of the local weekly. I'll get her head shot on the fax as soon as we hang up. You know Clarice?"

"Sure. She's been here and there for a long time. She was a columnist with one of the smaller news syndicates when Bettina was around. Very small circulation and the outfit was eventually snapped up by one of the larger fringe media companies and shut down. She's also pretty visible wherever she can be, but seems to have some writing chops. I think she's with one of the smaller daily papers in Northern California now."

"She says she's close friends with a whole string of celebrities and gives a bunch of producers as references."

"She probably knows them over the years. But Cassie…I'm not planning to leave the show. Just so you know."

"I do. But they don't. Especially Sherie who REALLY wants a shot!"

Meredith treated herself to a long, hot bubble soak in the elegant bathroom of her suite, a glass of good tequila and a quiet steak dinner. Raymond would arrive the next night and she was excited but needed sleep. She'd planned a couple of activities for his visit, including a promise to Ito they would get together for dinner on Friday night. Ito and Raymond had become good friends over a drug case involving a digital toy company—and Bettina Grant's murder—among other adventures.

"I should have a little information you'll want to know when I get there," Raymond told her by phone that night, his voice teasing. She stretched her lithe body long in the king bed and murmured, "That's not all I'm looking forward to when you get here."

We'll have Manhattan

"You should cut your hair—make it kicky—and highlights, too. Blondish-reddish. Nancy agrees with me!" Amanda Borkin's throaty voice sounded motherly and only slightly peevish. "Oh, by the way, Nancy says 'hello' and to tell you how much she's enjoying watching you," Amanda and Meredith were arranging themselves in their normal seats on the set moments before the show rolled.

Breathing deeply, Meredith chose to tamp down a snotty reply. Instead she said, "Good to know. But gosh with only three weeks left, no need. Nancy'll be back before we could schedule a color session! And thank Nancy for the compliment. Nice to have the person you're surrogating for approve of you." Amanda shrugged and began looking at the teleprompter. Everybody in show biz seems to want multicolored blondish-reddish hair, snorted Meredith to herself.

The Floor Director called, "Rolling" and the show was live again. The rest of the morning show went as usual—smooth flowing and on time. Hop-skipping through the post-show planning and other tasks, Meredith rushed out for a quiet, solo lunch to handle whatever work she had waiting on her desk at the hotel. She made a daily point of calling Sonia and periodically checking in with Russ at the media syndicate.

"Star lady," he greeted her on the phone.

"Not!" she responded. "I'm a journalist who covers media."

"Catchy title you've given yourself. Good idea. Now tell me how it's going over there at the NTS nature park!" Meredith gave him the latest news such as it was. Mostly talked with him about the rumors about her leaving L.A. and joining the *It's a Good Day* show.

"The show hasn't an opening and my joining it permanently has never been hinted and was never on my agenda." She told him about Cassie receiving resumes and Amanda Borkin's attitude toward her.

"Well, it's a very competitive town and everyone kind of becomes a predator. I've told you about the inner-circle politics around here. For me, I'd say the byword is watch your back and what's also in front as opportunity. In this business at your level, it doesn't show up on a job listing. There's a shadow in the distance and it's up to you to find the sources and define it."

"Ugh," said Meredith. "Where's Allan Jaymar when I need him?" She referred to a very old friend of hers, and of Russ. Allan had functioned as her representative, counselor and agent after Bettina Grant died. She'd not seen him in several months and realized she owed him a visit as soon as she returned.

"Where is he?" Russ echoed. "I'm told he's selling his house in Bel Air and he and Potty are moving into the Movie-TV-Music Country Farm for retirement." Meredith's eyes snapped open.

"No! He's my last vestige of the old life in gossip—across the street from Bettina's house. My solace. When and how'd you hear that?"

"Grapevine," chuckled Russ. "Actually, he called me to find out where you were staying so he could send you a letter. You get it yet? Obviously not."

"But that's clear out in the West Valley."

"You have a car. Set up a regular lunch," said Russ matter-of-factly.

Meredith was quiet for a moment, then spoke up, "Russ, you're not retiring any time soon are you?"

"Dream on!" he laughed. "You should be so lucky! Don't forget to pencil me in for lunch before you leave!"

"I'll have my person contact yours!" she quipped.

After they hung up, she cleaned up the suite and took a short nap. Raymond was scheduled to leave L.A. early in the morning and arrive in New York around five. So at that time, Meredith ordered a bottle of champagne and a cheese plate from room service.

At six o'clock there was a tap on Meredith's door. She took a deep breath and opened it to T.K. Raymond, his leather jacket over his shoulder, his drag-along case behind him. They both suddenly felt shy. "Hi, I'm here." He said.

"Me too," she responded and opened the door to welcome him.

"Nice home," he commented, looking around.

"Temporary, of course, but better as of right now." She put her arms around his neck and pulled his face to hers in a deep welcoming kiss.

"Let me get rid of this baggage and…" Raymond gasped, pulling free and tossing his coat on the couch as Meredith opened the double doors to the bedroom. He dragged his bag into it. "What amazing activities do you have in store for us here in the Big Apple?" he asked turning to face her. She sprang toward him and he saw the intended choreography as she leaped into his arms, wrapping her legs around his waist. They tumbled back onto the bed in a tightly clasped heap.

Their lips re-met but awkwardly as they disassembled. "It works in the movies," she laughed.

"Good enough for me," he snickered as he jerked up her t-shirt and she reached for the zipper on his pants.

Eventually the lights of the city twinkled from the windows and Meredith reached over to turn on the lamp next to the disheveled bed. "Is the cheese plate dinner? And can we have some of that champagne?" asked Raymond, raising up on an elbow.

"Cheese plate was supposed to be an appetizer but…there was, well, a better choice…dinner is actually supposed to arrive about…," a knock interrupted her words. "Now." She slipped out of bed, pulled on a hotel robe, closed the bedroom doors and retrieved the dinner cart.

☆☆☆

"Great scallops," Raymond said as they worked their way through the menu Meredith had ordered. Both dressed in hotel robes, the windows overlooking Manhattan providing a dramatic backdrop. "It's kind of like a movie set," Raymond joked.

"Only better," Meredith added savoring the effervescence of the champagne in her glass.

"You won't be disappointed when you get home and get grocery store wine in a water glass will you?" Raymond mused.

Shaking her head, Meredith said, "Nothing about home is ever a disappointment and speaking of home, how's Paco? And where's the surprise information you teased me with?"

"Paco is fine, ornery because you aren't there and he only tolerates me. He's staying with Norman at the condo. I think he prefers Norman to me. And, you may want to take notes on the info I have. Now or after dinner?

"Paco only prefers Norman to you because Norman works from home and is always around to pay attention to Paco. The cat's an attention-suck, you know?"

"I do know. Are we having dessert?"

"Just brandy from the mini-bar."

"Let's get it and move to the couch. My news is interesting and complex." He stood up and brought out two small bottles of rich amber liquor from the small refrigerator.

"Marty's been hot on this," Raymond explained, retrieving a file folder from his briefcase. "Finding junior Bota is like a complex puzzle." He lowered himself to the couch and spread out a series of papers on the coffee table. First, he handed Meredith a photo of a thirty-something man, a 50s-type male bouffant wave in his hair, already soft in the jowls but flinty, mean eyes. "Meet Junior. An older picture." She nodded.

"He disappeared about five years ago. He had a sheet of semi-minor infractions until then and a lot of law enforcement agencies speculating about bigger illegal involvement. He hadn't been quiet about his intentions toward Ronnie Milton and family. He and his entourage of young thugs were vocal about blaming—and avenging— Ronnie's mother for the embezzlement charges that took his dad to prison where he died. Coincidentally, the auto accident that took out Ronnie's parents was never really 'solved.' No proof that it was anything but poor driving on winding roads at night. So, five years ago, 'poof! Junior's gone. Think about time frames that Ronnie gave you.

"At first we thought he'd moved his own headquarters to the East Coast. Maybe to track Ronnie. But no sign of him anywhere. No driver's licenses, credit cards, nada. Ironically, his pals who thugged around with him in the L.A. area were all pretty much incarcerated in one place or another by then. Not Junior. So, Marty interviewed most of them and most had lost connection with him some years ago. But we did learn one thing, from one former friend: Junior was gay, but hid it very carefully. At that time, his cohort wouldn't have been very tolerant. Still…," Raymond almost gasped in the telling of the story. He took a sip of brandy and took a moment of silence.

"The only family we could find was Junior's paternal grandmother, Martha Bota, now in her late eighties and living in a nursing home in Eagle Rock. And, as her caregiver said, 'She's really fractured.' In layman's terms that mean crazy as a loon. But when we talked with her she gave us an important clue: he was using his 'real' name—Earwig."

"Earwig?" Meredith burst out in laughter.

"Hey, it's a 'clue,'" smirked Raymond.

"And you're a detective," Meredith added a finish to the sentence.

"When we looked at the visitor list for the old woman, we found an Elwin W. Manabota who had visited a number of times until about four years ago. We put that together with Martha's comment about his official name and it opened up the flood gates." He sat back and took another drink from the small glass that held brandy. "Not the worst brandy, but not the best either."

"Hey—you're in a hotel in New York. Not a fancy house in Malibu! Be respectful of the folks who are paying for this!" chuckled Meredith.

"Oh, I am. Please thank them for me," he smiled endearingly at her. "But, on with Sonny's saga. He apparently changed his name back to the original family name—Manabota—and went by his own official name again—probably to give himself some distance from his former life, or to go incognito. We don't know because the last piece of identification of him was a death certificate Marty called me about just before I left. Our researcher found it in Riverside County. An Elwin W. Manabota, aged 35, died of AIDS just about four years ago."

"Is it the same guy, the same as Junior Bota?"

"Hard to imagine a duplicate name with Elwin Winston Manabota. But, Marty's going to check it out with the former buddies. No other family. Junior's mother apparently named her baby boy his very 'fancy' name, as Martha would call it, eventually left and no longer seems to have a footprint. Possibly deceased. No siblings, no aunts or uncles, father and grandfather gone and grandma is in a world of her own."

"Does that mean Ronnie is safe now, no more stalking, no more danger?"

"We're waiting for Marty to check in with the old gang. If they even know. But the timing on it all seems to click."

"Ronnie and Father Paul will be happy to hear that. The story's over and so's the danger." Meredith flopped back against the couch and stared at the ceiling. "The end!" she closed her eyes and sighed.

Raymond reached over and squeezed her knee. "Well, probably. You know how stories spawn sub-stories?" Meredith looked at him.

"Martha," he said simply. "Her accountant apparently embezzled or stole the trust fund that was to have supported her at the nursing home where she currently lives. An upscale one, not a public assistance facility. She may have to move out."

"Where's the accountant now?"

"He died and his practice is closed. He had a partner and we're turning the situation over to the white-collar crime folks to investigate. There was money in the account—enough for a long time. Now there's not. Marty and I are determined to find out where it went."

"Wow. You guys are so nice. Maybe too nice."

"Yeah, considering Martha spat at us and then fell asleep. What a slap to the ego. Not even interesting enough to keep her awake."

"Speaking of keeping awake. My alarm goes off at three-thirty tomorrow morning and the driver arrives at four-fifteen. We should put the dinner cart outside and call it a night. Sorry for the early hour."

"Fortunately, I don't have to keep those hours," chuckled Raymond. "I'll send you off with coffee and a kiss and go back to bed."

"Uh uh," smirked Meredith. "You are coming to the show and will be in the first row in the audience. You aren't coming all this way to not see what's keeping me from home!"

"Spare me," murmured Raymond, standing up to his full six foot plus height, looking around the room, then pushing the dinner cart to the door and out into the hall for pick up. "Come on," he invited. "We have business to take care of before lights out!"

CHAPTER 39
SEPTEMBER 22, 1989
MANHATTAN
FRIDAY MORNING

Boy talk

Uh oh, thought Meredith as Amanda Borkin strode with focused determination toward Meredith's dressing room. T.K. Raymond had just been extricated from the confines of the studio security guard keeping him from making his way back to meet Meredith after the morning broadcast. Visitors weren't allowed without special permission and she had forgotten to leave his name. No harm, no foul, he was there now, complimenting her on her appearance during the show. Amanda noticed him.

"Who's this? A special guest?" asked the wily TV host, raising an eyebrow and looking coquettishly at Raymond. He quickly interjected. "T.K. Raymond. The L.A. part of Ms. Ogden's life." He extended his hand. She shook it.

"Seeing as how it's Friday, taking her home to L.A. for the weekend?" Amanda chuckled.

"Not really," Raymond answered affably. "She pretty much makes her own plans, but we thought it would be fun to spend the weekend here in the Big Apple. I took some time off."

"…off from…?" Amanda persisted, matching affability with Raymond.

"T.K. is chief of a high-profile detective unit in L.A.," Meredith answered, also with feigned affability.

"Ladies, I'll absent myself," Raymond quickly stepped in. "Meredith, I'm meeting Buster for lunch…." Taking a pen from the makeup table and his small spiral tablet from his pocket, he made a note and handed it to her. "Here's where we'll be at one. Join us if you can." He turned to Amanda, nodded his head and smiled. "Ms. Borkin. A pleasure." And he left.

"Certainly eye-candy and a gentleman, nice to wake up to," mused Amanda to Meredith.

"M…," murmured Meredith, then asked, "What's up?"

"Just wanted to meet your visitor. He seemed important." Meredith smiled, noncommittally. "Well, see you at the planning meeting in a little while," said Amanda as she turned and left.

At the planning meeting, Meredith was surprised when one of her suggestions was actually accepted for a topic on Monday's show. It was a rare development in a group that often shrugged off her ideas as "too Hollywood" or "not broad enough." The author of a segment was normally the lead researcher and on-camera discussant on a story. That often meant a busy afternoon frenzy to pull together interviews, artwork or videos or other material and work with the production assistant or director to make the segment ready for the next day's broadcast. In this case, Meredith already had parts of the story on hand and access to current video interviews from Cassie in L.A. Other materials were archived TV show clips easily accessed and by 12:30 she had the format sketched out with the director and ready to go.

"I actually got a lead story," she crowed at lunch with Raymond and Buster Boles. "I've been kept in my 'place' as simply a stand-in for the entire month since I arrived, except with the Trubo kid story with Rick. For sure after that. Like I need to relearn my place because the producer elevated me without the blessing of the rest of the show staff. Maybe your visit motivated…well, at least Amanda, if not others. You cut an impressive swath."

Raymond snuffed out an obscure, likely obscene, response. Buster tried to ignore the conversation. Meredith just smiled. The rest of the lunch was consumed by discussions of the two mysterious stalkers following Meredith earlier: the first to the church meet with Ronnie Milton and the priest, the second, the visitor who stopped by the hotel asking for Meredith the weekend before.

"I've got some really blurred security footage," said Buster. "Being a fancy hotel, they've had these cameras in place in a couple of locations—this one from the hotel entrance— for a while, but the quality isn't great. We maybe can enhance it but I'm not sure there's much there we don't already know about."

"Let's look at it anyhow," Raymond proposed. "Maybe something will trigger recognition in some way." He scowled and shook his head. Meredith agreed heartily and asked when. They agreed on the next day, Saturday morning before the day became a tourist journey for Meredith and Raymond.

"Good the big guy is here with you. Because, lady, you got a stalker!"

The possibility was on their minds Friday night when they met Ito who insisted on hosting them for a memorable New York dinner. He insisted on taking them to Windows on the World, the restaurant with the breath-taking views of Manhattan from the 107th floor of the World Trade Center.

"Something about weekends in New York that seems to suggest brilliantly twinkling lights and earthy street adventures," Raymond chuckled.

"We're all pretty lucky," Meredith mused. "For so many people, it's mostly earthy street realities not adventures. We get the best of it." All three acknowledged the truth in her murmur.

"I wanted to show you that I'm Mr. Cosmopolitan now," laughed Ito, offering a toast to the reunion. "I feel so comfortable in my position at UAM, but," he quickly added, "I'm always available to help solve a crime!"

"It's a long ways from Bright Leaf Lane," Meredith said softly, a touch of nostalgia. The three of them each fell into a momentary reverie about the home-based office in Bel Air where they'd all met under criminal circumstances six years before. Ito livened up the mood by taking them to a jazz club after dinner. With the mellow if melodiously discordant notes swirling around them, Ito crowed, "New York has so many entertainment wonders and what I like— so many you can walk to."

"Can I sneak into your suitcase and help you solve some crimes," he joked, saying goodbye to Raymond. They all knew he probably wasn't kidding.

CHAPTER 40
SEPTEMBER 25,1989
GREEN PARK HOTEL, MANHATTAN
MONDAY MORNING

New York, New York

"Can't be," groaned Raymond, cringing at the sound of the alarm buzzer. "No one gets up voluntarily at three-thirty. Turn the damn thing off!" He buried his head in the pillow and replayed the weekend, hoping the noise was a bad dream. It had been a full and pleasant three days that still lingered in his mind—even sleep strained.

On Saturday, he and Meredith had spent an hour with Buster in his office looking at the grainy video of the woman who had come to the hotel looking for Meredith. They saw little new, but it gave them all a better picture—blurred though it was—of the unknown visitor. In the afternoon, the couple took a run through Central Park, enjoying the verdant landscape, its pathways, trees and gardens starting to change colors on a crisp fall day. "Not Malibu Beach but pretty nice," said Meredith as they stopped at a bench to sit and take a breath.

"Lot of people," Raymond answered looking around at the weekend crowd with the same idea of enjoying a September day in the Park. That evening they explored a recommended eatery in Greenwich Village.

Sunday, they slept late, understanding "it'll be a while before either of us gets this luscious an opportunity again." As they lounged in the suite's living area, the left-overs of breakfast piled on the room service cart, Raymond sighed, "I can see how you can get used to this." Meredith looked up from the *New York Times* and laughed.

"Don't get used to it. If I joined the network, it would be business as usual and no more elegant lodging allowances or arrangements. I'd be on my own!"

Raymond looked at her intently, eyebrows raised as in question. "What?" she asked.

"Is that something you think about?"

She mothered the question, face furrowed in thought. Finally, "I guess I always think about it some," she answered quietly. "Not because of any desire to be on my own—alone— better word. But because 'alone' has been part of my life—most of my life. "

"We don't often use the word, Merri, but love is where I'm coming from," said the stoic man almost shyly. "How I feel about you and our life together. Whole, complete. I love you and I love us."

"And I've never done anything but love you, detective. Almost from the first New Year's Eve together. But I'm learning how to be 'us' and to feel totally engrossed in that. I need both your love and your help, which you always give. I'm trying to learn how to reciprocate." She looked up in uncertainty.

"Oh, lady, I can help!" he smiled, stood up and moved to sit next to her, folding her in his arms and hugging her.

"I'm a quick study," she murmured.

Later, they opted for a matinee of *A Little Night Music* off Broadway (Meredith had interviewed the director on the morning show and written an article on him), and Sunday night was again spent with room service in the hotel room overlooking the city's sparkle.

There wasn't much sparkle as he tried to open his eyes at the 3:30 alarm the next morning. "Turn the damn thing off," he growled.

"Can't," sighed Meredith. "It's a workday here in New York. Weekend's over." She sounded sad, rolling into him and pulling his body closer to her own. "Remember this," she commanded, hugging him fervently, head to toe, kissing him for a long while. She then turned back and swung her legs out of the hotel bed. He groaned again. "Shhh," she said. "Go back to sleep."

"Like that could happen," he snarfed, sitting up. Forty-five minutes later she stood at the door, dressed for the studio, a to-go cup of coffee in hand, tears in her eyes. "Hug Paco for me, have a good flight. And find my stalker."

"Just be careful," he implored. "Break a leg in these last couple of weeks. See you at the end of next week!" She kissed him lightly and was gone. He flopped back onto the bed.

He rolled over and attempted sleep again, but it didn't come. The weekend had been so full of highs and unpressured pleasures, he lay there running the mental films and smiling about those pleasures.

☆☆☆

As eight-thirty a.m. arrived on Monday, Raymond zipped his suitcase, then looked around the hotel suite making sure it was in order before he walked out the door and left for the airport. He somehow sensed things were changing and he felt a tinge of sadness and uncertainty about it. Some self-admitted fear that this chirpy, bustling, seductive New York was winning the race over day-to-day Los Angeles for his love's choice of future.

That afternoon, Meredith rode up the elevator to the room, slightly giddy from a good and successful day with the morning show crew. She had again won the approval of an interview she proposed for later in the week, and then scored the interview through the celebrity's agent. As she opened the door to the suite, she caught the slightest whiff of Raymond's shaving cream. It stopped her mid-doorway. The place echoed of emptiness. For a week she'd enjoyed the company first of Gloria and then the total immersion of time with Raymond. She was alone again and noticed how empty it felt. Strange, considering most of her life had been consumed with professional activities and commitments and aloneness had never much impacted her. This was a different kind of aloneness and she didn't quite recognize it. She immediately returned to the discussion with Raymond about "us" and the love of it. She could easily identify her feeling for him. But, as she had said, she was having to define what those feelings meant to a united "us."

CHAPTER 41
SEPTEMBER 26, 1989
WEST LOS ANGELES
TUESDAY MORNING

When we're old and grey

"Margo. Can I talk with you in my office?" Raymond's request was more command than suggestion.

"Sure," said the blithe red head special agent in charge of forensic corporate crime, looking up from her work. She walked into the glassed-in office of Captain T.K. Raymond. Interactions had been so strained between them she was quiet, respectful and demur as she took a seat in front of his desk.

"I know you don't work directly for me. And I know the atmosphere has been erratic since you joined us recently. Apologies. I'm not a very good fake philanderer, not a flirt as many men in this part of the country might be. But, if I've been offensive and stand-offish, I'm sorry. I'm in a committed relationship and maybe just don't even know how to deal with frivolous office banter with an attractive, flirtatious woman. Even one who saved my life."

She looked at him and smiled, surprised and not knowing how to respond. "So, what do I get from it?" she countered, raising an eyebrow. Characteristically flirtatious, she still didn't usually contend with the kind of history she had with T.K. Raymond, and didn't know how to respond to his candor.

"A desk in a great office on the west side of L.A. and pretty much autonomy."

"It's okay, boss," she said. "I get it and if I've caused you embarrassment or discomfort, my apologies as well."

He waved a dismissive hand. "No problem—and I'm not your boss. Bernie is. But, I do need your help." She smiled with a wily grin. She got that he needed a clear path to ask and accept help.

"What's up?" she asked dispassionately.

"You're a forensic accountant/corporate fraud investigator. I have a strange case that needs some digging and you're the best one to do it." He told her of the sad situation about Martha Bota and her disappearing trust fund. Margo listened, scowling.

"I hate it when people take this kind of advantage of truly helpless old people. Give me all the details and information and I'll look into it. It doesn't sound like it can be complicated. The opportunity was too available for stealing her assets, and there was no oversight." Raymond thanked her. She stood to leave, then turned to look at him. "Must have been a good weekend. You look ten years younger—long coast-to-coast flight and all." He blushed then smiled. She winked and walked out the door with a slight sashay.

CHAPTER 42
SEPTEMBER 27, 1989
MANHATTAN
WEDNESDAY

Yakity-yak

Trepidation wrapped around Meredith as she approached the elegant double doors of Amanda Borkin's flat on the 18th floor high above Central Park. She was ready for the promised column interview with the morning show host, had done her homework, but knew that Amanda was wily and manipulative. Meredith wanted a clean, deep look at the famous face, not a shellacked PR image. And based on what she'd seen over the weeks, that shellacked image was what nearly always marched in front of Amanda—wherever she went, whatever she did.

Wrapped in a lavender silk poncho over a sleek dark purple jumpsuit, her golden-red hair sleeked back behind her ears, Amanda welcomed Meredith in swooping grand style. "So this is my lair," she greeted in her well known deep throaty voice.

"Lovely. Impressive," Meredith murmured. Amanda offered wine and cheese nibbles. Meredith demurred in favor of club soda. "On duty?" Amanda goaded her, pouring the crystal liquid into her own glass.

"Something like that," Meredith smiled. The two settled themselves onto facing modern cream-colored leather sofas, clean lines in concert with the angular décor of the rest of the living room.

They quickly hashed over the morning's broadcast and Amanda took a sip of wine before soliciting, "Tell me about yourself, Meredith." It took the younger journalist less than three seconds to realize the strategy attempting to unfold. Ask your interviewer about herself, get her talking and when the piece comes out, make sure it's made known, "All she did was talk about herself, not me." Any discomfort about the final article has a good excuse and someone to blame for the misinterpretation.

Meredith smiled. "Not this evening, Amanda. This is about you and you have such a great background so let's start there. I see that you attended Wellesley College and studied English. How in the world did you find your way to being America's favorite morning show news host?" Amanda took a discrete sigh and a drink of wine, settled back against the cushions and told the story that Meredith had heard before but would start the conversation in the right direction. English major, no idea where to go with it, interned at a Boston public relations firm, heard about a weather girl opening at a local TV station, auditioned and got the job. After several years as a part of a morning show team in Massachusetts, she was offered the cohost position. Her producer-director boss who became her husband, moved to a larger station in New York and she was part of the package deal. The marriage broke up but Amanda was golden and moved into the *It's a Good Day* chair ten years ago.

"I feel like I've grown up in morning TV and grown old on *It's a Good Day*."

Meredith clucked, as expected, and shook her head. "Hardly an accurate statement from the 'Queen of morning TV,'" she said. Amanda snickered and drank some more wine as Meredith noticed most of the bottle was gone. Amanda must have prepped for the interview, too.

"Tell me what you know of your audience—the morning audience," Meredith asked. Facts and figures, some enlightenment before Amanda broke her own narrative and said, "One thing I know—they are loyal as long as you're loyal to them."

Meredith noticed Amanda's hands shaking very slightly—hardly noticeable, but evidence of nervousness and self-consciousness. It surprised Meredith. "What does being loyal to them look like?" she asked. The discussion veered off into more esoteric territory and Meredith felt the charge of adrenalin knowing she was getting a good story and a great inside view of the mercurial woman sitting across from her in the starkly fashionable apartment. Two hours later, the conversation had moved into eclectic subjects about on-camera demeanors, who had failed at that, Amanda's own foibles, and positive and negative set-side relationships. The subject of Amanda's cohost Nancy Igleton came up.

"I'm worried about her," Amanda said, picking at a well-manicured nail. Meredith looked at her in question. "And this is definitely not for publication. I don't think Nancy has her heart in the show anymore. It's a job and now with the baby and all, I'm afraid she'll just call in her role each day."

Meredith scowled and asked, "I don't see how that's possible with a process and production as intense as that show."

"She says she has no plans to 'sweat the small stuff'—weight, looks, preparation. The family has her entire attention now. It doesn't work for the presence she has through this show. The reputation and…well, style…and, as you say, as 'intense' as it is."

"And that worries you for many reasons?" Meredith probed, musing about Amanda's style reference and the pressure she, herself, had received to cut and color her own hair.

"Sure, a younger cohost might be brought in, or the producers may decide to let it slide and replace the whole concept with a new format…a million things that could disrupt…well, you get it." Now Amanda's eyes had taken on a darkly fierce glint and Meredith could see some defensiveness and a hidden warning behind it. Mostly because it was aimed directly at her. "Rumor has it that Cece and Tim are planning to expand the serious news coverage and want a more focused—'credible'—news person. I hope that will be me. I'm lobbying for it but…, and there are other changes in the wind. They seem to like the Hollywood presence…but they know I'll be a fierce opponent if I don't like their ideas.…"

"Amanda, you have to know they'll give you the best possible showcase. You ARE the show. You know that," said Meredith, as she wrapped up the interview before it could become personal or threatening. She knew better than to suggest to Amanda that the news position would likely be someone with bona fide news background, and, and…. The two women laughed casually as they reached the door. "You'll let me see the manuscript before publication," Amanda commented coolly, as though an afterthought.

"I think I mentioned before that's not the policy of the syndicate or my own column, but I'll check on any questions about accuracy. It'll probably be a couple of weeks before I release it. I'm also doing a full feature on morning shows in general. And I'll need some good photos from the PR department." Amanda didn't react to the answer, knowing full well what the response—and the resulting outcome— would be. Both women bid affable farewells.

When the massive double doors closed, Meredith walked abnormally briskly to the elevator and once inside, sighed hugely with relief. She'd survived the mama grizzly bear's den and only had seven more work-days to deal with before she was fully released from the obtuse threats.

Not the sound of music

Meredith mused over the couched threats in the final conversation with Amanda as she mothered the currently pressing ones from the mystifying "Duck." She continued to skirt the road, hiking along the brush as she continued her journey from the marina to whatever civilization was ahead. The scrapes and scratches on her palms and elsewhere burned and she occasionally dripped on them some of the water left in the bottle she carried. Amanda Borkin set aside, her main concern was over any potential threat from the strange man who plucked her from the ghost ship and dropped her at the empty marina. He'd given her no reason to assume he'd have second thoughts about her ride along on his apparent illegal delivery route that morning, but she was not stupid enough to assume he might not rethink the possibilities.

As if preordained, her roadside reverie was rudely curtailed by the muffled sound of a small engine—maybe motorbike or scooter—coming from the direction of the marina. Fearful of what or who would come with the sound, Meredith again crouched low into the underbrush.

Nothing but the truth

Crouching low onto the bedroom floor, Raymond peered under the bed and called, "Come on, Paco. Your dinner's ready. Stop pouting. If you will, I will. How's that?" No movement or sound from the dark tunnel under the mattress. Everyone seemed to know Meredith Ogden was missing.

At six o'clock Raymond got a call from Marty. "Every law enforcement facility and organization in the entire Suisun, Grisly and San Pablo Bay area is on alert. T.K., do you want to extend this to San Francisco Bay or further yet?"

Raymond sat at the dining table, phone clenched to his ear, and ran a hand over his face in frustration. "Not yet. It's not even 36 hours. It just feels like it. Let's hold and see what happens. Hopefully the studio security will track down more of the people who were on that damned ship visit and we'll get a little more insight."

"On another subject," Marty continued, "I caught up with Elwin—AKA Junior—Bota's former domestic partner. Junior walked totally away from his previous thug-hood. Felt he had to in order to live a quiet life as a happy gay man in those days. Part of that was also due to his diagnosis of the virus. He did tell his partner, however, that his father had had some involvement in the death of Ronnie's parents. He had no other information."

"That's good news," Raymond answered. "I can let Meredith and her Ronnie Milton fan club know they can breathe completely freely now. The bad news is—whoever was following her is truly following her and not Ronnie." He sighed. "Guess you should turn in a report on the cold case about Ronnie's parents. It was never solved. In fact, I'm not sure it was even left open. But make sure it gets updated."

Marty rang off. T.K. poured a glass of scotch.

R & R

"I'll buy you a scotch and treat you to a good lunch," said Billie Longmore who was waiting unexpectedly in Meredith's dressing room immediately following Friday's show. Meredith hadn't seen Billie since the trip to Montauk nearly two weeks before and smiled broadly when the older woman, stunning with her striking silver hair pulled into a bun at her neck and wearing a fashionably tailored suit greeted her.

"Nice surprise," said Meredith, closing the door to her private enclave off the set.

"I'm in Manhattan this weekend and Cece's got some work to do so I thought maybe you and I could hit my club and its spa tomorrow. Pool, massage, sauna—whatever suits your fancy. I need the attention and thought you might enjoy it, too."

Meredith idly noted her to-do list on the dressing table, then grinned. "Oh, you bet. That sounds divine. My weekdays have been filled to the brim with the long hours around the show and my own columns to write. Tell me more."

☆ ☆ ☆

Saturday evening saw a mellow Meredith after a day at Billie's private club—high atop a skyscraper in midtown. She had arranged on Friday to take an aerobics class in the morning, relishing the familiar burn and pound of the music in her bones and body, exorcising the stress and grind from her work in the Big Apple. The pool was indoors, but extended to an outer terrace with a view of the city, closed off when the weather was poor. It was not poor today but the two stayed indoors out of the crisp air, and then enjoyed a light casual lunch before sliding into the lower floor for a welcome massage. Billie had been totally hospitable and affable. No one spoke about *It's a Good Day* but they covered ground around modern news coverage, the life of a foreign correspondent, triggered by Billie's report that Rick Santaros was back in the field in Kuwait. Both women paused to talk about a news correspondent in war zones and especially the situation in the Middle East. They talked of the female war reporters, mentioning that Christiane Amanpour who'd been in Iran and Iraq, and was now following events in Eastern Europe; Anne Garrels who'd been expelled from a bureau posting in Moscow and then was a bureau chief in South America before taking on coverage of Eastern Europe. And the pioneers like Marie Colvin and Claire Hollingworth. Billie had stories of her own that fascinated Meredith. She asked permission to make notes as they talked. Billie was happy to comply.

By the time she was back at the hotel, Meredith was well rid of her fear about an empty weekend, and mellow from massage. And then Ito called inviting her to join him for "the best sushi in New York." How could she say "no?" She didn't.

"So, Boss, how's our Ronnie Milton case coming along," Ito asked, adroitly picking up a succulent piece of sashimi with his chopsticks.

"Not really a case, Ito. But certainly an investigation. We know that Junior Bota is dead, his only family, his grandmother, in a nursing home, mostly demented. And no other hangover vengeance. Just to make sure, Marty is visiting Junior's former partner to see if there's more to be learned. Otherwise, Ronnie's home free. Wherever he chooses that to be." Ito only shook his head.

"Anything else I can help with?" he asked, half joking, but more obviously half serious.

"No, not now, Ito. You have a full plate with your own job. And I'm just getting through the last week of this TV assignment and still trying to figure out the best exit strategy. Besides, most of my work these days is more in line with 'research,' not investigations."

He looked at her with a dramatic frown and said, "Oh well. I loved it when everyone was on the lookout for the truth about someone or something."

"Journalism is always about that, Ito. But not always about cloak and dagger."

"Or drugs and murders," he added with a wicked glint in his eye as they both ordered another glass of chardonnay.

Meredith was amused when she realized it was nearly ten o'clock when she returned to the hotel. A rare happening with a weekday three-thirty a.m. wake-up call. But tomorrow was Sunday and turning off the alarm setting and requesting no wake-up call was a luxury. She settled into the wide soft bed and placed a call to Raymond.

"Saturday night is the loneliest night of the year," he sighed long distance. "And all the while you've been out eating sushi with Ito. Not fair!"

"Barely a week left," she reminded. "Hang in there."

"I have some follow-up on the Junior Bota case," he reported later in the conversation. "Marty drove out to Redlands—

mid-way to Palm Springs—and interviewed a guy who was Junior's last partner/lover. He told Marty Junior had given up the chase against Ronnie before they met—about four or five years ago. That jives with everything else we seem to know about the situation. I think you can give Ronnie the all-clear."

"But what about Martha, the grandmother? Anything on what happened to her trust fund?

"Not yet, but Margo's on it."

"Ito would love to get involved. You know what a whiz he is at digging through numbers."

"And that's not a good idea no matter how you look at it. He's got a good job. He's in New York. Margo's a forensic accountant and I'd hate to complicate the office here any more than it is already. She's on it."

"Well…if you need back-up…." Meredith said quietly.

"Not with this particular issue," Raymond laughed.

As she turned off the light and pondered the day and the weeks in New York, Meredith came to a strange decision about Sunday and once again set the alarm.

Sunday in New York

The subtle, spicy scent of incense was somehow comforting as it wafted around Meredith in the sanctuary of St. Thomas Catholic Church in Manhattan. Sitting in the farthest back pew, she took in the light and rich warmth of the stained-glass windows, the somehow ethereal sense of the room. Distant, familiar recollections wended through her mind. She knew these sensual cues and they reminded her of elementary years in a girls' Catholic school. She'd just participated in the early morning mass, connecting with Father Duncan in this unusual way, for Meredith. Now she sat quietly as the last congregants straggled out the doors. Soon the tall, ebony-skinned priest returned to the interior and greeted her.

"An unexpected visit. A pleasure," he said extending his hand. She rose, took it and smiled broadly.

"I have some good news for Ronnie and I didn't want to disturb anything—and I wasn't even sure where he is staying now—but I did want to deliver it in person—at least to you. You're his messenger."

"Come on back into our outdoor sitting area. Weather's crisp, but a nice day." Father Duncan guided her to a rudimentary patio next to the cement playground, then excused himself to change from his service vestments into street clothes. As Meredith pulled together some wooden chairs and sat down, a presence behind her caught her attention. Ronnie Milton quietly sat down in the extra chair. "Hi, Miss Ogden," he said. He seemed cleaned up a little and certainly less stressed around his eyes and face. He smiled an almost-angelic smile. "I noticed you at the service and wanted to say hello and thank you." The priest quietly arrived and pulled up another wooden chair.

"Ronnie, are you back here living now?" asked Meredith.

The young man nodded. "I feel at home here."

"Well," began Meredith, "you can live just about anywhere you'd like. The danger and threats against you are over." She explained the information Raymond and Marty had uncovered. Ronnie's head dropped to his chest and he grunted a subtle sigh.

"I'm relieved," he said almost wistfully. "And I live here now. I'm about to start a new life phase, as Father calls it. Going to City College and starting to look forward. But I'm happy—and of value here. But thank you oh so much."

The conversation meandered here and there before Meredith excused herself. "Thank you both. It's not often we gossip folks get a chance to do some real good. And later this week I head back to California and home, for me." She handed both men a business card. "This is Buster Boles' contact information. He can help you if you get into trouble or are somehow harassed by anyone else." She pulled two more cards from her bag. "And this is me. If you're in California, please call—or just let me know how you're doing. I feel a little engaged in your journey now Ronnie. And Pastor, thank you so very much. I'm glad I came this morning. Your invitation and 'hospitality' have been empowering."

As she headed for the door, Ronnie quickly interrupted. "Miss Ogden?" He was blushing. "If it suits you, you can go ahead and write my story. But please don't mention where I am either in the city or the specific church." Meredith looked at him, surprised but sympathetic. He nodded. "Really. I know writing about people is your thing. It's my only way of saying thanks—for now, and that plane ride a long time ago."

"Thank you, Ronnie, I'll never endanger your life choice and anonymity," Meredith responded.

"You don't have to," he said. "Just don't say what city and what church. Is it a deal?" Meredith nodded, then hugged the young man. "Any current photos?" she asked, hesitantly, at the last minute.

"I'll take some and send them this week," said the priest.

"Sunglasses, non-identifiable baseball cap, nondescript background, but big smile," Meredith instructed. She shook hands with the tall man, squeezed Ronnie's arm and left, amazed. Her amazement lingered well into the afternoon as she assembled two other columns for release in the next two weeks. Her three-part series on morning television had gone well, including an unexpected phone interview with Nancy Igleton, plus quick conversations with other veteran morning show hosts who'd moved on to other endeavors, and with *It's a Good Day* producer Tim Felton. He'd been associated with other talk shows before his current position and had great insight.

"I have enough columns scoped out and written for the next six weeks," she told Raymond by phone that night. "Besides the morning TV series, I have a great collection of stories for another about female foreign TV war correspondents—a kind of historical piece that Billie Longmore inspired—a piece on Ronnie Milton, and one on a tough new movie shooting in the Bronx. Spent several days visiting the location and doing interviews. Now I can breathe a sigh of relief. And thanks to the various celebrities in and out of our show, I have several weeks' worth of celebrity columns as well."

"All the better for your return," Raymond answered. "I have a feeling you're going to need some time to adjust back to regular living here in sleepy caz-u-all old California." They both laughed, knowing better.

CHAPTER 47
OCTOBER 12, 1989
SUISUN BAY/HIDDEN HARBOR/MALIBU
THURSDAY

Bad B movie

5:00 p.m.

Meredith shrunk deep into the weeds and brush as she slowly wended her way toward her imagined civilization. She figured that if a motorbike came from the marina, it would have to return to it, and feared who might be riding it. Sure enough, about a half hour after the first inland pass, the rattling put-put of a small engine broke the silence, heading toward the water. Meredith slunk to the ground and rolled behind a tree, holding her breath mostly in terror.

As the small vehicle passed by and the sound diminished, Meredith glanced up to see only the back of the driver's head. But turning her own she could see inland that there might be a structure ahead. She stayed on the ground behind the tree for a good half hour until she felt fairly confident no one else was exploring the path. Then she scampered ahead, focused on the slight shadow she'd noticed a small distance inland.

I can't believe this, she exclaimed to herself. This is silly. It's 1989 and I'm living a drama that isn't even credible enough for a bad "B" movie. This is totally ridiculous. As the silhouette morphed into full view, it seemed like a gas station or some type of roadside store. She practically ran down the road, dismissing any concern about noises from the marina.

☆☆☆

In the handsome house on the bluff over Malibu Beach, the agitated detective attempted to distract himself by dealing with reports and paperwork from his office. He'd broken his concentration with visits to the kitchen for a snack, coffee, even went through a short workout in his make-shift gym in the space under a small storage overhang off the garage. He would have taken a beach run but was afraid to leave the house and the phone. He was beginning to intuit the worst, considering that it had been a day and a half since Meredith walked out the door and left for Suisun Bay. Too long for a simple "got lost," or a detour to spend time with a good story, but mostly too long for no contact to anyone—himself, Sonia, Gloria or even her East Coast bosses who had been casually asked about any contact with her in the past two days.

Who do you think you are?

"Meredith, you have a very important message," called out the show producer's assistant, holding out a pink message slip. "He said it was urgent." The show had just wrapped for the morning and Meredith was still disconnecting the mic and its wires. She accepted the slip and saw Russ Talbot's name and number. Then felt a fearful quiver in her bones. Am I in trouble? she asked, wondering about the urgency.

"What the hell is this column, Meredith?" came Russ's commanding but controlled voice. "It's really bullshit. You know that."

Confusion and instant defensiveness rose up as the first reaction, then Meredith talked herself to calm. "Back up, Russ. Which column and what's bullshit. I'm really confused."

"This week's column. It came in a little while ago and Todd red flagged it and brought it to me."

"Wait," said Meredith, working to control her shaky voice. "What's the subject? I'm still trying to put this all into context."

"Your take on Sal Mortensen, the new VP of Development for New Gold Productions! Call him a 'lovable but loathsome pedophile....' I won't go on." Meredith flashed through the subjects she'd covered in columns and especially the couple of back-ups she'd kept in case she fell behind in her writing schedule. She couldn't place anything she'd recently written about New Gold Productions. She suddenly worried that she may have screwed up her well-planned and, so far, well-managed schedule and calendar of columns.

"I...I don't think I've written anything about New Gold...but Russ, I have this week's column in my bag and was going to drop it off today. Can we look at what you have? You don't release until Wednesday. Let's figure this out. I'm totally mystified." Russ mumbled his approval and they agreed on an appointment at two o'clock. The rest of the morning show work and planning session seemed like swimming through cotton to Meredith as she anxiously anticipated the encounter ahead.

Walking into Russ Talbot's office at UAM she felt her knees go soft. Russ never before had demanded her presence or raised his voice—or suspicion—over her work. She was so shaken by the thought she had trouble convincing herself that it wasn't a mistake she, herself, had made. But she couldn't sort it out. She saw Todd Lingren, the managing editor for the syndicated services sitting in a side chair and knew things were tense.

The column in question sat on the edge of Russ' desk and he pushed it toward her, his face grim, eyes squinted in anger. "This can't be you!" he said with a snarl she'd never heard from him before. She picked up the print-out and began to read it as she sat down in front of the desk. Her eyes grew wide and her heart pounded as she read words she would never have written even in her most defiant way. But there was her name and the normal syndicate submission format, dated today and sent from area code 213. L.A.

"I've never seen this before, Russ. I swear I didn't write this. I cannot recall ever interviewing or researching this guy or this company. Items here or there in the old gossip days, but never…where'd you get it?"

"Came in by fax, as usual," answered Todd. "But a day early. At first, I started proofing and copy editing, automatic…because I almost never have to do much with your copy. And then I took a close look at it. There are allegations in there, name-calling— all the things that bring out the attorneys. At first, I just thought I'd run it by legal. That's a typical matter of course. But then it just wasn't a sound presentation, sound arguments or allegations without confirming sources. That's when I brought it into Russ." Both men looked at Meredith.

She thought for a moment, then looked closely at the copy again. "This isn't our office phone or fax number. It is a 213— Los Angeles area—but not ours. And this is not Sonia's day in the office. Maybe it's the fax number from the weekly newspaper office she also works at. I'll call her." Russ pushed the phone toward her. She picked up the receiver, pushed a button for an outside line, and punched in Sonia's phone number. She asked the answering party for Sonia and waited anxiously.

"Did you, by any chance, fax a column for me to the syndicate today?" She preempted any unnecessary conversation when Sonia answered. "Huh. I didn't think you would. Do you know if we have any article or column past or future about Sal Mortensen at New Gold Productions?" She put her hand over the phone to tell Russ and Todd that Sonia carried a thick binder with just about everything past and present in case a question like this came along when the assistant was not in Meredith's physical office. They all bided their time for a few minutes until Meredith abruptly refocused on the phone. "Whew. But someone did. Any thoughts about that?" Meredith listened, said, "Thanks. Fill you in later," hung up the phone and pushed it back toward Russ. She shook her head. "Nothing."

"Strange," said Russ. "There's one thing more, though." He picked up a pile of three photos and handed them across to Meredith. "These were sent—also from L.A.—to three of your big outlets. Boston, Kansas City and Detroit. Take a look."

The photos were wire copies obviously taken on two different movie sets that showed Mortensen interacting affectionately with youthful stars from the films. Innocent candid shots at best, but damning in context with the article. "They were sent independently with a note 'to accompany this week's column.'"

Meredith could only shake her head, confused. "We never send photos unless someone asks—usually through your offices. Who would do this? Honest to God, Russ. I didn't. Here's my column for this week. The whole thing is about a sci-fi movie shooting here in Riverdale. About suburban locations and so on." She pulled the manuscript from her bag and handed it to Russ. He looked it over, then placed it side by side with the false column.

"Format matches but the font, of course, is different. Margins slightly different from our usual style." He looked at Todd, looked again at Meredith, then added, "I think we have some kind of intentional deception or fraud going on here, Meredith. Who wants to discredit you?"

"I haven't any idea, or why?"

"Well, here's what we're going to do. First, we're going to alert the three papers to disregard the photos. A mistake. Then we're going to release your real column as usual. And we're turning this over to our legal department to investigate. There's some nefarious behavior here but I'm not sure what—likely fraud…I don't know but stealing someone's identity this way is somehow illegal…."

"Especially over the phone lines…interstate…" added Todd.

"But the biggest issue for me is not only how they did it, but why?" sighed Meredith. The voice of Buster Boles suddenly came to her, "Lady, you've got a stalker." She told Russ and Todd the story.

"In that case, the police need to be involved," said Russ. "And, Meredith, I'll give you the contact for our legal folks when I get them later today. Don't you know someone in 'high profile' policing in L.A.?" He smiled cryptically, breaking the tension. "You can pass those contacts along because I think you can get that ball rolling."

"In about five minutes," Meredith affirmed.

CHAPTER 49
OCTOBER 2, 1989
WEST L.A./NEW YORK
MONDAY – WEDNESDAY

Who's that knockin' at my door?

"What the hell?" spat Raymond on the other end of the line. "A fake column under your name? Jeez Meredith, you do fall down some rabbit holes, don't you?" He heard her murmured affirmative.

"Give me the phone number. Also the return address from the post office packages that the photos were sent in. And I'm sure the authorities involved in New York can collect those packages and check for fingerprints. Although by now, with all the hand-offs, there may be a lot of them on the envelopes. But, worth a try."

Meredith sunk back into the hotel bed and felt a dark cloud wrap around her. "Do you recall Buster's assessment: I have a stalker?"

"Yeah but this is really different. I need to think about this. Let's work on one thing at a time. I'll get someone working on the fax number and then the return address as soon as I get it. Have you heard anything from Buster, speaking of the round guy?"

"No," said Meredith. "Apparently whoever was following me has taken a hiatus or really did fly back to California and gave up whatever the quest was. Maybe just a fan follower from the morning TV show."

"M-m," Raymond's distracted voice came across. "Let's talk tonight," he broke in. "I need to get on this. See if you can get that address as fast as possible. You don't want any more of that happening." She agreed and hung up.

I'm a good Catholic convent girl who likes to write about glamorous people and interesting subjects—so how have I become such a trouble magnet? She asked herself. Stalkers? Murders? Drug dealers? Who'd ever think the movie and TV worlds would deliver up such complex matter? She decided to spend the rest of her time in New York, three and a half more days, just writing up the column materials she had, wrapping up what little other business in the Big Apple and doing her bit on the talk show. And, being quiet and rested.

By Tuesday she had passed along the bogus photo envelopes' return addresses—each one different—and connected the L.A. PD through Raymond with the legal department and its designated investigators and law enforcement partners. She'd called Buster to report in and suspected he was keeping a close eye on the situation again.

In New York on Wednesday, she had a long lunch session with Russ and agreed upon a new contract that had expanded her syndicate client reach by more international clients, which upped her income. He encouraged her to put in a little more time on Cassie's show in Los Angeles. "You have some national presence now. The network here did some promotion on your taking Nancy's place and you have a coast-to-coast presence. We've got some plans for the L.A. show so take advantage of it. And, let Cassie have the benefit of your presence—that is, if you're not moving here to become big time on NTS!"

"That, I doubt," Meredith snuffed. "Getting up at three-thirty every morning—any morning— is against my religion."

"You can work that out with Cassie, or whoever's in charge," he directed her. They talked about the fraudulent column and the progress the various authorities were making in identifying the sender of the fax and photos, but so far not much had developed. Raymond's people had managed to identify the source of the fax number and found it to be a hotel administrative office where a guest no one could remember had used the fax machine for an emergency document, paid cash and left. They were still checking the return addresses from the mailed packages.

"Kerfuffles," Russ smiled. "I told you to avoid them. But Meredith, they follow you like flies to cotton candy."

The pleasure of your company

"A real SOB," snarled Margo Flaherty, standing over Raymond's desk. He was studying the report in front of himself and she was tapping her foot. He shook his head as he read along.

"Predator," he affirmed.

"I hate people who take advantage of old people who cannot care for themselves," she crowed. "This sleazebag accountant just up and moved Martha's money into his own account—along with a half dozen other nursing home client's money—and then distributed it into about a dozen accounts around the U.S. and in Belize. And almost no one noticed, except for the places they lived who were supposed to be paid for their loving care."

"Great work, Margo. Can we reclaim any of what's left of Martha's fund?"

"Not easily, but we'll get it. I promise. More easily than having to find her a new decent home. I've got this, Raymond. The funds are frozen now and we'll get them recaptured and the sleazebag where he belongs. He won't need a trust fund. Lodging comes with bars and three meals a day."

It was a productive day so far. Only noon. Raymond had spent the past two days cleaning up the house, putting things in order and even checking out the Brentwood condo where the two young students had moved out, their college programs sufficiently completed so they could move on. Paco was brushed, fed and attended to and Raymond was anxious to have his lady back in view and in the fold, likely safer than she had apparently been for the past six weeks. She was booked as usual on the three p.m. flight from New York.

CHAPTER 51
OCTOBER 6, 1989
NTS, NEW YORK
FRIDAY MORNING

…Uncle wants YOU!

"Mr. Longmore would like you to stop by his office before you fly out this afternoon," the secretary said to Meredith at five fifteen in the morning as Meredith was being made up for the show for her final appearance. Meredith's eyes shot open in question. "Probably just to say thanks and goodbye."

The day before, Meredith had caught up with Ito for coffee in the UAM syndicate building's deli to say goodbye and update him, candidly and confidentially, on the fraudulent column. "I just want you to keep an eye out and an ear toward anything you might hear anywhere about someone trying to discredit me or…well, anything that sounds pertinent to this weird situation. This is between us. Please don't say anything to Russ. We're all puzzled." Surprised and concerned, Ito promised to do so. They embraced in a fond farewell.

The last of Meredith's appearances concluded with hugs and good wishes as the show ended. Lots of "hope to see you back here soon," "maybe you can join us more often," and similar comments. She made a quick exit to the network programming chief's office although she was earlier than invited. There was time before the start of the last planning session with the show staff and crew, but since she wouldn't be participating in the program they were working on—Monday—she didn't mind being late to the conference. She would, however, not be willing to be late for her flight to Los Angeles. Many of the cast and crew were taking her to lunch and she would leave for the airport from there.

Cecil—Cece—Longmore greeted her into his opulent glass and maple office, closing the door behind her. "Thanks for taking a few minutes, Meredith. I won't keep you long. I know you have a full day and a long flight. Sit, please." She did. "I hope you've had a productive and positive experience with us," he practically mewed.

"I did, Mr. Longmore. Thanks so much. And so many thanks to Billie and your hospitality in Montauk and time I was able to spend with her last weekend."

"Our pleasure, for sure. And it's Cece." She nodded. He folded his hands on the desk and looked intently at her. "Most people don't know that Nancy Igleton has given us notice to leave the show in January to freelance and be a...well...fuller-time mother. It wasn't really unexpected. We've kept a close eye on your integration into the production, your creative ideas and contribution, and we've done some audience testing on you over the past few weeks and found a very positive response...," he slowed to catch her reaction. "So I'd like to advance the idea and the offer for you to become a permanent part of our *It's a Good Day* show." He looked at her kindly.

She blew out a deep breath. "I'm a little overwhelmed," she said thoughtfully squinting her eyes. Internally she told herself, crap! This wasn't a decision I wanted to face. Oh well. "I've learned so much and enjoyed the expansion immensely. But I really do have to think about it. I need to talk with my significant other who's really L.A. based. And with Russ Talbot because I can't imagine not writing some of my own work, Cece. It's the heart and soul of me."

"We certainly respect that and actually would want to set this up to make sure you can continue your national column with UAM. And are open to talking about how to accommodate your homelife. I know it's heavily California-based so we'd make some accommodation for that."

Meredith wondered what kind of accommodations could ever be made to replace the unique role Raymond held in the world of specialized and celebrity crime. Or he held in her life. But she said, "I'm flattered, Cece. I can't tell you. And I am so impressed by the show. I will need to think about this. Some time to talk to people and kick it around."

"Understand that, Meredith. Confidentially, we're making some big expansions of the show, and some major changes. It will be a lot more exciting visually and content-wise. Expanding the time for another hour each morning, adding an exterior set for audience and visitors to interact with the hosts. You've shown us your creativity and expertise. It feels like you'd be a great fit."

Meredith felt her mouth dry and at the same time her resolve shaken. She stood. "I'm expected soon at the planning session, but Cece, I'm so flattered and I need some time to think about this and to talk with my quasi-agent, Allan Jaymar. I'll be back in California this evening. Maybe we could talk next week."

"Of course, we can. Maybe come into New York the week after to discuss the details," he said in an assumed close to the deal. He handed her a folded note page. "This is a start for a discussion. And give Allan my best. I haven't seen him in years but he's the finest of the finest."

"I know, Cece." She stood up to leave, tucking the note in her handbag. She reached across to shake hands. "Thank you so much. Hi to Billie. And I'll talk with you next week."

"Oh, Billie said to tell you she has some ideas on a place to live…if you should decide to join us."

Meredith barely walked through the last meeting and the luncheon at a trendy Manhattan pub with most of the gang from the show. Mostly she wanted to get to the airport and get home.

Going my way?

6:00 p.m.

The "store" she had seen was a ramshackle place that boasted fishing gear and some groceries. When she rushed to the door, it was closed, apparently only open on the weekends when yuppies brought their boats to the small inlet to sail.

Frustrated and frantic, she banged her hands on the windows and ran to the back hoping for someone working in the unopen building. Defeated, she had slumped against the wire-reinforced door as an older rust-colored station wagon pulled into the parking area. A weathered grandfatherly-looking man stepped out of the car hurriedly and began to clean grime from the windshield with a towel. An older woman sat in the passenger seat and a young girl in the back.

"Excuse me," said Meredith.

The man looked up from his window cleaning and when he saw her said, "Are you okay miss?" She stood up and started over to where the car was parked when the woman passenger quickly opened her door and stepped out—as if to shield the others from a dangerous person. Built box-like with curly grey-brown hair and a well-lined determined face, the woman asked, "Who are you?"

Realizing how bedraggled and grit-speckled she was, Meredith held up both hands. "I've been accidentally left behind at the marina. I have ID that I'm reaching for. I'm not a threat." She dug into her tote and removed the small leather flip wallet that held her press pass from the *It's a Good Day* show. She flipped it open and held it out. The woman cautiously stepped forward and looked at it, looked up at Meredith and back to the ID, then said, "Well lord-a-mercy. You sure don't look like you do on TV. What're you doing here?"

"Long silly story," Meredith said, tucking her wallet back into her bag. "But I desperately need a phone. Is there another shopping area or gas station close by?"

"About two miles down the road and another mile to the left. I'd offer you a ride," the man said, "but we got to git my granddaughter to the airport, as quick as I clear the butterfly off the windshield."

"She lives with us but is going to Escondido to visit her momma for a long weekend," the woman chimed in.

"How nice," smiled Meredith, then was struck by the situation. "What airport are you going to?"

"San Francisco International," said the woman.

"Could I please ride with you? I'll pay for gas or your time, but I'd so appreciate the lift. Maybe I can get home."

Grandmother and grandfather looked at one another in indecision, apparently seeking consent or not. The teen in the back seat snuffed, "come on, we gotta go!"

Pizza time

Raymond had ordered an extra-large pizza a while before, guessing he'd be eating alone and might enjoy a fulsome meal. Hoping a full stomach meant an occupied mind. He still felt shaken from the realization that the mystery of Meredith was still unsolved. She'd only been home from New York four days when she headed to the ghost ship press event in Northern California. And his imagination, generally well-grounded and pragmatic, had seen an international story on network news about foreign correspondent Rick Santaros, reporting from Kuwait, and Raymond talked down his surprise reaction. Jealousy? Suspicion? Envy? Hardly any of them deserving of the focus of the unflappable T.K. Raymond.

Paco regarded him from atop the refrigerator and he reached up to tickle the ear of the big grey feline. Unable to quell his unease, he walked out the patio door and down the steps to the beach and further to the water edge. The lights along the curving beach and distant commercial coastline twinkled. He took some solace in their glow. Making his way back up the steps he heard someone at the front door. A soft rap, then another. Dinner.

He opened the door to the fleshy face of a teenage pizza delivery driver. Behind him appeared the bedraggled figure of Meredith Ogden. Raymond thrust some bills into the hand of the pizza messenger, grabbed the oversized box and, as the boy left, stared at Meredith, who simply stood on the porch unmoving. A stunned moment passed before she shyly asked, "Can I please have some of that? I haven't eaten since yesterday morning?" Her first verbal volley about food didn't surprise him.

Raymond pushed the door open and pulled her into the living room by one arm. She semi-stumbled in, then slumped forward, her forehead resting on his shoulder. "Hi," she whimpered. Raymond dropped the pizza box on the door-side table and let her rest for a moment, realizing she was spent, disheveled and...well...disoriented. Her puffy jacket lay in a soiled heap on the floor, her hair lank in its pony tail, jeans grimy with mud and un-designer-styled snags and rips, make up long ago gone.

"What can we do to make this better?" he asked carefully.

"Shower. Food—pizza, PBJ, steak. And a glass of tequila. After that, we can talk about it." He took her gently by the shoulders, turned her toward the stairs to the master suite and guided her to the first step.

"You take care of the shower," he said. "I'll take care of food and we can both handle the tequila." She turned robot-like and headed up the stairs, dropping items of clothing as she plodded upward. Raymond picked up the jacket and the bulky discarded tote bag, noticing Paco the cat, who'd jumped from the refrigerator top, following Meredith up the stairwell, softly yipping in a feline-style bark all the way to the top.

As soon as he heard the shower start, he put the pizza in the oven to heat and called Stan Smallet at the home phone number the studio marketing chief had given him. "She's here," he said in a near-whisper. "I'll know more later and will call you first thing tomorrow morning." He heard Smallet's exasperated sigh of relief.

"We'll all sleep a little better tonight," said the veteran executive.

"True that," affirmed Raymond, hoping it was true. He repeated the call to Sonia who insisted on coming into the office the next day. "Just make it a little later," he advised. "I doubt she'll be on deck early." Then he mused that some things don't change. Food was particularly high on his lady love's mind.

Bedtime story

10:30 p.m.

Only debris remained from a large pizza, a half-gallon of rocky road ice cream and a half glass of tequila. Raymond picked up the remnants of the unexpected, enthusiastically devoured, meal and wiped down the table and kitchen. Meredith had unraveled the story in almost flat, unemotional cadence. A surprise to Raymond who figured she'd be too tired to talk until after sleep and some distance. But the last of the adrenalin trickled through and he began to hear the frustration and weariness taking over.

"…the 'store' was really a small marine boating shop," she had explained, "fishing stuff, some foul weather gear, snacks. But the marina was basically dead during the week so it was really only open on the weekends," Meredith had explained, damp hair clinging to her neck, wrapped in her favorite old Mickey Mouse pajamas and faux bunny fur slippers. "All that walking and mucking around in the mud and bushes…and no phone available. No human on site."

After she had approached the older couple in their rust-colored station wagon and requested a ride to the San Francisco airport, the woman asked, "Where do you live?"

"Los Angeles," Meredith answered.

"I can drop you at the first terminal," answered the man, "but we can't tarry. We're just going to make Patsy's flight as it is. We're likely to hit traffic. If you want to come along, get aboard. We gotta go." Without another word, Meredith opened the back door and climbed in next to the sullen teenage girl who barely looked up.

"Patsy, we got a TV star riding with us. Tell your momma about that!" said the grandmother with a great amount of pride. The teen looked at Meredith and nodded. Ninety long minutes of answering questions about what it was like to appear on TV, Meredith nearly tumbled out of the brown station wagon, voicing profound thanks, and rushed into the PSA terminal. She looked for the bank of public phones when she saw the flight schedule board and that the Los Angeles bound flight was scheduled—in five minutes.

She rushed up to the ticket counter and the agent told her, "If you rush to the gate right now, you can make the flight." Meredith pushed her credit card forward, grabbed the ticket handed to her. She ran to the gate, seemingly miles down the jetway, dodging travelers pulling carry-on bags, coming and going, and apparently not as rushed.

"One minute more and you'd be out of luck," the gate agent told her as she gasped a thanks, out of breath, then hurried down the ramp to the aircraft. And to the very last seat in the very back of the plane. She sighed heavily, sorry that she had not had time to call anyone, especially Raymond, to tell him of the situation. And that she felt dank, disheveled and even odorous after her long ordeal. She made her way to the airplane restroom in mid-flight and shuddered when she saw herself in the cramped mirror. Besides fatigued purple moons under each eye, there were smudges of dirt on her cheeks from her grovel through the underbrush, hair hanging against her face as if she'd come through a steam bath. And clothes that were so weary and crumpled she wished she had even a t-shirt to refresh herself. Instead, she washed her face thoroughly, brushed her hair and pulled it into a fresh pony tail, then swiped some lipstick onto her parched lips. I hope I'm not too offensive to my seatmates, she told herself as she squeezed back into her row.

She felt an Atlas-worthy weight gradually melt away, adrenalin slowly ease from her body and a profound weariness grasp every part of her being. Filtering in and out of sleep, she found herself talking to her long-gone mother and then to one of her college boyfriends, then her deceased father and late uncle. Am I dreaming? she wondered. Hallucinating or just crazy? The jet bumped onto the tarmac at LAX, taxiing to the gate, and Meredith struggled to focus attention. As she merged with passengers leaving the aircraft and flowing into the terminal, the throng of people in constant motion and lights glaring along the jetway were jarring. Meredith reminded herself to breathe and keep moving.

Phones. The mission for so many previous hours. She found she hadn't the mental acuity to look for a phone bank and also move toward the lobby. When neon signs appeared directing passengers to the taxi areas, she made the decision to keep moving with a new mission: home. She curled into the back of the first yellow cab in the pick-up line and gasped out the address to the driver.

"What about Duck and the motorbike?" asked Raymond, carefully, circling back to the one unresolved threat.

"I didn't stay to find out." Her voice had become soft and thin, weary. She looked at the outside rim of her hands and showed him the purple bruises from the beating both had taken on the closed shop windows, the scrapes and gouges from her fall in the woods. He cleaned and dabbed antibiotic cream on them and bandaged a few. He knew there would be much more discussion about the entire dramatic event over the weekend, but for now, Meredith had said enough.

Later, as he closed up the house for the night, he glanced at the refrigerator top and saw it empty. He knew where its resident would be. Snatching up clothing items—hat, jacket, scarf, jeans, socks, turtleneck—discarded along the stairs and into the generous master bath, he dropped them into the laundry hamper, thinking maybe the trash container would be a better choice. But that's Meredith's decision, he thought.

And surely enough, there were two blanket-covered mounds in the wide king-sized bed: One curled tightly on her side breathing steadily and clearly in a far-off somnambulistic world. The other, a small mound tucked into the back of the larger one, also asleep but rattling with a contented purr. It would be a full bed for the night, Raymond thought, as he stripped off his own clothes and crawled into the empty side.

CHAPTER 55
OCTOBER 15, 1989
MALIBU
SUNDAY MORNING

We have re-entry

Raymond was surprised to see Meredith up and dressed for exercise on Sunday morning. She was off to the early class at the fitness club she'd belonged to for years in Santa Monica. He could see some of the normal verve had returned to her eyes, energy in her actions.

Two days before, on Friday, Meredith emerged in late afternoon, and then with little conversation. Raymond had gone to work about ten when Sonia arrived for most of the day. He returned to a napping female who rose long enough to eat piping hot chili and a full baguette of garlic bread for dinner, doze off in front of the TV for about an hour and return to bed.

Saturday had been more subdued in the household than Raymond could remember it being since they'd moved in. Meredith wandered in a semi-daze until he packed her off to lunch at their favorite seaside seafood diner and she began to interact with the activity around her. The familiarity of the place and the need to respond to the servers and make decisions began to restore reality. Still, at home, she mostly attended to necessities—laundry, grocery lists, and occasional note-making in her office. TV and pasta dinner that night readied her for early sleep. He was wise enough to leave her to her own choices. "Maybe that's what being older means," he chided himself.

"I need to do this," she said early the next morning, Sunday, ready to exercise, gulping down coffee, crumbs from a hastily devoured bagel in the sink. "I have to get my body and soul back into gear. You could come along...." So he did. It seemed the smart move and he was ready himself to use the fitness center's extensive workout equipment to bring back his own sense of grounding. It had been a long three days.

Sunday evening, they walked slowly and quietly along the beach. As a heavy breeze whipped around them, the sea tumultuous and large, the fragrance of shore plants in the air, Meredith finally spewed forth her anger, frustration and fears over the tumultuous two-days of craziness. "They just left me and didn't even notice...how sick is that?" "Stupid phones were torn out..."

"And I was so lame I couldn't even keep from hurting myself!" She looked at her hands, already healing, and began to cry. Raymond put an arm around her as she sniffed and they walked along the shore. "And you always said I walked into the fire too often...I thought this was to be a quick bayside visit to a floating movie set...nothing's ever as it seems...."

Wasn't me

Marty Escobar's notes

"I wasn't worried about Meredith Ogden. I was too busy herding those foreign press assholes around. That French guy nearly drove me nuts." Terry—movie publicist.

"Wasn't my job. We swept the place down just before Matthew Morgan began his little promotional talk and made sure the launches were in place and everyone got off safely afterward. Picked up the folding chairs and loaded them in one of the boats and we were gone." Bill Kuhlman—ghost ship guide.

"I told her she didn't have to listen to the spiel I was going to give because she'd heard it before. She said she'd go 'off to the side' and work with her notes. I never noticed her again. My presentation was only about 10 minutes." Matthew Morgan—Producer, Shadow of the Wave.

"I remember hearing something about Meredith moving from the Oakland group to the SFO group, but the whole bunch was so noisy and disorganized, kind of took

the exodus from the ship on their own. I think it was Claude the French journalist—I just remember the way he pronounced Meredith's name. Not much else. I guess I lost control. I have to take responsibility." Nate the Intern—press trip coordinator.

"I have no idea who was on my launch. The studio folks were handling that. I know my group was the 'Oakland Airport' gang but who they were, no idea." Skipper of launch 1.

"It wasn't my problem, although I have to say everything seemed confused as we left the ship. My passengers, I was told, were the ones who would transfer to the van to SFO." Skipper of launch 2.

"The only person I really knew was Terry, the studio publicist, and I had always planned to come from and go back to the Oakland Airport." Kevin Toll—film distributor executive for North California area.

"It was quite a visit. The ship was awesome, but all I knew was Meredith Ogden came in from Oakland and I assume went back there. I didn't see her after Matthew started his presentation and I wasn't on her launch." Clarice Duncan—local media representative.

"Spectacular set visit. Loved it completely. But I only vaguely remember Meredith Ogden. Fine looking woman, as I recall. But she wasn't on our launch when we left—we were the bunch headed for SFO but some of the guys changed from the Oakland destination, I think. Never noticed her as we assembled to leave the ship." Cyril McAdams—British journalist.

"Claude, the French press guy, asked me to tell the launch driver for Oakland that Meredith had changed to the San Francisco group—going to the San Francisco airport. Said he was passing along a message but I don't

know from whom and to whom except the launch pilot and he didn't seem to care. Check with Claude. He may know more." Fritz Wagner—German magazine writer.

"And where's Claude?" asked Marty, Raymond's entertainment industry crime specialist. The meeting in Stan Smallet's office had been underway for a half hour with a handful of the same folks who had met the week before to try to unravel the disappearance of Meredith Ogden. Nate, the studio coordinator, said nothing, still embarrassed about losing control of the process.

Smallet winced, shrugged and shook his head. "Still haven't found him. He's the only one of the entire group we haven't had a conversation with. He apparently told Nate and the German journalist that Meredith was switching airport destinations. But we don't know when she told him that or even if it was Meredith, herself."

"Doesn't his office know where he is?" pressed Marty.

"No. He was on 'vacation' and used the trip here to branch into personal travel. We're all looking for him. I'm sure he'll turn up soon, though. He has to sooner or later."

"Well, the important thing is that Meredith's back and safe. I can't wait to hear the saga," said Terry, a long-time colleague of Meredith.

"Won't we all," sighed Marty.

"And we have some restitution to make to Meredith for her discomfort. Please assure her—and Captain Raymond—that we're still focused on this," Stan Smallet said in his best deep executive demeanor. Marty wondered if Smallet knew the connection between Meredith Ogden and T.K. Raymond.

"I'll be interviewing Meredith soon," Marty commented as he packed up his notes. "Let's see if she remembers anything else."

CHAPTER 57
OCTOBER 16, 1989
MALIBU
MONDAY

People aren't always who they say they are

In her home office, Meredith was grappling with her own devils. Cecil Longmore's secretary was on the phone, bitchy and angry. Still gaining strength and energy after her ordeal the week before, and even after a quiet weekend of R&R, Meredith wasn't ready for the New York attitude again. She shut her eyes and worked to not shout at the woman. The shrew Gestapo-femme actually knew more about the pending mystery than Meredith did.

Friday afternoon, Meredith had faxed a well-constructed letter to Longmore thanking him profusely for the job offer on *It's a Good Day*, but explaining that although she had thoroughly enjoyed and felt at home with the cast and crew, her home was in L.A. and after deeply exploring her own career wishes, she'd determined that her path was more focused on written and print journalism rather than broadcast.

Her letter fax was not well received. Especially because a special delivery letter supposedly mailed by her had arrived two days before, accepting the job and outlining some parameters. Meredith, surprised and confused, had no knowledge about the postal letter until Blanche told her of it. And Meredith was now working to prove to both Longmore and the G-femme, his assistant, that she had neither penned nor sent the first letter. She shuddered in a sense of déjà vu at how this same kind of subterfuge had occurred only a couple of weeks earlier with the phantom column she supposedly had written. Fear out-nudged puzzlement and anger. In frustration, she called Raymond to ask his expertise and advice, suspecting the issue had again become a legal one requiring law enforcement attention.

Raymond made the call to Longmore, personally, and asked his help in clearing up the mystery of the fraudulent communications. He again repeated a familiar request: "Please try to avoid anyone else handling the letter. Place it in a plain fresh large manila folder along with the envelope in which it arrived and anything else that was associated with it. A colleague from New York law enforcement will come by to pick it up in the morning." Raymond's office had already introduced the bogus faxed column into active investigation.

Longmore wasn't happy. He'd already drafted a contract and alerted his top-level staff about the possibility of Meredith coming aboard. He felt vulnerable and embarrassed. But he also worried that the fall-out from the perpetrated scheme would impact the network in some legal way, and perhaps even damage its reputation.

"I don't understand what this could be about or why someone would want to wreak this kind of confusion, even potential damage," he told Raymond.

"Nor does Ms. Ogden or those of us here at the special unit of the L.A. police department," Raymond spoke into the phone, careful to keep his professional distance and demeanor, not sure if the executive knew of his relationship with Meredith. "Can you think of any event, situation or even conversation that might suggest someone was unhappy with Meredith or had any reason to put her in your cross hairs?" Longmore did not. Raymond cautioned him to put the package containing the letter and envelope under lock and key until a police investigator retrieved it.

"And I would urge discretion," he instructed Longmore. "The less anyone but you, my law enforcement colleagues—both here and in New York— and your legal eagles know about this, the more it will allow us to investigate without unneeded interference." Longmore grumbled his agreement and said he was turning the situation over to the network's legal and security division. Raymond clicked off the call and immediately put in another to a complimentary division of the New York Police.

"It's complicated," he said to Detective Simmons with whom he'd worked other cases and who agreed to look at the situation.

"Most everything about you coasties is," chuckled Simmons. "It's the special protocols for the 'special' people," he said in his customary growl. Raymond smiled at the other end of the line. He knew that in spite of his grumbling, Simmons always enjoyed tracking through celebrity-involved cases. They gave the older officer a 'special' patina in his department. "And, of course you want the lab folks to find everything they can by tomorrow, right?"

"Like always," said Raymond with an affable tone.

"'Kay," said Simmons.

CHAPTER 58
OCTOBER 16, 1989
BEVERLY HILLS, CALIFORNIA
MONDAY

What's the skinny on this?

"This is a bona fide shit show," said Gloria, Meredith's best pal who was also an attorney. "You've wandered into dangerous, illegal and life-threatening story threads before, but this is very different. I have to wonder what your astrological horoscope must look like these days. Snagged a berth in the top rate morning show, scored a bunch of new column outlets from your terrific reputation with the news syndicate, new Malibu digs, hot boyfriend, etcetera, etcetera…, but these character assaults coming in like a hailstorm."

"The movie on the ghost ship said it for me…*In the shadow of the biggest wave.*" It made her think of the slick French journalist Claude something-or-other who said it on the ship. "Suisun, New York, even around here in L.A. Just waiting for it to crash down on me—but what is it?"

"Have you and Raymond gone over this?"

"Yes. Hard not to when I'm in the middle of it, and he's looking into the most inflammatory issues first—the ones that require more police or law enforcement oversight. But, I'm concerned about my raw legal exposure," said Meredith. "I'm not responsible for any of the misdeeds—or mistakes, to give a benefit to the doubt—but I might be perceived to be."

"I'd love to tell you you're overthinking it all. The syndicate and the network legal minds will be working with the police on this, but let's play with it a little anyhow, because anyone can sue these days for just about anything," said Gloria, going to the white board in the modern glass and steel conference room in which they had headquartered themselves. "At least we'll have some kind of picture to work with," and Gloria began to write.

- *Someone unknown followed you in New York—to a meeting with Ronnie Milton, also Father Paul Mercer.*

- *Someone unknown showed up at the hotel while you were away and wanted into your room but failing that, waited for you in the lobby, then left before you arrived.*

- *Someone unknown wrote an article under your name and faxed it from L.A. to your N.Y. employer to be distributed as if by you to newspapers and news outlets across the U.S. and several other countries.*

- *Someone unknown wrote a letter of acceptance for a job offered to you and sent it from a Los Angeles address to your potential employer in New York.*

- *Several people acted on a rumor started by someone unknown that you were leaving the L.A. TV show to accept a permanent position in New York.*

"And this is really a long shot because we don't really know if 'someone' actually 'did' this…," interjected Gloria, then wrote:

- *Someone unknown perhaps was responsible for leaving you stranded on a derelict ship after a sponsored visit.* <u>*In any case, the studio is responsible for any fallout for you.*</u>

"I don't know that anyone did that on purpose," Meredith insisted, looking intensely at the list. "I made a copy of it all. Let's go get some coffee and noodle this."

"Let's go have a martini instead," said Gloria, picking up her notes. She wrote a large "Do Not Touch" on the top of the white board. On a piece of notebook paper, "Do not enter" which she affixed to the conference room door as they left and she locked the door.

In a small cubbyhole bar off a nondescript diner about four unfashionable blocks from Gloria's very-fashionable Beverly Hills office, the two women huddled over one of only five tables, theirs in a corner with no windows. One other person sat at a small five-person bar.

"I like it here," muttered Meredith, pushing an olive into her mouth. "It's so private and quiet." Gloria nodded her agreement. "It seems like the adoption of Trey is going very well," Meredith changed the subject. "He's such a nice and cute kid."

"Yeah," mused Gloria. "It's an adjustment but it's working. Of course, he's a little sad and distant. Losing a dad will do that. And, we've had to set up some rules and boundaries—as much for us as for him—but you were right when you said now was the best time to bring a kid into the household. George and I are both at a point where we can ease back some on our own work, and also afford to put into place some of the support we can't offer ourselves. Trey's doing great at school, but again, it's a private well-run school. I'm actually grateful right now. Talk to me when he turns 15!" She took a drink of her martini. Then looked at Meredith, "But you're evading the subject. Who's out to discredit you? Who wants your ass?"

Meredith shrugged. "It's one thing to talk about it. Another to live it," she cringed. Gloria continued to gaze intently at her. "Raymond asked the same question but it's taken time to think about it. This is the first time I've actually been focused enough to look at it without cowering and walking away. For the moment, let's set aside any celebrities or studio or network people who didn't like what I wrote. No one has accused me of lying, so for now, let's take that off the table. This feels more personal." She looked at the list she'd jotted from the white board.

"Mean, vengeful," muttered Gloria.

"These are names that have no real grounding—just off the top of my head, going back a long way, okay?" Gloria nodded. "Fitz, my deceased fiancé's sister-in-law—hated my connection to the family and Hollywood. From Bettina Grant's family and the whole murder time—Vivian, Bettina's ex-husband's fiancé who was arrested, Larry Grant, Bettina's ex-husband whose cushy next life came apart when we solved the murder, and Bettina's daughter Lea who once resented me because I was a star—instead of her—in her mother's eyes—but that all seemed to dissipate. I think that's all water under the bridge, Gloria. All those folks seem to be happily resettled in new lives after a half-dozen years.

"So, more recently? Well, lots of super-sensitive people at Global International over the whole ghost ship episode, but I think that's a separate issue and no one person seems to be to 'blame' for that. Just a general overall screw-up. And, it happened after the first stalking episodes."

"Frankly, Meredith, it's not in the studio's best interest to take you on, anyhow. In fact, we should talk about what you might want in the way of restitution later," added Gloria.

Shaking her head vehemently, Meredith went on, "Much later. But…someone associated with Ronnie Milton? Although he's been very friendly and happy and no one—family or friends—has been involved or impacted by clearing his path. The show? Well, Hy—Hiram—the assignment editor who tried to assault me in The Hamptons? Can't see it. Don't think he remembers it. Rick Santaros? I can hallucinate and imagine that he was pursuing me romantically. That's kind of the sneery rumor among a couple of the show people, but I swear it wasn't the situation at all. He's in the Middle East and has long forgotten our on-camera feature.

"Amanda Borkin, my short-term co-host. She never seemed to like me or trust me. Sneered at me a lot. But she's the queen of her daytime TV realm and I'm really no threat." Meredith squinted, trying to think of any event that might have prompted retribution from Amanda. "She hasn't even seen my articles so she can't be angry about anything I wrote. Other than not letting her see it pre-print."

"But if she dislikes you enough to do this, pushing you through rumor to a full-time position with her wouldn't be in her best interest, either, would it?"

Shaking her head, Meredith said, "Nope. Then there's Raymond's newest staff member. The infamous Margo Flaherty. He insists she's calmed down and is just one of those inherently flirty women."

"History there?"

"Yeah. But not as much as you would think, but apparently she might or at least did for quite a while. Of course, she did save his life in New Mexico. But still, too obvious. And she's too smart—a seasoned law officer—to be so nonprofessionally blatant."

Both women focused on their drinks for a few minutes, then Gloria murmured. "There is more than one legal consideration going on here, Meredith. There are serious law enforcement issues—definitely stalking, probably identity fraud or theft, and there's probably an issue of interstate communication fraud or similar. It's not my area of law, but I think Raymond, with his legal background and departmental expertise will be more knowledgeable. And the media companies have attorneys who will know exactly what's at stake. And because state lines were crossed, it might require the feds to be brought in. Whew, let's take a break and talk about Global International for a minute."

"Let's not," sighed Meredith. "If I consider 'retribution' it's kind of like being on the payroll of one of the world's largest film studios. And that means special treatment. Some journalists might relish that. It's too much responsibility to think about right now."

Gloria nodded and asked, "So, you recovered from your adventures on the bay and in the woods yet?"

"Mostly. I had lots of time for thinking and planning," Meredith began. "I feel like it's time to make some new inroads, maybe look beyond the immediate horizon. I'm thinking about selling the Brentwood townhouse after all these years...."

"There's a surprise. Why?"

"No decision yet. It's always been my backup in case—just in case. But you remember Beverly Tompkin from school?" Gloria nodded. "Her daughter Margie has been living there with a roommate for the past year finishing off a special program before graduation from UCLA. They just moved out. But a few weeks ago someone broke into the place and spread their underwear all over. Nothing taken or anything...just...well underwear."

Mouth open in surprise, Gloria asked, "Who and why?" Meredith shook her head. "Well executed. Raymond sent some-one over but no prints, nothing. But the neighbor, Norman, had seen someone nosing around a couple of times."

"Huh. Still sounds pretty personal to me," said Gloria, noting the time on her watch and getting ready to stand up. "What other new plans are afoot? Raymond involved?"

"Raymond is always involved," laughed Meredith. "Have you ever known anyone as steadfast and sturdy? Hardly a waver in the face of challenge."

"What does that mean?" pushed Gloria, suddenly remembering the pricey carrot being dangled in front of her friend from the *It's a Good Day* show in New York.

"I'll let you know when I know." The two picked up their belongings and left the tiny cloistered enclave.

"Where are you parked?" asked Gloria.

"In the high-priced lot under your building. Someone keyed the paint on the Mustang door a couple of weeks ago. I just picked it up and wanted to keep it pristine!"

"It's always something, isn't it these days," commiserated Gloria.

Just the facts

"Out!" yelled the production assistant and Meredith once again found herself unplugging a microphone from her blouse at the end of a morning show—this one in L.A.— and thinking about the next appointment that awaited her. Cassie O'Connell strode quickly into the studio and did a fast look around.

"Wow— we pulled this off pretty well didn't we?"

"You'd think we really were sitting on an elegant patio on a mountain overlooking the glamorous desert empire," cooed Meredith, looking around at the wide-open sky in the background photo of palm trees and a view of the exotic Coachella Valley around Palm Springs. "This scene was perfect and the perfect setting to interview Sonny Bono."

"Well, we didn't have the budget to take the show on location to Palm Springs but Sonny's heading up the new Palm Springs Film Festival—so this was the next best thing! It kind of looks authentic and it's a pretty neat celebrity story, if I do say so myself." Cassie beamed as Sonny, Palm Springs Mayor and former RnB music star, came over and thanked her. He'd told them how many directors and producers he had lined up for the first ever event and that "big stars like Sinatra" would eventually be part of the celebrations.

Meredith smiled, waved quickly to the team and ran out the door. In her car she used a soft tissue doused in makeup remover to wipe her face clean from the extra screen image enhancers. She mused at how luxuriant it had been to have a dressing room adjacent to the set in New York, and someone to make sure her face was what it needed to be even after the show. Running her fingers through her hair, she dumped the theatrical tools into their carrying case and started the car.

She had a command performance at Raymond's office to meet with a member of a Sheriff's Department in the Suisun Bay area. She couldn't recall which one. Raymond had called her the afternoon before to tell her she needed to be at the unit first thing the next morning. "Can't," she said. "I'll be on camera from eight until ten."

"Right afterward, then," he conceded. He told her it had to do with "the guy who pulled you off the ship and then dumped you at the abandoned marina." She gnashed her teeth. She wanted the legacy of the infamous Duck to be over. And she still felt more appreciation for him than angst now because he had been willing to rescue her and put her ashore safely. No one else had even looked her way, stupidly waving her red flag, that morning.

Driving quickly to Raymond's west Los Angeles offices at ten-thirty, she entered the small, tight conference room, fitted out in utilitarian wooden chairs and table, and was nearly puffing in her haste. A large, wide but firmly built man in a beige and khaki uniform stood up, straight and tall and regarded her with kind eyes. They shook hands. "Meredith Ogden, this is Sheriff's Deputy Frank Alcorn," Raymond introduced them. The two tall men seemed to crouch around the compact table. Meredith leaned back and took a deep breath. It had been a busy morning.

"We'd like to hear more about your experience in Suisun Bay on the mothball ship, but especially with the man you identified in your report as 'Duck,'" Alcorn began.

"Let's see," Meredith began, sitting up at attention. She recounted the entire movie set visit to the ghost ship and then what had transpired after Duck had found her and taken her from the ship. The deputy probed with numerous questions, looking for building descriptions, identification of any other individual, but Meredith had seen none.

"We'd like you to tour the same route with one of us and see if we can find the various stop-off spots and maybe do a look into some photos. Tomorrow or the next day would be most helpful. Time is valuable in these investigations," he reminded. Raymond watched the interaction without interrupting.

Meredith shook her head. "Deputy, I truly understand the importance and intensity of this exploration, but what are you looking for? Drugs? Guns? Has he done anything wrong?"

"We have too much drug interaction in these out-of-the-way waterside locations," he explained. "They're off the grid and trafficking isn't easily tracked. We'd just like to talk with Duck. And, you've seen this guy full face."

"Well, I've just been on a very rigorous and actually depleting excursion up in your area. And six weeks of very demanding work schedule beginning at three-fifteen every morning plus commutes between New York and L.A. I've had some vertigo and even nausea since the sleepless, foodless and liquid-deprived, ship rolling days and I'm not feeling much like getting on another plane and going back to Suisun Bay. I'm sorry." Raymond gritted his teeth, torn between his frustration at Meredith's denial of the cop's request and his knowledge of the truth in Meredith's response. But then she continued.

"Maybe this will help and get me off the hot seat. I'm on just too many of them right now." She reached for her bag and pulled out a post-card sized packet of photos, then her small Minnox camera. "These may be helpful. More than me trying to guide you through little inlets and hidden streams that I will never remember. I was oblivious by the time I got in his boat." She fanned the photos out on the table and began to describe each one. "This was his boat. Here's the only identifying number I saw…this is the first dock and building we went to—that's Duck walking up the ramp…Here's the second location…." The last two photos she set out separately. "This is Duck from the side as he sped away from the little marina where he left me. He has some kind of tattoo on his neck. But this one is full face from the front. I'm surprised he didn't see me taking it but I thought it was a good idea to have some idea of my rescuer—and my abandon-er. Will these help?"

"You recognize any of these places, Deputy?" asked a much-calmer Raymond.

The big officer nodded. "I do. These are very helpful. Why don't we do this, Ms. Ogden. Let me take these back and see what we can learn from them. If we need you to come up to the site, we can arrange it after you've had some time to decompress." He looked at Raymond who nodded in affirmation. Meredith audibly sighed with relief.

"I do want to say one thing, officers. This man, Duck, while maybe some kind of law-breaking reprobate, was nice enough to detour from his duties—lawful or not—help me off the ship and out of my problem—and when he realized I needed official help, at least dropped me at a place that was safe and had some services. He didn't know the phone was not working. Normally, with that, my drama would have been resolved. So, I can't condemn him totally." She took a quiet breath. "And, do we even know if he's broken any laws?" Both detectives didn't respond. She reminded herself of the motorbike on the road, then gave herself the out that he was there to check that she was doing okay. Or not. If it was Duck.

Frankly, she thought to herself, Duck is the least troublesome thing going on in my life right now. Maybe when everything else settles, I can wonder more about all of that. Right now, he's on his own. And I'm hungry for lunch and have to get down to real work.

Who's asking?

The wind was brisk but the sun was high and balmy as Marty stepped out of his car in front of the house on Malibu Beach. He loved the location and had been a guest there often—casually as a guest and as a colleague for work sessions. But this time seemed more official as he walked up the steps to interview Meredith, a task that Raymond would normally have handled informally. But the criminal incidents under investigation needed to be "by the book" and more formal.

"Holly crap," said the detective as he entered the house. "About that earthquake up in Northern California—Loma Prieta. Isn't that where you were on the ghost ship?"

"Yep," Meredith shook her head seriously. "I know there was a lot of damage in that area—especially Vallejo—but not sure how it impacted the fleet. Wow, what a difference five days made!"

"Sorry to intrude, and I know this is awkward," said the tightly built detective framed by swarthy skin and a crew-cut. He shifted uncomfortably in the overstuffed side chair at the small worktable in Meredith's home office. He looked down to his notes and nervously thumbed through them.

"Cut it out, Marty!" Meredith commanded. "It's not the first time we've fumbled through the haunted forest of an investigation."

"Yeah, I know. And, Meredith, we already have most of this information but just needed you to confirm it—or expand on it. Okay?" She nodded. Marty then went through the outline of the two problems: the bogus column and the fake letter to Longmore. They reviewed time frames and locations when and where the items were faxed, dates mailed, received, information within. Meredith, herself, had conflicts or alibis in every case.

"Are the Feebs coming in?" she asked hesitantly, knowing how much local law enforcement disliked the intrusion of outsiders.

Marty shook his head. "Above my pay grade." Finished then, Marty packed up his papers and stood to leave. "Just out of curiosity, what made you visit the ghost ship location anyhow? The way you describe the junket, it didn't sound like there was much to gain for your story?"

"Mathew Morgan is the one Hollywood producer who has the inside with the military. Most of the big productions involving war machinery, aircraft, ships…Morgan is usually orchestrating the relationship. I wanted to know more and this movie seemed like an interesting visual one to use as an example."

Marty thought for a moment, brow furled. "Did you get the story you needed—the inside scoop on the military and Hollywood?" Meredith had to laugh as she nodded affirmative. When she bid Marty goodbye, she changed into workout clothes and headed to the fitness studio. She needed an aerobics class to shake off the stress and frustration that had her mind and body locked up tight.

And then I have to get back to work, she vowed. I've been way too distracted, and don't have the luxury of being undone! But on her way along the Coast Highway to the Santa Monica fitness spa, she came to Sunset Boulevard and on the spur of the moment, made the turn toward town. She followed Sunset as it snaked through the west side communities, past her own Brentwood landmarks and eastward to Bel Air. Up Roscomare and along the meandering streets, she made the turn onto Bright Leaf Lane and pulled up in front of the elegant home and portico belonging to Allan Jaymar. She glanced down at her workout clothes and chuckled that Allan had never seen her in her most serious "work" clothes. She pulled on a sweatshirt and made her way to the etched glass front door. Allan opened it with a surprised grin when he saw her. "And look who's on our doorstep! What a lovely afternoon treat," said the older gentleman, sweatshirt and jeans clad himself, not his usual natty portrait. "Potty come here. We have our wandering girl as a surprise guest."

As they entered the wide foyer, Allan's decades-long partner Potty—Parker—appeared from another room. Meredith was shocked to see that the portly egg-shaped man, former well-known character actor, was about half the size he'd been the last time they'd visited. She knew about the stroke he'd suffered a few months earlier and the intense treatment he'd undertaken to return to a somewhat normal life.

Potty stepped forward, both hands extended to clasp hers. "Good heavens what a gift you are! In the midst of all of this…," he glanced around the room, "it's nice to have your light!" Meredith hugged the man—gently—and said, "Wow, Potty. You said you wanted to lose weight this year. Took it a little far didn't you?" They all laughed.

"Done and done," affirmed the old actor, bald with a fringe around his lower head and ears.

"We're all impromptu today," Allan mused. "Come into the kitchen. Most of the furniture, I'm afraid, is already moved or gone. It's dismal in here these days but we look ahead only a few days to the nifty new digs we'll have at the Farm. Come and have some tea. We may even have some lemon cookies." The empty rooms, void of their lovely oriental rugs, unique and artistically chosen, perfectly placed art, comfortable—often overstuffed—furnishings, caused Meredith to discretely blanche. "We're moving to the Movie-TV-Music Country Farm, as you know," Allan went on. Meredith mentally squeezed her eyes shut, trying to block out the emptiness. She thought of the many times she had sat in these welcoming rooms, sharing triumphs and concerns. How they had reached out to be of help and comfort when needed. Situated across the street from Bettina Grant's former home where she and her colleagues had all once worked, it was a place of support, comfort and care in some of the most vulnerable times of her life. Now the stolid residence was only blank walls and doors to empty rooms. She lounged back in the kitchen chair around the glass top table with Allan and Potty. "I was afraid I was too late to say goodbye to the old girl!" she mused looking around, then sighing.

"Wait until you see our beautiful new home," said Allan in his most accommodating voice. "More compact, but it was time to weed out too many years' worth of unappreciated collectibles," he smiled. "And the view from our place at the Farm is simply wonderful, isn't it, Potty?" His partner nodded enthusiastically. "Rolling meadows out there in the golden foothills of the west valley. Horses in the distance…."

"And plenty of help and support. Even meals provided. We can cook when we want to, but not all the time," chuckled Potty. Allan accommodated with a gentle smile.

"So what's happening in your lane on this crazy freeway?" asked Allan, leaning forward on the table and grinning at Meredith. "Russ and I spoke a week or so ago. Sounds like some really bad stuff going on." Meredith took a deep breath and told him the full litany of events.

"Well," Allan said with a scowl. "I know the various media companies are on it, but I also know your detective will be all over these issues…but, the bigger one is your choice of career paths. I know you've turned down the NTS morning show, but knowing you, it's not gone completely from your mind." Then, for the first time, she mentioned a new offer from Cecil Longmore and NTS for a place on the *It's a Good Day* show. It was generous and far-reaching. They talked of the professional catapult ahead if Meredith stepped into the role offered, and how that would change her public and industry exposure.

"You're the first and only person I've told," she confessed. "I couldn't say no—outright. After all the consternation and drama, the fact that he still came back with another offer made it more important—at least to him."

"And you?" asked Allan. "Obviously you weren't ready to say a definitive 'no.'"

"You know me, Allan," said Meredith gazing at her hands, and picking at a thumbnail. "I've been fortunate so far, being in the right place at the right time and making stellar decisions that were available to me. But I've always been ambitious and it's hard to turn that off. The money, prestige and momentum that would come with a permanent berth on the *Good Day* show would be really difficult for a hard-nosed—driven—professional woman to turn down."

"And yet?" the seasoned eyes regarded her.

"The downside, Allan," Meredith reasoned, "is if it didn't go well, it'd be hard to restart or correct. Who would want a failed talk show personality?"

Potty snuffed a chuckle. Allan spoke up, "The air waves are full of those. Once promising news anchors on one network now heralding shows on another. But is TV what you want? You already have more entre than you can handle now, it sounds like," said Potty. "You've always said you wanted to be 'in' Hollywood, not 'of' it. Would that credo be compromised by becoming the celebrity instead of writing about her?"

"Now's probably a good time to think about those elements you said you would take a bullet for?" suggested Allan with a wink, reminding her of her comments from a much earlier conversation.

"One: My own integrity," she had said. "I want my family, friends and colleagues to know I'm a good and true person, one who cares honestly…about everything. Allan, Potty, you're part of that. Two: T.K. Raymond…and maybe…my cat Paco. Three: My passion for writing and the ability to follow it."

"Of course, priorities and relationships change…," Allan added. "But it's always good to review them…."

Blushing, she thought about it for a minute and then said, "Thanks, Allan. You've reminded me of some basics I'd forgotten somewhere in the grassy woods around Suisun Bay and in front of the cameras at NTS New York studios. Gives me a starting point, at least." Breathing out heavily she looked around again. "How can I help *you*?"

"We have lots of hired help, Merri. None of us should be hefting boxes and couches—not even you with your healthy glow and strong-woman outfit! But come and see us in our new home. It's only a little farther from Malibu than here but the same old gents will be there to welcome you!"

"The cosmopolitan fellows are about to become gentlemen farmers!" crowed Potty. Allan lifted a skeptical eyebrow.

"And I'll put on my cowboy boots and straw hat to come and visit you often!" Meredith laughed. She didn't share her feeling of sadness that blanketed her as she first entered the grand house and saw the empty shell of a home. Nor the sense of final loss as she glanced across the street at the former Bettina Grant place before driving down the lane. There were no more excuses or other natural opportunities to revisit Bright Leaf Lane. As Allan put it, "A chapter closed." She headed to the last class of the day at the fitness center and focused on ditching her sorrow in the heavy beat and dynamic movement of aerobic dance. For now.

CHAPTER 61
OCTOBER 21, 1989
MALIBU
SATURDAY

Brain trust

"We have company," Raymond announced, sparked with excitement, as Meredith burst in the door from her Saturday morning aerobic workout. She paused and looked around to see Ito walking out of the kitchen holding a cup of coffee.

"He brewed it," said Raymond. "I wouldn't dare touch the pot with him in the house." Ito's coffee—and culinary skills—were legend among the circle that was borne from the deceased Bettina Grant's world. Meredith dropped her bags and ran over to the grinning visitor, tossing her arms around him for a hug.

"You just love me for my coffee," he said. She punched his arm.

"I didn't expect to see you this soon. And not here in California. What's happening?" The bespeckled pixie-like face grinned wickedly. Raymond smothered a laugh.

"I did some detective work in New York and thought we could brainstorm over this false column and your—um— supposed acceptance of a position on the morning show."

"How do you even know about that?" asked Meredith, picking up the coffee cup and taking a long appreciative sniff of the aroma.

"I'm good friends with Russ's secretary and she knows I'm also good friends with you. I heard about it and did some digging through the press departments of several institutions."

Meredith pondered for a few seconds, looked knowingly at Raymond and then laughed. "You always have been psychic, Ito. This afternoon Sonia, Cassie and Gloria are coming over to dig around in this whole thing with me and Raymond. Everyone has a little piece of information or insight. So, your timing is perfect! But did you just fly in—on a red eye?"

"Yes, but I slept all the way. Russ sprang for first class. He wants this cleared up, too. He told me to take a day to surf and be back on Wednesday. I had a lovely breakfast on the plane. Well, an okay one. And I've already showered in your amazing guest bathroom. And T.K., thank you for inviting me to stay here!"

"I'd never hear the end of it if I hadn't," chuckled the tall detective.

☆☆☆

"The brain trust has arrived. Be afraid, Ito. Be very afraid," mused Raymond as Cassie, Sonia and Gloria milled around the dining room table, settling in for the investigative meeting in the late afternoon. Ito bustled in and out of the kitchen, setting out banana bread and apple slices.

"You don't have to do that, you know," Meredith chided him.

"It's like old times," he said. "I am compelled to make sure everyone is comfortable. And…," he added proudly, "I am part of the investigation team with important information." Meredith nodded with a big smile on her face.

The air was lighthearted but still curious as everyone assembled around the extended table. Meredith began the conversation, thanking them all for participating. "Each of you has some small piece of information or ideas here so maybe we can assemble a complete picture instead of puzzle pieces. First, I have some perspective from Allan Jaymar." The name brought instant attention and focus. "He said one very important comment that I'm bringing to the conversation—again. 'My dear, you have a serious stalker. And stalkers don't give up too easily.' What does he or she want as an outcome?" Meredith looked around the table. "Let's start with the bogus column. Who and why?"

"But the letter of acceptance seems to be also associated with the column's timing and secretive method, somehow," added Gloria. "The intent must be to snag you into some kind of disfavor, make you look incompetent or foolish? They came to your primary work centers—the news syndicate—and probably your next most weighty professional outlet—the morning show network."

"And I got news of both developments before they happened," said Cassie, "with resumes and sideways announcements that Meredith would be leaving our show here in L.A.—and hopefully the news syndicate—to go to the morning show."

"It wasn't the first time Russ at the syndicate has been pestered by would-be replacements—first for Bettina and more recently Meredith," Ito spoke up. Meredith looked his way, her eyebrows raised in surprise.

"Pestered how and by whom?"

"Well, let's see," said Ito as he flipped through his notepad. He listed five names of people applying to be considered for columnist positions: Cecelia Markam, reporter from the *L.A. Spotlight* tabloid for Bettina's column six years ago and again two years ago in general inquiry; Clarice Duncan six years ago as a syndicate replacement for Bettina, then last month—she was working for a small paper up in the San Francisco Bay area; Sydney Fairbank from the *Sacramento*

Bee as a general inquiry last year; Bob Boquist from TV 17 in Kansas, general inquiry; Sherie Silberman from that little Beverly Hills tabloid in the past month."

"Both Duncan and Silberman approached me as well," said Cassie.

"Clarice Duncan actually went over Russ's head to the President of the syndicate, pushing the fact that true Hollywood news and gossip isn't included in the syndicate's package now with you only interviewing celebrities but mostly writing more in-depth features," murmured Ito, feeling a little self-conscious. "But Sherie is the niece of Amanda Borkin. And she apparently was working Cecil Longmore for a spot, not on the staff of the morning show, but as Nancy Igleton's full time replacement. Amanda was pushing for some kind of assignment for her. Sherie's done some commercials." Cassie nodded, affirming the information about commercials had appeared on the resume the young woman had submitted to her as well. Meredith's mind was in deep near-shock mode. Amanda's animosity toward her suddenly made sense although Meredith could not see a neophyte commercial actress as a key figure on such a heady program.

"How do you know all this, Ito?" asked Sonia.

"I'm good friends with the publicist on the *It's a Good Day* show," he said demurely. "She did some digging for me."

"Let's make lists of people who've been involved in any way with each of these situations and examine the cross-over," suggested Sonia.

"How's married life?" Ito asked her suddenly, remembering her life change.

"Good. Great—anything else you have to add here?" He shook his head, and reached for an apple slice.

"I know the name Clarice Duncan," Sonia continued. "She applied for Meredith's job with Bettina years ago. Was kind of arrogant as I recall, acted as though it was a foregone conclusion. When she didn't get it, she pestered Bettina for a couple of months afterward."

"I never knew gossip was such a dearly valued profession," snarked Meredith.

Raymond sat at a corner of the table and slouched back in the chair. His mind was in motion, though, Meredith could tell. He spoke up hesitantly. "Cecelia Markam is a familiar name to me, but not for all the reasons you'd think. She was arrested a couple of years ago for prostitution—high class stuff—in a sting. But was bailed out and more or less rescued by a 'benefactor.' A well-known agent, unnamed, but…had a very good attorney. I was assigned the case as high profile."

"Who else is involved in all of this we don't know about," laughed Gloria. "And what else—besides the infamous leave-behind on the ship—do we need to look at?"

Meredith waved her hand and answered flippantly, "Well, there's the underwear escapade break-in at the townhouse in Brentwood. And the nasty keying of my car. Two people following me in New York. They could all be independent…just coincidental."

"But all the TV and fiction detectives tell us 'there's no such thing as coincidence,'" laughed Ito.

"We're showing the sketch and bad photo of the New York stalker or stalkers to several people with actual contact with the mail fraud, and to Meredith's former neighbor Norman who caught a glimpse of the Brentwood B&E perpetrator," Raymond followed up. "Probably a dead end but you never know. Hope to have more in a few days."

"Well, Raymond, I think someone needs to talk to Clarice, to Sherie and to the other one, the prostitute. Hard to believe that case would link through Meredith to you, but…."

"…stranger things have happened," the detective finished the sentence.

"So, Raymond has his assignments," Meredith wrapped up. "Cassie, how about following up with both Sherie and Clarice as if there might be an opening on your show? Maybe you can learn something new. Ito and Sonia, keep asking questions around the center of this stuff. Sonia, keep track of us all and start the parade to the martinis?"

"But what about the mystery of the ship hostage?" asked Sonia.

"I think that's just a master fuck-up by the intern who let go of the traffic control for the press visit," sighed Meredith. "We're still waiting for the French journalist guy but I don't think there's anything but mismanagement involved." Everyone tsked, winced and shrugged, starting to collect any papers around them and thinking about martinis at sunset on Malibu Beach.

Everyone except Raymond, who caught their attention in his laid-back stance with a deep resonating hum. "Not necessarily," he spoke up. "It seems like young intern Nate dropped the ball, but I spent an hour with him earlier this week and have his notes. He was pretty organized and stayed to the plan, managed to shift things when it was necessary. It's all in his on-site notes. There were a couple of diversions, but he drew arrows at the time indicating those switches from one launch or group to another. He had an arrow indicating Meredith's switch to the SFO group but could not recall who gave him that information. The news of Meredith being left behind threw him. He's brooded about it and taken full responsibility but until we can talk with Claude the French journalist, we still don't have the last connection as to how Meredith was overlooked."

"Let's check back in a week," said Sonia. "I'll be the point person for this group. "I want this solved. We all have a pretty good situation, we'd like to keep it, and it's all connected."

"And I'm cooking tonight," Ito chimed in, "for those who can stay." He rattled off a menu that Meredith had no idea how he'd assembled. Barbecued steak marinated in sake sauce. Asian style fresh vegetables, also roasted on the barbeque, fried rice. And a butter cake with ice cream for dessert. "T.K. is manning the grill."

"George is bringing Trey over in a few minutes," said Gloria, referring to her husband and their new household addition.

"Bob is in the neighborhood," Cassie added about her husband.

"And Art will be coming in also," added Sonia, news to which everyone was thrilled. No one had spent much time with the groom of their long-time colleague.

"You sure Ito?" asked Meredith. "We can all go to the Sea Shack."

He looked at her deplorably. "Go fix some drinks and appetizers. Hors d'oeuvres are in the fridge," he retorted.

Raymond put an arm around Meredith and whispered in her ear, "I laid in a store of vodka, vermouth and tequila."

✩ ✩ ✩

"So it seems like this Malibu haven is winning out over the New York stairway to heaven?" asked Raymond, wrapped tightly around Meredith, curled into the big bed on the second floor of the house late Saturday night after cleanup from the houseful of guests. With the surf sounding outside the window and the moon showing on the water, thick linens and covers tumbled around them, he carefully murmured "I really have wondered if you might take the plunge into big time TV, in New York."

Savoring the firmness of his body and the familiar spicy scent of his skin, she wrapped herself into his embrace and sighed. "Home, Raymond. Tonight was family night with everyone I care about. And this, right here, at this moment, is home."

CHAPTER 62
OCTOBER 22, 1989
MALIBU
SUNDAY MORNING

A house is not a home

An overcast sky and huffy breeze pushed back against Raymond as he ran along the beach early Sunday morning. His usual morning workout. Hair ruffled against his head and face set against the blow. As he jogged through the thick sand, his mind focused on Meredith's affirmation of "home." He'd never really given much thought about what the word meant. Like most, he'd just accepted it as a cover term for—the house where I live, the place where I park my car, where I eat meals, where I move to and from most of my life activities. In younger days "home" had a more resounding context than it did after Lili's death and Will's growing up.

With Meredith, "home" seemed, again, more psychological—Zen-based, maybe, where he defined, fueled, recharged and reveled in contentment and worth. His most valued possession. Glimpsing ahead to the house he called home, he trudged toward it and breakfast when the idea of predators crept into his thoughts. Threats—the appeal of New York-based TV stardom for Meredith, his own demise in the line of police duty, Rick Santaros (he wondered), and a myriad of other made-up scenarios. He shook his head to clear the picture.

☆☆☆

Disruptions in her own home base were also on Meredith's thoughts as she curled up on the sofa, wrapped in her soft robe and sipped a cup of coffee. She listened to the wind meander across the water, the beach and slightly stirring the patio chairs as she considered the sale of her long-time townhouse residence in Brentwood. Allan's pending move from his decades-old home base came to mind just as the patio door blew open and Raymond huffed in, puffing from his workout, wiping his face and neck with his sweatshirt.

"I was thinking I'd cook breakfast this morning…," he began.

"Great," crowed Meredith. "You cook! I've already made batter with bananas! Homemade pancakes!" He wasn't surprised.

Paco regarded the scene from the top of the fridge and moved his tail so not to get it caught when the door was opened.

Head shots enclosed

"Why do you think you would be a good addition to our morning show, Sherie?" asked Cassie. The young woman sitting primly across the desk straightened her back and subtly adjusted her blouse, then smiled broadly.

"I've done a number of commercials and get excellent feedback from my directors and agency. And on-air television has always been my goal—and I think it's my aptitude. When I heard an on-camera opening was coming on *Morning Coffee* here in Los Angeles, it seemed a perfect opportunity." The young woman spoke well, perched in the simple wooden chair in Cassie's small, utilitarian office, and focused with intentional sincerity. A slender, open face with large eyes, a pert nose and wide, rich mouth and long, stylish blond hair, Sherie Silberman struck Cassie as the perfect intern.

"I understand your dream" said Cassie, "A lot of us have experienced it—and some realized it. But, you're young with very limited experience. Do you have any news experience? Current events are key to our show."

"Not exactly," murmured Sherie, looking down at her hands. "But I wrote some stories for a newsletter for my sorority house in college. And Aunt Amanda said I could learn news easily on the job."

Nodding her head rather than laughing at the casual assumption that becoming a news professional was a quickly-learned skill, Cassie murmured, "Mm…I'm curious where you heard about a potential on-camera opening here on *Morning Coffee*?"

"First, I'm a pageant girl—been on stage and presenting—since I was five. I was first runner-up to the state Miss American Teenager contest. I studied drama in college. And…," she hesitated, her voice dropping to a conspiratorial low, "…well, my aunt is Amanda Borkin. She told me she thought Meredith Ogden would be moving to New York and, well, you know…Aunt Amanda's show and all. She said this was a good starting point. And I'm dating this actor who's on a TV series. I went to a movie screening with him and some woman in a group we were talking with said Meredith Ogden was leaving your show."

Cassie's brain snapped to attention. "Oh. Of course, Ms. Borkin. But who's the other person—the local woman at the screening. Who was she? Did you get her name? Just curious. Very few people know about this possibility."

Sherie shook her blonde locks. "I don't think I ever heard her name. She seemed to be a reporter or some kind of maybe-gossip columnist. But I don't think she's from L.A. though. She sounded like she was in town only for a couple of days. And she was with some guy—Fred Banner—Barter—something like that. He was apparently an executive with one of the important trade publications."

"Mm," Cassie pondered, instantly recognizing Fred Barton, one of Meredith's closest friends. "Well, Sherie, we have your commercial videos and will review them. But please be aware that right now there is not an on-camera opening, but if something opens in the near future, we'll surely consider you."

The perky blonde looked at Cassie sideways, conspiratorially. "I know this isn't public knowledge" she practically whispered. "So thanks for giving me this opportunity to talk with you. I know it's a big change. My contact information is on my resume. I hope we get to talk again."

"Indeed," nodded Cassie, standing up and reaching forward to shake hands with the young woman. As the perky interviewee left, Cassie grabbed her coffee cup and felt ill from the discussion. But she quickly picked up the phone to call Meredith.

CHAPTER 64
OCTOBER 24, 1989
WEST LOS ANGELES
TUESDAY

Money on the table

At the office of the Special Profile Investigative Unit, T.K. Raymond was brought up short when Margo Flaherty stormed into his office and slapped a set of documents on his desk.

"Got him!" she snorted. Raymond looked at her in shocked surprise. "We found Martha's money!" Raymond, pulled out of concentration on other matters, stammered for response.

"It'll take a little while to reclaim it and get it to Martha's account. But it's such a slam dunk. No one even tried to hide the fraud. Can hardly believe it was allowed by the banks. But when no one else is watching, it's real easy to steal someone's worth! Damn!" She slapped a hand down on Raymond's desk. He jumped. Then scowled.

"How can we keep Martha in her nice nursing home? All that legal mumbo jumbo could take years."

With a coquettish grin, Margo said, "If I solve that problem for Martha, will you love me forever?"

He thought for a moment and said, "No. But I'll appreciate your skill and tell the folks who need to know. Tell me how you'll solve the problem."

"Much of this whole fraud mess started right here in L.A. at a local bank near Martha's home. The banker didn't realize what was happening and as we went through the steps, he felt terrible. Remiss. He said he should have kept better tabs on the situation but didn't notice it was happening. I say, maybe that's the truth. But, he's willing to make some extra efforts to cover Martha while the official gears are being turned. How long? Up for negotiation. There are some other government branches that need to be involved, but at least we've got everyone's attention, and no one suggests Martha's shit up a creek now—pardon my French." She comically batted her eye lashes at Raymond.

"Put the whole thing in detail and triplicate—or more—in a report." She pointed at the thick stack of papers on his desk. "Ah—got it, thanks. And…."

"…And I'll wrangle the whole thing. How's that?" She winked at him. He rolled his eyes and nodded.

Idle chatter

"Wow, Musso and Frank," exclaimed Fred Barton as Meredith waved him over to the table where she sat. "Feels like either an announcement or an emergency," he chuckled as he slid into the booth. One of the long-time Musso waiters was immediately at their table in service. It was the Musso and Frank legendary tradition. The restaurant was a Hollywood legend—still a favorite with insiders. Decades old tile flooring and décor, servers in white shirts and ties and aprons.

"Wedding, funeral, new job, won the lottery?" asked Fred as he adjusted the napkin in his lap. Meredith just laughed. The two had been friends over many years and jobs. Fred, originally her boss, the publicity director, at the network where she began her Los Angeles career. Responsible for her connection and subsequent job with Bettina Grant, and her ultimate career. Meredith was Fred's substitute date when he didn't have a current starlet girlfriend, also his occasional stand-in therapist and close friend.

"Nah," she shrugged. "Just some gossip and some quick questions." While they ordered she briefed him on the strange incognito assaults and stalking. He flinched and ordered a beer. "Entre nous," she reminded him.

"Yep," he affirmed.

As their sandwiches arrived, she hardened up on her own primary questions. "Fred, you were at a screening last week with some dark-haired woman, maybe a journalist?"

He looked up caught off guard, puzzled. "No. I went to a screening by myself. Who's trying to couple up with me now? Oh, those starlets."

Meredith laughed at his continual self-image of the playboy. "No one, but a young woman we met recently said she was at the screening and in a conversation group with you and a journalist who seemed to be from out of town who mentioned that I was leaving Cassie's show to join *It's a Good Day* in New York. We're all surprised by that rumor since it's not even been decided yet and no one is even supposed to know it could be— could be—in the works. We're wondering who you all were talking to with that information."

Scratching his head, Fred wrinkled his nose and pondered the question. "Well," he began, "I think you must be talking about Clarice Duncan. It was such a drive-by conversation. And now that you mention it, I guess it is a little surprising. At the time, all I thought was that you were already connected with *Good Day* and I hardly paid any attention. There was also an actor, Ted Milgram, and his date, a freshly minted young wanna-be."

Meredith closed her eyes and nodded her head. "Okay. Makes sense. Do you remember anything else she said?"

"I hardly heard that, but I honestly wasn't listening. Clarice has pestered me many times for a job on the paper. I tend to tune her out."

"Not a quality product?"

"Don't know. Won't know. I hate pains in the ass and she's one. I don't see her on our staff." He looked at Meredith with puppy dog eyes. "So, are you leaving us for New York? And am I the last to know?"

"Fred, you'll always be the first to know anything worth knowing about me. Let's just say, probably not. But if so, 'I'll have my person call your person.'" He exuded a sigh of relief.

"I think you dodged a big bullet by being in the bay up there on the old mothball fleet when you did instead of a few days later. Wow—lots of destruction," he said as an aside. She nodded. "And when am I gonna be invited for a drink on the patio of that spiffy house in Malibu?"

"I'll call you, myself, on that one—in the next two weeks. And you can bring Angie, who everyone says you're about to marry. Now who's keeping secrets?" Fred blushed uncharacteristically and stammered. "Oh, stop it," Meredith grinned. "Eat your sandwich. Then tell me all about it."

What're your goals?

Cassie kept an eye out the window of the restaurant-diner, watching for Clarice Duncan to arrive. She wasn't sure what the woman might look like now. She hadn't seen her, personally, in a few years. Cassie had made a quick trip to Oakland to meet with the "candidate" for the presumed opening in the *Morning Coffee* show who lived in San Francisco's East Bay and worked for a local there. Cassie was nervous. Clarice may be a suspected character terrorist, but she was also an active and known member of the Hollywood journalism community. Even though Fred Barton called her a "pain in the ass." She opened her purse on the seat next to her and checked the small recorder.

Soon a thin woman, gaunt of face, entered, a fashionable dark purple raincoat covering her tall angular body. Cassie recognized the face immediately but also thought about the disguised figure that they had all puzzled over. The height was right, the thinness. The rest had obviously been a disguise at the time. She waved Clarice over to the booth where she sat.

"Hello," Cassie said as she stood up and offered her hand. Clarice accepted it with a bony hand and shook it energetically, then shook out her two-toned blond hair as if to rid it of debris. As the waitress arrived with menus, Cassie added, "thank you for taking time and the drive from Hayward."

"Thank you for flying up from L.A.," the throaty woman responded. "You won't be sorry." Cassie smiled and already worry set in. The stress of her mission was heavy and she knew she had to succeed—however that looked. The two chatted casually for a while until lunch arrived.

"Let's cut to the chase because I know we both have a distance to travel to get back to work," Cassie opened. "As you pointed out, Meredith Ogden may well join the *It's a Good Day* show soon. After their interest and invitation to sub for Nancy—and rumors that Nancy will leave, it's obvious there's a connection and potential joining of forces. It's a logical step for Meredith."

Clarice nodded and stirred her fork around in her salad. "Yes. Obvious but also in Meredith's best interest. She's been the best at chasing her own dreams—sometimes to the detriment of others, but in this business who wouldn't?" Clarice replied without sounding rancorous. "And her spot on *Morning Coffee* would be open?"

"Well, you are direct," chuckled Cassie. "Let me say, 'perhaps' it will be open because neither Meredith nor anyone else has told me this was all happening."

"Oh, believe me it is," stated Clarice with no hesitancy. "I know she's already sent a letter of acceptance to Longmore at NTS."

"How do you know that?" asked Cassie, keeping her voice neutral, and gazing at her lunch partner.

Smiling conspiratorially, Clarice said, "I know." Cassie chose not to charge into battle just yet. She asked the eccentric woman more questions about her own qualifications and background. The answers were well sculpted, scripted and rehearsed but held little substance for a job in front of the cameras on a popular metropolitan TV program.

"And how are you still connected to the L.A. entertainment scene from up here?" asked Cassie.

"Well my readership here is quite substantial, and growing, and the studios and network appreciate that." She paused for a moment, considering her own answer. Then added, "And I have maintained some very strong contacts. For example, the producers of *Darkness in the Alley*, you know Bill Wedgewood's film shooting in New York, invited me to location in Manhattan a couple of weeks ago. Full pop—first class air, Waldorf for two nights and all the interviews I could collect. Bill's an old friend. I have several of those who still understand my hold over a substantial number of readers."

Cassie nodded. "So what is special about what you would bring to *Morning Coffee*, different from any other well-qualified face?" asked Cassie.

"For one thing, I'd fight tirelessly to help the show, to be creative, to put it first over anything else. I'd be loyal." Clarice poured hot water from a small ceramic tea pot into her cup and with her well-sculpted nails that matched her raincoat, she bounced the bag in the steaming liquid.

Cassie nodded at the answer. "How so?" she countered, motioning for the waitress to refill her own coffee.

"For one thing, I wouldn't be looking for something else the whole time. I wouldn't be jumping over barrels and hoops to find the next better job...."

"...like Meredith?" Cassie ventured.

"Well, sure. Look at her track record. And who she's left in the wake of her trajectory."

Cassie fought to keep her eyes from snapping open, she kept the theater. "Like who?"

"You. Me—I was supposed to be Bettina's legwoman when you left all those years ago. But two days after I was offered and accepted the job, Meredith pushed me out. Same thing when Bettina died. Russ Talbot promised me Bettina's spot and presto! Meredith had a new gig, and Russ wouldn't return my calls. There's so much more. But this isn't about past history. It's what I will bring to you now and in the future. One thing's for sure: I won't be spewing gossip that could get us sued!" Cassie threw her a confused scowl. "Another time, another story. A Meredith story. But for later."

"I have all your information, Clarice. And I need to be very clear and straight forward. This is not a job offer yet. These changes have not happened yet and this discussion is confidential and really in advance of some expectations. You do understand that, right?"

"Yes, of course," responded a dramatically demurred Clarice as Cassie paid the check and both women gathered their belongings to leave. Placing her ultra-round fashionable sunglasses on top of her head, Clarice added, "I'll be in L.A. day after tomorrow. Maybe we could have a drink. Are you going to the *Immaculate* screening? Studio's doing it up big. Reception at the Beverly Hilton."

Cassie mentally slammed through her calendar and the possibilities—and dangers. "Okay. I may know more by then and if you've forgotten anything that would give us a full picture of who you are, bring it. A video of one of your on-camera gigs would be helpful. And you know, thinking about what you said, Meredith's surely been on a fast track and there is a lot of history in her wake." Cassie added, reluctantly, but in an effort to cement the relationship, "We do have to remember that being respectful to her if this on-air change happens will be important. She has a lot of fans."

Clarice sniffed derisively. "Sure. How about Friday 4:30 at the Wing lounge, around the corner from the Hilton. We probably shouldn't be seen together—among the industry, you know? My treat?"

Cassie accepted, anxiously waiting to exit the appointment. Clarice left quickly. Feeling soiled by the encounter, Cassie slowly walked out the door, then nervously checked the recorder.

With a little help from my friends

The tension in the room was almost palatable. Meredith's "brain trust" hovered around the conference table in Gloria's Beverly Hills office. Anxiety and anger lay heavily over the group. Gloria's secretary set out a tray of mugs and a large coffee urn on the side credenza. By the time Gloria called the assemblage together, everyone was holding a full, steaming cup.

Sonia spoke first. "Not to bury the lead—that's journalism talk—let's cut to the chase: we've located Clarice Duncan in too many situations associated with the assault on Meredith to be coincidence. We need to lock that down." The group, again, including Cassie, Meredith, Gloria and Sonia, all fingered the notes Sonia had provided. "And, Sonia continued, "get it under control."

At that moment, Raymond entered the room, quietly edging in the door, always somewhat intimidated by this group of powerful women, and not wanting to disrupt the conversation. "Raymond," Sonia called out. "Good that you're here."

Sonia then summarized what they knew as fact. Clarice knew about the letter of job acceptance to Longmore, made reference to the phony column containing fake and damning information about Gold Productions, clearly inferred that she had a "strong" dislike for Meredith and made a point of trying to discredit her. "And was enlisting Cassie to join her diatribe against Meredith." Everyone nodded.

Sonia lifted her coffee to her lips, took a drink and then went on. "There were other coincidental episodes that seem to have set off Clarice. The initial one was after Cassie left Bettina years ago and two days before Meredith showed up to interview. Meredith got the job. Clarice approached Russ Talbot three or four times over the years—once when Bettina died, but again, Meredith got the slot. And on and on...."

"And I should mention that when she started jamming on Meredith yesterday in Oakland," Cassie interjected, "her eyes nearly popped out of her head, she was compulsively tapping her finger on the table and I think a knee was bobbing up and down. She kind of went psycho."

"Meredith, have you ever had a one-on-one run-in with Clarice?" asked Gloria.

"Silly story from years ago," Meredith began. "Back in the early Bettina Grant years. I was on a press junket to Mexico City with her and another journalist. She was with her smaller syndicate then. It was a major, but the last movie role for Felicia Landrom, capping off her amazing career everywhere—movies, TV, stage, etc. The studio somehow ended up with one too few hotel rooms and no others available so Clarice and I had to share a room. She was livid. She was worried I would overhear her filing her column on the phone or would read over her shoulder when she was typing it. She asked me to stay away from the room for about ninety minutes the last night of the trip so she could file—read—her column by phone to someone recording it. I was fine with that. The whole crew was in the bar watching local singers perform. No problem. But when I did return, she had not only locked me out, wouldn't answer the door or the phone. We had to get the manager of the hotel to open the door. We were afraid she had dropped dead or something. But no, she had her sleep mask on, ear plugs in and feigned sleep to keep me out of the room. Profound apologies the next day—with a wicked glint in her eye.

"I've run into her from time to time since. The studios and networks seem to allow her some leeway and let her come to some events, interview some stars...."

"Probably only part of the puzzle," Gloria took over. The door quietly opened again and a new, weathered face, entered the room. Raymond quietly welcomed the newcomer, then stepped into the discussion circle and apologized for interrupting.

"There are a couple of additional facts you all should know. First, most of you know Norm Tallyure from the L.A. FBI office." Norm stepped forward and said hello to the group, then began to explain his presence.

"I'm always impressed at how adept you all are at getting to the heart of a problem and protecting your own. We've seen your work before. But, there are a number of serious legal issues here concerning whoever has perpetrated these frauds through the mail and fax. We need to know more and are stepping up to help unravel it. But, it's serious and more than a pesky harasser. You need to let the professionals handle this. This time it is in your own best interests."

"More information," Raymond continued, "I had a long conversation with Stan Smallet a while ago. He finally tracked down the elusive Frenchman, Claude, the journalist who went AWOL on vacation—to the wine country. We had a long conference call, the three of us, and Claude said he was asked— by Clarice— to tell the Oakland launch driver—and Nate—that

Meredith was switching to the SFO group. He had to stretch to remember her name but he was clear she was a local 'smalltime' journalist. And I.D.'d her photo by fax. He was the one who passed the message along."

The room was quiet as contemplation set in. Raymond saw Meredith's hands ball into fists on the table. She stared into them and he could tell her teeth were gnashing. "That's why I spent the night on the rusted hulk hearing ghosts?" she spat out. "Clarice Duncan?" The assembled turned to her. Raymond instinctively felt her fury and hurt. He wished he could hold her or at least put a consoling arm around her but knew it would embarrass her.

"How do we stop this? Now!" pushed Sonia.

"Wait, wait, wait!" the venerable older FBI agent growled. "This is not a TV show. You're all so damn…collegial…and confident. But this woman now has an escalating history of violence toward Meredith. With things like the damaging of her car, break-ins at the apartment, and God knows, the stranding on an abandoned battleship. Whew!" he puffed, "Not a mystery for Nancy Drew. My behavioral profile people tell me that she's capable of going off the rails and in the worst possible way at this point. And that it's most likely a personal vendetta— vengeance—leave her to the professionals. We don't want anyone to get hurt!"

"But we already have her contained," countered Cassie. "I'm having drinks with her tomorrow night to talk about opportunities to replace Meredith and…"

"…and?" asked Raymond.

"Well, supposedly to avenge her for all the misdeeds she's done to Clarice. That's the inference. And after, there's a screening that she, Meredith and I will be at. I plan to carry my recorder along in my bag."

"And what? Confront her at the screening with Meredith in tow? You're setting her up as bait? To push Clarice Duncan over the edge? And then what?" Tallyure stared at the three, sitting next to each other at the table. "Citizen's arrest?" He shook his head.

"Hey, we've done pretty well so far," snapped Cassie, her short, tousled brunette curls bouncing as she addressed the FBI chief. He'd seen that look from her before in the New Mexico case. "Maybe you folks could help us out!" Three female heads looked intently at the two lawmen.

"Look," Raymond stepped in. "Norm, these folks aren't shy nor fragile and they've been in the fire before. You know that. Maybe they have the edge on this. If Meredith confronts this woman and if it pushes her too far, the onus is on us all to stop the process before it gets violent. And your group can surround the activity to make sure everything happens safely, as it should, and ends appropriately—for all concerned."

Tallyure rubbed his forehead, troubled. He sighed and nodded. "We'll need warrants...." Raymond moved quickly to organize a plan of action.

I bet you think this is about you

Cassie arrived early at the Wings Wine and Cocktail Lounge around the corner from the Hilton. She felt on high alert and uncomfortable with the wire device the feds had affixed to her torso and chest. She wore a plain black sheath with a pencil skirt and a flared jacket to cover any suspicious lumps or bumps. Quickly approaching the bar, she ordered a club soda with lime, figuring she could pass it off as a gin and tonic. She chose a quiet booth and settled in. When Clarice arrived, she waved her over.

"Looking good," she smiled at the tall woman whose hair somehow suggested a styled fright wig sprinkled with glitter. The waitress arrived. Clarice ordered an old fashioned. "How was the trip?" opened Cassie. Clarice shrugged.

"Same old, same old." Her drink arrived and she took a sip. They talked about the movie that was about to be screened. "So, what's the story with YOUR show?" Clarice burst out, looking intently at Cassie. "Do I get the job?" Cassie shuddered internally but continued to stay calm on the outside.

"Clarice, it's only been two days since we last met—the first discussion. Did you bring your videos?" Clarice pushed a thick package toward her. "I've pushed Meredith for an answer,"

Cassie explained, sipping her drink, frowning. "So Meredith. Says she's 'close' but not finished negotiating." Her explanation was greeted by a bold slap on the table and an audible "Grr."

"No surprise," muttered Clarice. "Dangle everyone in limbo and then drop them over the cliff."

"Yeah, well. But I do need to remind you we're only in discussion here, I am not offering you anything right now. Tell me you understand that." Clarice, whether chastened or acting, nodded and picked up her drink. "Clarice?" prodded Cassie. "Do you understand that?"

"Yes, of course. Saint Meredith. We hang out until Meredith tells us we're screwed."

"Wow, Meredith Ogden can be a spoiler, I can't deny that," uttered Cassie, "but how come you dislike her so vehemently? What's all this anger and angst?"

Switching to a lighthearted, dismissive voice Clarice said, "She's just been too much with us. Me, for sure. I've written articles for her, sent letters, done everything I can to make room for myself. Tried to move her out of the way again and again. I'm always the also-ran. Sometimes, like now, I think maybe I might just choke her and silence the wench for good." Cassie tilted her head and stared impassively at the woman.

"Kidding, just kidding," Clarice bubbled. Then, "Let's go to a Hollywood party and a screening, what do you say? See all the pretty people."

Cassie agreed, picking up the check, taking a silent but huge sigh of relief. "See you there." Clarice bustled up and out of the lounge, leaving Cassie to finish the transaction. As she signed the tab and picked up her bag, she said quietly into her chest and the wire there, "I know I should have pushed her harder, but she scares the hell out of me."

CHAPTER 69
OCTOBER 27, 1989
BEVERLY HILLS
FRIDAY NIGHT

Stars shining above you

The after party for the screening welcomed guests into a dramatic intergalactic bubble. The room was darkened except for stars glittering in formation overhead, a giant, glowing moon behind a small combo playing jazz in mellow tones. Well positioned spotlights illuminated the bar, food tables and each guest table. The studio lighting experts had made a magical astrological wonderland.

"I feel like someone out of a Star Trek movie," whispered Meredith to Cassie as they entered the party. "We just have to watch out for the Borg!" Cassie snickered. The evening progressed, both anxious for it to be over. Both now self-conscious and aware of the wires each wore.

"And I thought longline bras were uncomfortable," murmured Meredith. The soft swirl of her black skirt and flowing blouse hid the mechanism she wore and was a more subdued adornment to her usual colorful self. She gazed around the room frequently, observing the various guests and where they chose to sit. Looking for Clarice. Looking for signs of the undercover agents. "What are we supposed to do now?" she whispered to Cassie, who initially shrugged. Then, spotting Clarice, cozying into the table where Fred Barton and his friends sat, she thrust a thumbs-up to Meredith and excused herself, headed toward the bar, passing visibly by Clarice's table and greeting Fred and others as she passed. Watching the drama unfold, Meredith felt her nerves begin to seize. This could be the moment of truth.

Cassie stood at the bar ordering a glass of chardonnay and making small talk with the server. Suddenly Clarice arrived at her side. "Nice party, isn't it?" She purred.

"Party is way better than the movie," mused Cassie, turning her back to the bar and looking directly out into the room. "Look, I don't want to waste any more of your time, Clarice. Meredith just told me she has turned down the New York job and is staying where she is." She could feel and almost hear Clarice balloon into high tension.

"That can't be true. I saw the letter she sent to NTS accepting the offer."

"I don't know what you saw or where but she said she's already had the conversation with the people there and turned it down. How'd you see that letter, by the way?" Clarice seemed to be caught in slow motion, stammered something unintelligible, turned and stormed toward the exit. Cassie slowly let out her breath, dropped her head and stood silent for a moment. She made her way back to the table where Meredith sat, watching intently.

Clarice had scuttled out of the party room, through the hotel lobby and into the night. Cassie saw her waiting for her car at the valet stand, frowning sharply. Tiny camera in hand, Cassie slipped around a corner and shot two photos of the woman as she waved her car over and handed the valet a tip.

"Now what?" asked Meredith, back in the party room.

Cassie shrugged her shoulders and pointed to her chest. "Ask them."

As the party wound down, the two women stood to leave not wanting to be the last stragglers. "Going to the ladies' room before we hit the road," Meredith said, heading into the side hall where the restrooms were located. Cassie waited in the ballroom, wondering about the presence of an undercover agent. As Meredith left the ladies' room door, a strong hand grasped her upper arm and she also felt small spikes piercing sharply into her neck as she was pulled through the short hallway to an unmarked service entrance.

"Clarice! What are you doing?" she gasped, unsuccessfully trying to wrench her body free as they stumbled outside into the empty rear loading area. Meredith struggled, starting to scream, but dimly remembering the strategy and how this very act played into their plans, she kept nerve-numbing quiet. She fervently hoped someone was listening and following.

"You just can't help yourself, can you?" the angular face spat out. The fingernails on Meredith's neck released but instantly it was replaced by the pressure of what Meredith knew to be a revolver.

Too shocked to do anything but mumble, searching for a comeback, she finally gasped, "What are you gonna do? Shoot me? Kill me?"

"I hope so, that's the plan," snarled Clarice, "something I should have done years ago."

"What have I ever done to make you so nasty to me, to do the hurtful things you've done?"

"Where shall we start?" growled Clarice. "How about…well, you took two major jobs that should have been mine, but honestly, your worst sin was getting me fired from my former news syndicate out of Chicago! "

"What? I never even knew your editors or anyone there," retorted Meredith, puzzled but working to stem the terror she felt. "Your news syndicate was bought out by another one and they closed down the West Coast operation, including your column. I had nothing to do with that!" Her captor's hand pushed the gun harder into Meredith's neck.

"Good story, but I know you had the execs from the movie studio that took us to Mexico ban me from all set visits and trips after that stupid little hotel room mix-up. You went directly to the head of the studio—that night—and he wrote a letter to my editor telling him how evil I was."

"The head of the studio happened to be in the hotel bar with the other folks from the company when I asked for help to get into OUR room at midnight and you wouldn't let me in. It took the hotel manager! I didn't do that. You did. But this all seems so much bigger than that!"

"Bigger? I couldn't get a Hollywood job after that! A gossip professional whose gossip no one wanted hear…."

"Gossip was changing, Clarice. The old-fashioned columnist idea was—and is—over. Why your column and office were shut down…not my fault…."

"And now I work for some Podunk regional newspaper and beg for Hollywood to notice…I'm not going to genuflect at the altar of Meredith Ogden anymore. No one will have to…."

Meredith jerked away from Clarice's iron-fisted grip, twisting behind her—just as a strong hand grabbed Meredith's other arm and pulled her to the ground, then quickly enfolded Clarice's body, trapping her arms. With very little tussle, the gun dropped to the ground. A tall, well-built, stunningly attractive red-gowned Latina woman looked around as two other male party-garbed agents appeared from around the building and stepped in to handcuff a struggling, spitting and snarling Clarice Duncan.

"You sent that phony column under my name, full of lies, to Russ—the bogus letter of job acceptance to Longmore, broke into my apartment, keyed my car and worst of all—stranded me on that god-awful ship. What? Did you think no one would ever find me until there was nothing left but a decimated or mummified skeleton? How dare you!" snarled Meredith as she was pulled to her feet and firmly thrust to the side.

"Well you wear cheap underwear!" retorted Clarice. "I found them in your townhouse!"

"Not even mine, the girls using…."

"Sh-sh-sh," directed the begowned agent. "The story is over." She guided Meredith to a bench along the building wall and firmly lowered her onto it. Cassie came running out of the building. The area became a beehive of law enforcement specialists. Raymond emerged and walked over to Meredith. She sat hunched forward, head drooped, elbows resting on her flouncy cocktail skirt, chic copper blonde hair style wildly askew, eyes shut, totally frozen. Raymond carefully placed his hand on the small of her back and rubbed softly. She twisted her head and looked up at him.

"Can I take this damn wire off now?"

Look what we did

"We did this," exclaimed Sonia, reading the local L.A. newspaper article reporting the arrest of Clarice Duncan and the respective misdeeds that led to it. "So many crimes!"

"Alleged crimes," reminded Gloria the attorney. The ensemble of Meredith, Cassie, Sonia and Gloria sprawled on Gloria's patio. Normally, they'd be in the pool, but it was a chilly November day. The women were wrapped in sweaters, sipping hot chocolate. With a little rum mixed in.

"And now there's even assault with a deadly weapon, attempted murder…and…I'll bet that FBI honcho is eating his words now," Sonia went on. "The guy in New York who saw your stalker remembered the purple, spiked fingernails and the huge round sunglasses. So did the hotel desk guy and the person who sent off the faxed article."

"I can tell you about those fingernails—they are like tiny blades. I still have the wounds in my neck," interrupted Meredith. "But now I just wish the authorities kept the lid on it a little tighter. I'm embarrassed having all this information about me out there."

"Well, after the six weeks on *It's a Good Day*, you already had a start at celebrity notoriety," mused Sonia. "And now maybe you'll be more visible anyhow through the plan we're looking at between the show here in L.A. and *Good Day*." Russ and *Good Day* producer Tim Felton along with Cassie had come up with an idea to include a combined segment about Hollywood comings and goings twice a week. The interactive coast-to-coast banter between the hosts of both shows, which included Meredith on the west coast, would strengthen the appeal of both shows.

"Just so I don't have to get up at three-thirty in the morning," groaned Meredith.

"Your segment would be at seven-thirty. Rational hours for any working girl," snarked Cassie.

"But however it works, not until January," Meredith yawned. "God, I'm tired. Lots to do between now and Christmas. But I think I need a complete breakdown before then. I think I'm still seasick and dizzy from the adventures on the ghost ship."

"Well, get over it," said Gloria. "I know you've got a couple of trips scheduled and Raymond's kids and grandchild coming to visit. Better gear up." Meredith sighed and Gloria rose to fetch more rum.

Good bye yellow brick…well, you know

The townhouse's emptiness swirled around Meredith as she looked around the home she'd known for a decade or more. Purchased as a haven of quiet and privacy, the two-story then fashionable place was a gift to Meredith by way of a life insurance policy bequest from her fiancé, Fitz, who died way too young. The rooms had seen the rise of Meredith in her career, various lovers, Paco the cat, break-ins, a few plumbing problems, and the entrance of T.K. Raymond upon the murder of Meredith's boss. Raymond initially was a frequent visitor, then a resident. And then he had wooed Meredith into a new handsome home on the beach. After keeping the townhouse for two years after the move, mostly empty or for last minutes need for alone time, Meredith finally decided to release it and the memories. The place had sold in two weeks and was due to close, with new residents moving in the next morning.

Pulling a bottle of chilled chardonnay and a paper cup from her bag, Meredith opened it and poured some of the golden liquid and sat down on the carpet in front of the fireplace. She let the echoes and memories flood around her and reveled in even the saddest or most frightening moments. As she lit the gas logs, she glanced to the kitchen, gazing at the dent in the top corner of the refrigerator from a bullet aimed at Raymond by an intruder in the middle of the night two years before. The refrigerator also seemed lonely without the big grey cat named Paco sprawled on its top. Now he was fine with his new "home"—the bigger fridge in Malibu. She thought about Allan's elegant and welcoming Bel Air enclave, now only walls with life's accoutrements packed for delivery to his new Country Farm retirement digs. "Home is here," he said, pointing to his heart, "and all that lives within that domicile."

Home is wherever I hang my hat, she mused. "Home" before Hollywood—Seattle as a child with two centered and loving parents. After her mother's death from breast cancer which had followed her father's fatal heart attack two years before, her last view of that home was through the rearview mirror of the van she and Gloria had loaded up and drove back to their apartment at Northwestern University in Illinois. House sold, new paths ahead in her senior year.

Alan's credo came to mind, "What you love in your heart is what makes a 'home.'"

A light tapping at the front door interrupted the reverie and she heard keys in the door. She had invited Raymond to share the last few minutes in the now-pristine, primped for new owners, abode.

"Sure you want company?" he asked hesitantly, but carried a large pizza box and a bottle of champagne.

She laughed. "A guy with a hot pizza in his hand? How could I say no?"

"Knew that," he said as he shrugged off his jacket, opened the pizza box and chuckled that both had thought to bring wine. He joined her with another full paper cup and sat down on the floor next to her.

"First, some news," Raymond began. "They found Duck's boat—pretty sure it's his—smashed and washed up on the shore near Suisun—victim of the earthquake. No sign of the guy and still no ID on him." Meredith felt a little relieved because the strange guy had done her a big favor getting her off the ship. "And Marty visited Martha in the nursing home, told her about her money and that she didn't have to worry any more about her future there. She snarled, then farted," Raymond chuckled. "But he said she murmured 'thank you' as he left the room." They laughed and then fell silent.

"I'm wondering why Clarice chose your townhouse here," he pondered, "instead of Malibu to harass you. The break-ins, and spying around?"

"Raymond, she never knew I had moved out. She still believed this was where I was living," mused Meredith.

They talked about upcoming holiday plans. In the past year Raymond finally met Magda, her "almost mother-in-law," in Palm Springs. The dignified older woman treated them to lunch in a trendy desert restaurant and shared stories with Raymond like old friends. After a pleasant afternoon and as they rose to leave, the white-haired maven gave Meredith a classic thumbs-up on Raymond. "Thanks for introducing us," she said. "You need—deserve—a one hundred percent wonderful life of love, family, kids…."

"Whoa," Meredith had cautioned with a grin, holding up an extended palm. "Not too much of a good thing. Nothing is one hundred percent, so one thing at a time."

"If and when it suits," corrected Magda with a wry grin.

Later, in the fading light of the blank townhouse, Raymond gazed into the fire and said, "You seem to be focusing your life on our place in Malibu. I hope that's right."

"Our?" she answered, tone low and quiet.

"You know I wouldn't have bought it if there was any chance you wouldn't be sharing it with me. It was a gamble."

"And a great deal," she chuckled. "You couldn't turn it down, Raymond."

"But when you were in New York, I really had the sense of what it would be like if you weren't here. Wouldn't be my first choice."

"No place else I want to be but here," she said.

"I was worried you would head for the Big Apple," he admitted somewhat hesitantly. "A big carrot for you. And I know you got a later, bigger carrot offered."

"Where'd you hear that?" she probed.

"I have my sources."

"Even if I did get a bigger offer from NTS, I'm here now."

"I can see where it would be super appealing. Money, high-stepping life, exposure, open doors to the wonder of TV, movies and all they bring."

"I have most of that now, Raymond." He smiled at her. "I think I told you before," she murmured. "Home…," she pointed at him and then herself. "This is home and it's where I want—no, need—to be. Even this…," she waved her hand around pointing at the townhouse. "It's just a place to store clothes, underwear, shampoo, food and a cat."

They began to reminisce about the townhouse. The break-ins, the shots fired, Paco as the king of the realm, the vandalized underwear strewn about the place. "She said I wore cheap underwear!" Meredith pouted as they opened the bottle of champagne, the chardonnay depleted.

"But we know better," said Raymond reaching for her, "and we can prove it…."

At some point, Meredith awakened groggily from a messy sleep. She was curled on the carpet, covered with her jacket, one leg draped over Raymond next to her. Raymond breathed heavily in a deep snooze. She raised up on one elbow, noticed the empty pizza box and two empty wine bottles. "Ugh," she thought, feeling a vice squeezing her head and the thickness of her mind, the cotton in her mouth. And the fact that she had no clothes on. She looked at her watch and panicked. Five thirty. Escrow was closing at eight. The new owners could likely be arriving in two and a half hours.

She pushed herself up, headed dizzily for the bathroom, collecting items of clothing all along the way. Then she recalled, they had decided to de-christen the place room by room. Even the kitchen? She wondered. Then wondered, how and where? Glad Paco wasn't around to judge.

Cleaning herself up as best as she could without towels, soap or any other necessity, she heard Raymond stirring downstairs. "Get up, lazy!" she demanded. "We have to get out of here!"

"What time is it?" he gasped.

"Five-thirty a.m.," she announced and instantly felt a bit nauseated, herself. "Yeah. Too early but the new owners may be here in less than two hours!" Raymond groaned and assembled his long body as he worked to leave the floor.

"Clothes," she said, handing them to him.

"I thought we were going home last night," he murmured. "Looks like we didn't." He looked up the stairs to the master bathroom and slowly made his way there.

Funny, thought Meredith, there's a full, smaller bathroom just around the corner here, but old habits die hard. The upstairs bath is OUR bathroom. She began picking up the left-overs from the night before and checking to see no debris was left behind for the new owners.

As they stood at the front door, Raymond looked at her and asked, "Are you sure you're okay with this? One hundred percent?"

"Well, nothing's ever one hundred percent, but it's too late now if I'm not, but yes. It just seemed like the time. And Magda gave me her blessing to do it."

"Can you drive?" he chuckled.

"Can you?" she countered.

"Let's hope so! See you at home. I need coffee."

She took one long, last look and murmured a "thank you" to the townhouse, to Fitz and to the good years. A tear trickled down her face as she started the Mustang and headed for Malibu.

All the things you are tonight

The unfractured image in the mirror said she had caught up with life and things had stabilized. Meredith upswept her hair into a striking style, checking out her artistically applied makeup. She'd learned a lot of tricks from the makeup experts on the New York show. It was still one of her favorite nights—Gloria's elegant Christmas party. Tuxedos, caviar, filet and lobster, a softly pulsating jazz ensemble, and many personal friends who saw each other maybe only this once during a year. The party at which she first connected with Raymond six years before. Her dress was the same sparkling long-sleeved top with the sequined swoosh skirt she'd worn that first time. Cleaned and lovingly stored in the "special clothes" closet, surprisingly, it still fit. She smiled wickedly to herself.

Raymond's tall figure appeared behind her in the mirror and he placed a hand on her shoulder with a gentle squeeze. She smiled at his gesture, but also at his figure still sleek and awesome in Armani. "A present for you from my mother. Early Christmas. She gave it to me when I drove down to see her last month. And she's looking forward to all of us being there for

Christmas. But...." He handed her a small white box. She gingerly took off the top to see a beautiful set of earrings, sparkling blue sapphires set in sterling silver. Large enough to be a significant accessory, but elegant enough to be subtle. And they worked well with her dress. She stubbed the rods into her ears and looked up at him.

"They're beautiful."

"They were hers in her 'high-stepping' years, as she calls them. My dad gave them to her. She said she could see you wearing them well and proudly."

"I will," murmured Meredith as Raymond leaned over to kiss her tenderly on the neck. She placed a hand over his resting on her shoulder and thought about all that was to come.

"I recognize the dress," he said.

She smiled and nodded. "I told you this dress would live to dance again," she chuckled. Then silently gave thanks for what brought him into her life and felt some trepidation for what she had to tell him. She had chosen the holiday celebration at the Masners' because, years before, the party had ignited the relationship they still shared. They seemed to accelerate it every year at the same event. Something about it seemed right.

☆ ☆ ☆

When they arrived at the artistically sculpted iron door of the Masners', it was opened by a liveried butler welcoming them to a sparkling wonderland of holiday lights and décor. Then, an eight-year-old Trey Masner, hair deftly and fashionably cut, dressed in a well-tailored mini-tuxedo and standing next to his aunt Gloria Masner, warmly greeted guests. In a deep blue velvet gown, the sleekly coiffed brunette grinned widely and wickedly at Meredith as she introduced her young ward. "Welcome to our home," crowed the youngster in an apparent well-prepared script. "The group is gathering in the patio area," he motioned toward the sound of the music. Gloria winked at Meredith in a kind of conspiratorial code.

"There's a picture I never thought I'd see," chuckled Raymond as the couple made their way into the elegant expansive sunroom and patio where the party activity was taking place.

"What? An eight-year old in the Masner household?"

"Yes. These two always insisted they're not the parenting type," said Raymond.

"Well, Gloria says the new 'family' situation is going very well and she's turning into a well-suited mom. Something I never thought I'd see. But apparently they're quite content. As Gloria put it, she and George are so well grounded in their work and economically at this point that they can take more time and focus away, give the child a life they couldn't have in their twenties or thirties. And the energy of a young person in the house seems to be kind of energizing for them."

"Energizing? How so?"

"Well, taking George and Gloria out of their years-long habitual patterns, opening them up to new adventures. They're planning to visit Yellowstone over Trey's spring break. Neither of them would have planned that on their own. And they're both volunteering at his school a couple of hours a week, seeing new things, gaining new perspectives."

"So, you're saying it's been good for them?" Raymond raised an eyebrow and turned up his mouth in a slight grin.

"They think so," Meredith said as they sidled up to the bar and ordered drinks. Meredith looked around at the festive cocoon surrounding them—almost old fashioned in its nod to big-time Christmas. Twinkling lights, flickering candles, music and evergreen trees, wreaths and swags throughout the house.

With Christmas a week away, she and Raymond talked over plans to meet with Will, his wife Sophie and their son Kit, arriving from Seattle and joining them in Laguna Beach where they would all stay at the Ritz Carlton and visit with Raymond's mother. She lived in a pleasant nearby assisted living home and would join them at the resort. After Christmas they would drive north back to Malibu where the young family would visit with Raymond and Meredith for two days. Am I really standing in the role of grandmother? she asked herself and then silently laughed. What irony!

☆☆☆

The evening evolved. He snagged Meredith by the arm and pulled her onto the dance floor. She was reminded of the magic of their first evening on the same dance floor. Soon they circled back to their own seats, then headed to the smorgasbord table.

"George seems happy," said the detective. "And by the way, I need to tell you about a couple of small changes at the department. We're promoting Marty—sort of—to be more of a direct assistant to me. The new guy who came in last year in the celebrity/entertainment unit will work with him. But Marty'll take some of my administrative tasks—paperwork—and I'll take more time in the field. I miss it."

"Huh," Meredith said in vague surprise. "So, your brush with the studio big wigs got your investigative juices flowing again? My sabbatical on the ghost ship actually had some good outcome?"

He smiled. "Well…just keeping the big wigs in the game. Margo Flaherty is also moving to offices in Los Angeles instead of ours on the west side." Meredith's eyes widened in question, not stating the obvious. "She's a valuable and really effective agent, but most of her cases are in downtown L.A. and she'll be supported by folks there in her own genre."

"And she's made you crazy," murmured Meredith with a smile.

"And that," he smiled. "I worked this out with Bernie on Friday. But it's costing me."

"Costing you?"

"Margo's vacant cubicle is now reserved for Bernie when he wants to work out of the west side. You know how he loves this side of town."

"Oh," smirked Meredith with a nod. Then a smile "I better lay in a stock of good bourbon for him and you'd better introduce him to the Sea Shack's calamari—if you haven't already." They moved to the food table, filled plates, chatted with their tablemates and finished the meal. "Let's walk over by the pool," suggested Meredith. "I need to move around after that rich food." They walked hand-in-hand to the quiet side of the property, the lush garden framing them as they talked idly.

George Masner began rounding up friends for his annual Christmas billiard competition in his well-outfitted pool room. He spotted Raymond and Meredith across the property and made his way there. He could see a deep affectionate embrace evolve into animated conversation with some big smiles and also some deep consternation on the faces.

"Surprised me, too, you know" he overheard Meredith's comment to Raymond. "Nothing—even those—apparently are always one hundred percent!" They both laughed nervously.

"T.K.—Teke! Ready for me to beat your ass in billiards?" George interrupted. Raymond saw him approaching and seemed visibly pulled between two forces, looking back and forth to each.

"Go beat the socks off all those guys," said Meredith waving her hand dismissively, solving the dilemma. "There's lots and lots of time for this conversation." She ran a hand over her swept up hair and looked back toward the party for Gloria and Cassie as Raymond turned away.

The tall Armani-clad detective breathed deeply and made his way, caught in deep thought, around the swimming pool perimeter to join George. "Looked like a heavy conversation," his friend commented.

"Well, yes and no. Heavy and lighthearted—considering I just learned that, next Christmas, my grandson, Kit, will be a year and a half old, about a year older than my daughter... probably...yet she'll be Kit's aunt. Half-aunt?"

"Well, damn!" said George.

ACKNOWLEDGMENTS

"Do murders and crimes really happen in movie-making?" a reader asked skeptically. Soon after, she was the first to note that Meredith Ogden's last adventure, *Sunset West*, with a death on its remote film location in the New Mexico desert, was published only a couple of months before a real-world tragic death on the New Mexico location of the movie, *Rust*. *Sunset West*, however, was suggested from a 1970s film that shot in Arizona and suffered the death of a crew member. *Shadow of the Wave* was influenced by breath-taking personal views of the now-absent ghost fleet of San Francisco Bay, and the challenging life decisions that face us all, including upwardly-mobile Hollywood journalists. While Meredith's dramas are "inspired" by real-life Hollywood-land happenings, they are also imagined, and, a lot of creative folks have suggested some additional sparkle. Among them wing-woman Deborah Baker, also Linda Dozier, Teri Morisette, Peggy Normandin, Jim Vincler, Nancy Vincler, Barbara Wilson and Butch Wilson. Buffing up the shine, kudos go to Susan Wagner and Dana Barnum.

And never last and certainly not least, endless appreciation for Dixon Smith's imaginative mind as a story developer and keen eye toward drama, punctuation and grammar. And patience. It takes a family.

And you, readers, are part of the family of friends belonging to Meredith Ogden. Thanks for your loyalty, interest, comments and suggestions. Visit my website

pennystories.wixsite.com/penny-smith-books

ABOUT THE AUTHOR

Penny Pence Smith began writing professionally as a teenager for the local Indio, California, daily newspaper. Later, after college graduation, she covered the entertainment industry as a movie magazine editor, as assistant ("legwoman") for a well- known gossip columnist, feature correspondent and bureau manager for the *New York Times Special Features Syndicate*, and as correspondent for the *Hollywood Reporter*. With a Ph.D. in communication, she has taught journalism and communication at UNC Chapel Hill and Hawaii Pacific University. Her *Under a Maui Sun* and *Reflections of Kauai* were best-selling tourism books in Hawaii.

Check my Author Page on BookBub for news about future Meredith Ogden adventures and other books: pennystories.wix site.com/penny-smith-books.